YOUN

THE ANNIVERSARY EDITION OF HERMAN CHARLES BOSMAN

*Planning began in late 1997 – the
fiftieth anniversary of Bosman's first
collection in book form,* Mafeking Road *–
to re-edit his works in their original,
unabridged and uncensored texts.
The project should be completed by
2005 – the centenary of his birth.*

GENERAL EDITORS:
STEPHEN GRAY AND CRAIG MACKENZIE

Already published in this edition:
MAFEKING ROAD AND OTHER STORIES
WILLEMSDORP
COLD STONE JUG
IDLE TALK: VOORKAMER STORIES (I)
JACARANDA IN THE NIGHT
OLD TRANSVAAL STORIES
VERBORGE SKATTE
SEED-TIME AND HARVEST AND OTHER STORIES
UNTO DUST AND OTHER STORIES
A CASK OF JEREPIGO
MY LIFE AND OPINIONS

Herman Charles Bosman

YOUNG BOSMAN

The Anniversary Edition

Edited by Craig MacKenzie

HUMAN & ROUSSEAU

Cape Town Pretoria Johannesburg

erman Charles Bosman was born near Cape Town in 1905, but moved at a young age with his family to the Transvaal, where he lived for most of his life. He was educated at Jeppe High School and the University of the Witwatersrand, where he trained as a teacher. As a schoolboy he published around twenty pieces in the Johannesburg *Sunday Times* and also wrote for the Wits student magazine. A selection of these pieces makes up part of this volume.

In 1926 he was posted as a novice teacher to a farm school near Zwingli in the Marico District of what was then the Western Transvaal. This position was abruptly terminated in July when he was arrested for the murder of his step-brother at the family home in Johannesburg. While serving a four-year sentence (his death sentence was commuted), he resumed his writing career, smuggling at least one piece out of prison and publishing it under a pseudonym ("In the Beginning", reprinted here). Upon his release he embarked on a career as a journalist, often providing most of the copy for the short-lived periodicals he and fellow journalist Aegidius Jean Blignaut repeatedly launched. A selection of these items makes up the bulk of this volume.

In 1934 (the cut-off point for this collection) he left for London, returning only in 1940 after the outbreak of war in Europe. His first novel, *Jacaranda in the Night*, appeared in 1947 and was followed in the same year by a collection of Oom Schalk Lourens stories, *Mafeking Road,* and, two years later, his prison memoir *Cold Stone Jug*. He died of heart failure in 1951 at the age of forty-six.

Contents

Introduction

WITH one exception, all the pieces included in this selection of the work of Herman Charles Bosman were written between 1921 and the end of 1933, shortly before he left for London. The volume therefore represents a gathering of young writings, completed well before Bosman's more settled and mature phase of the mid-1940s, which saw him move into a very productive period culminating in the publication of *Jacaranda in the Night* (1947), *Mafeking Road* (1947) and *Cold Stone Jug* (1949).

Bosman's earliest recorded piece ("The Fowl") was published in *The Sunday Times* of Johannesburg (in May, 1921), followed closely by sketches in *The Jeppe High School Magazine* in July and December, 1921; the latter are reproduced in the companion volume to this one, his *My Life and Opinions* of 2003, where they appear as annexures to an essay he wrote later about the onset of that career of his "in the writing line."

But as fundis of Bosman's work will know, Mitzi Andersen of the University of South Africa has recently collected and assembled *Herman Charles Bosman: The Prose Juvenilia* (published by Unisa Press in 1998). This elegant pamphlet brought to public attention the contributions young Bosman, still a schoolboy bumping up his pocket-money, made regularly to *The Sunday Times*. Andersen reproduced some sixteen sparkling pieces of his from that source, all in the vein of the fictional humorous sketch: nine of these are duplicated here as a sufficient sample, together with two others Andersen overlooked or chose not to include (for full details of the first publication of each item, see the Notes on the Text). Written as parodies of now forgotten models, they are a beginner's squibs, knocked off with rattling good humour. Previously 'Saki' had done such blithe pieces for *The Morning Post* of London, notably about Reggie the Johannes-bourgeois who brought such a Cape-to-Cairo quality to the Carlton Hotel.

As a supplement to her selection Andersen also included some pieces written by Bosman once he was no longer a juvenile, technically speaking. An example is his early humorous playlet, "The Urge of the Primordial", first carried in the October, 1925, number of *The Umpa*, the Magazine of the University of the Witwatersrand's SRC, by which

9

date he was a full-time student there and a regular contributor to such miscellanies. Evidently one of the prime topics of undergraduate discussion was how your 'Jim Fish' was to measure up to the expectations of one Clements Kadalie, the noted National Secretary of the Industrial and Commercial Workers' Union, who was making headlines at the time and whom conservative whites dreaded as the bogeyman braggart who was to pull down white civilisation in Africa.

Andersen also omitted from her compilation, or failed to find, several non-fictional pieces Bosman contributed to *The Sunday Times* during the same period of 1921–23. A complete run of back numbers is held in the newspaper stacks of the Greater Johannesburg Public Library as well as in the Rand Afrikaans University library, where the upstart's progress may be followed in full. One suspects that the obstacle to scholars hitherto has been the fact that he contributed under a number of phoney names. In the *Jeppe High School Magazine*, after a tentative 'H. C. B.', he had begun with the first of these – 'Ben Eath' – which is rather well known; as this Ben Eath he appeared through most of Andersen's selection. But Ben Eath was only one of three of Bosman's Bens: there was 'Ben Africa' to come (author of the coyly sexy piece "In the Beginning", smuggled out of Pretoria Central Prison to appear in *The Sjambok* in 1929), as well as 'Ben Onion' (whose extraordinary

Herman Bosman
(seated right) with
young cousins
(National English
Literary Museum)

10

analysis in "Pride of the Reef" was in *The Sjambok* a year later, once the budding ironist was out on parole). A note on this 'Onion' (pronounced o-naai-on, with the stress on the second syllable). Probably this was Bosman's nod of acknowledgement made to the influential ghost-story writer, Oliver Onions, whose collection of short stories, *Widdershins* of 1911, had had such an impact on the florid imaginative style of his fellow schoolmates. From Onions comes Bosman's early habit of using overdetailed descriptions, encrusted with outmoded vocabulary (for example, Chaucer's "whilom"), in pieces that suggest subterranean horrors of which only the true, Beardsley-like artist has a special understanding. Rather disdainfully, that artist never bothers to clarify, or to allow his work to arrive at any proper resolution (examples of this include "The Man-eater" and "Heloise's Teeth").

But *The Sunday Times* was then a lively affair and its editor, J. Langley Levy, kept Bosman well within the conventional parameters. For him Bosman came up with some humdinger nom de plumes to which Andersen seems not to have tumbled. How else was he to earn the usual fee (of one guinea per hundred words), which was not peanuts to the cash-strapped, jocular adolescent behind the mask? One of the earliest of these was 'Will-o'-the-Wisp', who produced "The Needle Test" and "The Dagger" in July and September, 1921. There was the inimitable 'Ferdinand Fandango', whom Aegidius Jean Blignaut in his book on Bosman mentions as one of the labels the plural prodigy had invented; Fandango came up with the satires of South African history as taught in school and of our cricketing habits, reproduced here. There was also one 'Vere de Vere Tornado' no less, author of a rollicking injunction on the vogueish way to keep fit at gym. Once Bosman had reached varsity, he chose 'Pedagogue' as an alias (contributing his sassy "From a Student's Diary").

What is also not commonly known is that, after his short spell as a teacher in the Marico District and the subsequent rather long gaol-term, Bosman continued to contribute to *The Sunday Times*. By 1930 he had settled on using his mother's maiden name to cover himself; in effect as 'Herman Malan' he made a fresh start. He did so with "The Professor" (in *The Sunday Times* in November that year). This begins a sequence of factual-seeming Depression tales. (Other examples are the items Bosman mentions as having given to Stephen Black – "The Night-dress" and "In Church", which are included in the *Old Transvaal Stories* volume in this Anniversary Edition.)

So the supplement of *The Sunday Times* in Johannesburg of the mid-1920s onwards, it would be fair to say, was the most important literary seedbed in town. To it many famous names of the day contributed (Leonard Flemming and Hedley Chilvers), as well as several jaunty characters who were to become permanent members of the Bosman circle: Blignaut himself, his brother Ney, Bosman's own younger brother Pierre and their cheerful associate, Ehrhardt Planjé, are examples. Both Blignaut and Planjé would become Bosman's editors in due course. Yet at *The Sunday Times* the literary tone was not exactly progressive: Levy made a point of preferring the somewhat orthodox, upcoming Sarah Gertrude Millin over the late Olive Schreiner, thought of as still contentious on racial issues, whose posthumous pieces, letters and so on her husband Cron was assiduously publishing. While Oscar Wilde was treated distantly, the opinions of the violently reactionary G. K. Chesterton held sway.

To some extent the Bosman group tried to duck out of the firmly British–South African orientation of the paper by discovering for themselves how to read American. If there was one single book which influenced them all, it was J. A. Hammerton's *The American Short Story* in the Masterpiece Library, noticed extremely favourably and at length in *The Sunday Times* on 3 April, 1921. The unnamed reviewer (if, indeed, it was not the avid fan, Bosman himself) adumbrated several points that were to come up over and over again in Bosman's subsequent career. There was admiration for the psychological skills of Edgar Allan Poe, the atmospherics and delicacy of Nathaniel Hawthorne in his short works and the rambunctious effrontery of Mark Twain. There was Ambrose Bierce to come to terms with, several of whose motifs would prove useful in early Bosman stories, right through to the city-slick essay-excursions of O. Henry himself. Nor did Bosman ever forget the lessons taught by that errant Englishman who took over another British dominion as his own – Stephen Leacock, settled in Canada. In fact, on 1 May, 1921, the local *Sunday Times* pulled off a much publicised coup by signing up Leacock himself as a contributor; from that date (the very day of Bosman's debut), twice a month, he sent in his wise columns of "clean, healthy humour." Evidently he was held in such esteem by South African readers that he was featured on the very front page. Alongside J. H. Amshewitz's piercing cartoons (frequently of General Smuts as some daffy medieval crusader), the Leacock columns certainly made an impressive display. Another such cartoonist, H. E. Winder, brought out from England to embellish the sports pages, would join Bosman and Blignaut in their publishing ventures in the 1930s.

Then, if there was another central tome that influenced the young Bosman, it was a popular, fat, red-spined volume of 1908, most probably held in the Jeppe High School library, entitled *The Golden Humorous Reciter*. There the zestful schoolboy could discover, apart from gobbets of Twain, Leacock, Onions and the other witty authors mentioned above, some lesser known favourites, whom Bosman likewise cited for ever after. There was Max Adeler (whom he always remembered and spelled as Adler) with his excerpts from *Out of the Hurly-burly*; there was the garrulous chaffer, Artemus Ward; and there were bits of the *Condensed Novels* of Bret Harte. That *Golden Humorous Reciter* set the appropriate limits to Edwardian gusto: to paraphrase the introduction, their version of humour was to avoid everything which might offend religious feeling, or offend the refined sensibility; it was to be warm, as all-embracing as the sunshine, and to bathe its objects in a genial and abiding light. Needless to add that, once rebellious Bosman and Blignaut struck off from the constrained world of their schooldays and of *The Sunday Times* in order to establish their own alternative line, they went at it hammer and tongs to offend the prevailing morality in every single respect.

Entrance to the school, used to illustrate Bosman's reminiscence,
"Jeppe High Revisited" (The S. A. Opinion, Oct., 1946)

They had reason to do so. For example, by 1923, in Leacock vein, *The Sunday Times* would have a go at stimulating local humorists by holding what nowadays is scarcely credible: a 'Houseboy Competition.' This called for hilarious true anecdotes about the gaucheries of 'Jim Fish' in from the bush, finding himself adrift among the better adjusted manservant class. Bosman's taking up of this theme in "Johannesburg Christmas Eve" is a brilliant retort to the smug chauvinism encouraged by the regular press. Napier Devitt and C. Selwyn Stokes, both understandably the butts of Bosman's contempt later in this collection, produced suitably bad-taste and demeaning items about their inept 'boys', only to be somewhat stopped in their tracks by an actual one of them: H. D. Tyamzashe. Tyamzashe took exception to their wretched quips about 'drunken natives' and so on, as one might imagine. He would also rather soberly try to put some other such racist slurs to rest in the pages of the other humoristic journalistic venue in town, *The Sjambok*.

The Stokes–Devitt stream of South African writing would eventuate in the *Veld Fire: An African Omnibus* anthology which Bosman reviewed so tersely, although it must be said that that effort did contain work by some writers of great merit (like Fay Goldie and Frank Brownlee). Stella Blakemore receives the same dismissive treatment (and then had to reinvent herself as 'Theunis Krog', the highly successful Afrikaans-language author writing for young adults). But Bosman was not to rest on this matter of the official South African mainstream of creative writing; in 1949 he put out his own reply, the *Veld-trails and Pavements* anthology which proposes the more liberal tradition which has since become the canon (of Schreiner through Pauline Smith, in effect to himself).

As Bosman never fails to acknowledge, the origin of the alternative humorous press for his generation in South Africa was *The Sjambok*, that journal edited by one Stephen Black (1880–1931). Formerly a phenomenally successful actor-manager, who authored his own popular comedies about the foibles and snobberies of South African society, Black had by then been edged off the stage by the boom in cinema, specifically by the advent of the talking motion-pictures Bosman and his cronies so enjoyed. From 1929, often appearing in his "Have You Heard" pieces as the 'Straatlooper', Black put out his weekly, rather acid commentaries. On Black's death in 1931, Bosman took over this role directly (when he was not busy as Herman Malan) in his "By the Kerbside" and other columns. As already mentioned, Black had the temerity

14

to publish smuggled-out pieces by Bosman while the latter was a convict forbidden to publish from his cell. He also published Blignaut, Planjé et al, together with other stalwarts like W. C. Scully, R. R. R. Dhlomo and a poet called Theodore Hermann van Beek – all in *The Sjambok*, for the predictable pittances, with D. C. Boonzaier installed as the political cartoonist to rival Amshewitz. For obvious reasons Black and Bosman had hardly ever met (Black did not move to Johannesburg until after Bosman was behind bars). But when Blignaut as editor revived *The Sjambok*, after *The Touleier* episode, as *The New Sjambok*, on 18 July, 1931, with

D. C. Boonzaier's cartoon of Stephen Black, The Cape Argus, 9 Feb., 1929 (National Library of South Africa, Cape Division)

Herman Malan continuing as his literary editor, he made a point of paying fervent tribute to their predecessor. By the 24 August issue of *The New Sjambok* Blignaut was writing:

> We have had many letters congratulating us on our fine tribute to the memory of the late Mr Stephen Black. A number of people have come forward with the suggestion that we should organise an annual pilgrimage to his grave to commemorate the birth of 'the Friend of the People.' Such a movement will have the hearty support of thousands and we can visualise the day when people will come from the farthest corners of South Africa to do homage to a fine character, a great man. We shall be pleased to sponsor the proposal: one shall regard it as a rare privilege to take the lead in perpetuating the memory of a man who loved us all.

Nevertheless, Bosman's own obituary of Black, printed on 7 November, 1931, adopts a more cussed, flippant tone and rather focuses on one unfortunate 'Miss Cohen.' (She was Black's mistress, the Englishwoman Marjorie Cohen, who had also contributed to the original *Sjambok* religiously.)

Two of H. E. Winder's covers for The Touleier
(Greater Johannesburg Public Library)

The Touleier of the Blignaut–Bosman team that intervened between the two *Sjamboks* was launched with Vol. 1, No. 1, in December, 1930; for a while it overlapped with Black's *Sjambok*. A full-blown literary review, with sensational covers by Winder in art deco style, *The Touleier* ran for another four numbers until May, 1931, by which time it had generated sufficient debts to have to start up again as *The African Magazine*. Then Vol. 1, No. 1, was the only issue of that effort. Bosman's "The Artist" in the second issue of *The Touleier* set the tone. In the next three of March, April and May, 1931, he kept the ball rolling with the "By the Kerbside" columns, from which a substantial sequence is presented here. Some items in them are really thinly disguised advertisements, funny write-ups surely intended to generate sympathetic sponsorship for the journal. Rather than evidence of the abandoned joys of the Jazz Age, they are documents of that Great Depression he describes so well and which saw to it that one spritely publishing venture was doomed. Replete with running gags (see Professor Carey and his manipulator occurring three times), Bosman persevered, like O. Henry, in his New York of Africa (as he remarked), and in the footsteps of Addison and Steele.

Following *The Touleier* as a supplement came *The New Sjambok*, printed in newspaper format, then another revival of an earlier Black publication, *The New L. S. D.* (from which the selection from the "Masters. . . and Others" columns is taken). After *The New L. S. D.* came *The Ringhals* (see "A Nun's Passion") and *Mompara* (of which only one number survives), followed by various revivals of those. Where a run is interrupted or incomplete, the serendipitous researcher often has a second chance, however, because, to the dismay of the bibliographer, with *The New Ringhals* in 1934, and even *The New Sjambok* again and a reversion to *The Sjambok* in 1938–39, Blignaut was wont to reprint several pieces unrevised and sometimes (with titles changed) more than once. An instance is Bosman's "The Gag", credited as by 'W. P. Jacobs' – surely a reference to the writer of such short stories with snapper endings, W. W. Jacobs. "The Gag" must date from much earlier in Bosman's career, although for us it first appears in *The Ringhals* of 20 October, 1939. That was just before Blignaut himself dramatically gave up and left for London, in his case to undertake his war service.

But the truth is that, with the departure of Bosman for overseas, the generative genius had gone out of the alternative South African press. Blignaut admitted to the loss caused by the exit of his young compadre (in a piece in *The Sjambok* of 18 August, 1939, called "The Grandeur of Africa's True Sons"), when he paid his respects in his usual overblown fashion to Bosman and another of his ilk, Roy Campbell:

THE NEW SJAMBOK

Vol. I. No. 2.   JOHANNESBURG, SATURDAY, JULY, 25, 1931.   PRICE 3d.

NOW FOR THE TRUTH

We wish to thank the public heartily for the enthusiastic welcome they extended "The New Sjambok." It has made us feel that our fight in the cause of morality strikes in with the feelings of the majority of our nation. We know that we shall bring about sweeping changes and become a still greater power in the Union by taking counsel of our readers.

We have now acquired our own press and are no longer in daily concern of being murdered by every stray upstart.

Our 100,000 readers can do a great deal to advance our interests, which are also theirs, by supporting The Sjambok Printing Works.

THE NEW SJAMBOK PRINTING WORKS.

Our prices are the most reasonable in Johannesburg. And everyone that supports us is assured of the co-operation of our 100,000 readers

All kinds of printing done - from a visiting card to a novel in six volumes. 'Phone 7814   67 Simmonds Street Johannesburg.   P.O. Box, 3942

17

it will always be remembered to our utter shame that we let these immortal poets go hungry in England. But it is fine to think that at a time when we worshipped little gods made of gold, these two young men, starving and suffering on the alien benches by the Thames, yet sang golden words to unfettered symphonies. Their songs will live for always in a miracle of cadences, and some day our little gods of gold will be hammered into shrines for them. That will be their triumph.

MOMPARA.

Herman Malan, the poet, sitting on a mine-dump. He says

'I am glad that the Rand gold mines were discovered and worked --- the sand-dumps are so soft to sit on'

And so we have reached the natural cut-off point for this volume: the going into voluntary exile from South Africa of Herman Charles Bosman, still in his twenties, early in 1934. He set off for London to seek his future, having no plans ever to return. Undoubtedly one of the factors weighing on his decision to turn his back on his home country was the reception accorded that hot piece called "A Nun's Passion", subtitled "A Xmas Story", carried in *The Ringhals* of December, 1933. The ensuing trial for blasphemy notoriously had both Bosman and Blignaut back in gaol, and for the umpteenth time, on petty charges. Bosman's abrupt departure shortly thereafter is likely to have been prompted by his sense that the Bosman–Blignaut partnership was going to end badly. A further spell in prison would surely have dealt a final blow to his already fragile mental state.

As for Campbell and William Plomer of *Voorslag* before him, for Bosman colonial society had proved itself only too constricting. Out of his lost African dominion, Bosman felt, he might enjoy the freedom of expression he needed to mature his talent. He intended to be more than a merely promising rebel, out on the fringes of the literary world of his day; he meant to measure himself against the great adults of that British Empire which challenged him.

Young Bosman is divided into three sections according to genre – stories, sketches and plays – with the pieces within each section arranged as far as possible by date of publication. The two novella-length works ("Romance: A Sequence" and "Johannesburg Christmas Eve") remained unpublished in Bosman's lifetime, the sources in each case being undated typescripts. The first of them has been placed at the end of the story section, both because it is clearly a more mature effort and also because this fits the movement from very brief 'storyettes' to progressively longer pieces. "Romance: A Sequence" would also probably date from Bosman's first reading of Damon Runyan, whose collection *Guys and Dolls* appeared in 1932.

A considerable proportion of this collection consists of new material – that is, previously unpublished or previously uncollected pieces (in eight cases, attribution has only now been made). Accordingly, a perusal of this volume will mean – even for Bosman cognoscenti – an encounter with an almost unknown figure. This young Bosman is certainly precocious: his first appearance in South Africa's major weekly newspaper (which in the 1920s boasted a circulation "five times larger than that of any other Transvaal weekly") occurred when he was just sixteen, and he went on to publish nearly twenty other pieces there before he left school. Later, as a young journalist freshly out of gaol, he was to provoke prim 1920s and 30s Johannesburg society with stories dealing with incest, blasphemy, eroticism, misogyny, obscenity and other graphic horrors like cannibalism.

De Lancey's illustration for "The Man-eater" (The Touleier, *Apr., 1931*)

It is worth noting that several of these items were written under the rubric of Black's days, 'Life as Revealed by Fiction', which encouraged such journalists to approach their copy as *writers*, writing rawly about their immediate world. So, instead of observing the conventional distinction between 'fact' and 'fiction', writers working in this vein produced a kind of transgressive, borderline genre – to which virtually all of the pieces here, including the experimental plays, belong.

The sheer extravagance of Bosman's use of pseudonyms also suggests that he was trying out various personae in these stories: sly parodist; eroticist; provocateur; hard-boiled writer dealing cold-bloodedly with the seamy sides of life. The young man who emerged from prison in 1930 was no doubt disturbed – and more than ready to launch a barrage at polite society. In London, where some hard lessons in life tempered his devil-may-care attitude, he was to achieve a moderation and distance. From there he was to pour out his longing for South Africa in a series of memorable stories, beginning with "Veld Maiden" in December, 1934, and ending with "Martha and the Snake" in October, 1937. That in this short space of time he produced some twenty stories about the veld, sixteen of which were later to appear in his classic *Mafeking Road*, attests to the chastening effect of an alien environment that was coldly indifferent to his poetic presumptions. But the apprentice still had to get to that point, and his pieces gathered here – sometimes callow, sometimes unsettling, always provocative – were part of this necessary process.

To round off this selection the uncut text of a piece of his written upon his return to South Africa from his long European visit is included. One of the so-called "Texas fragments", his "Johannesburg Christmas Eve" is an example of the kind of retrospect the mature writer was to produce about the period of his early manhood in the vulgar Johannesburg of the Twenties. Presumably it was planned as the opening section of a novel, in which a wide span of characters was introduced and the major plot-lines were got underway. Nevertheless, incomplete or not, Bosman's "Johannesburg Christmas Eve" stands on its own well enough. In it he achieves the historical perspective he had so desired, whereby he could bring his lost days back into an impressive perspective.

Making the near-forgotten forever memorable.

Stephen Gray and Craig MacKenzie
Johannesburg, 2003

David Butler as young Bosman in A Touch of Madness, *2000,*
directed by Nicky Rebelo (photo by Mark Morrison)

The Fowl

P EAL after peal of laughter rang out into the stillness of the afternoon air, as the driver, rocking from side to side in his innocent mirth, sent the taxi through the streets at a tremendous rate. On we rushed madly, spinning round corners on two wheels, driving panic-stricken pedestrians to the side of the road. Suddenly we swerved, turned right about, and sped in the opposite direction back to town, the while the chauffeur gave vent to his glee.

"Hi!" I cried, as we jumped round another corner, "what's the matter?"

Convulsed with merriment, and with difficulty suppressing another roar, he shouted back: "I wonder where the warders think I am. By now they must be searching all over the asylum for me."

Regardless of consequences, I jumped.

Having sorted myself, and discovered that there were no bones broken, I set off back along the road we had come, and had walked some distance, when an infuriated farmer rushed out, dangling a very emaciated-looking fowl, which, he heatedly explained, I had run over in the motor-car. As we were both splendid talkers, quite a large crowd had soon collected to hear our fluency, whereupon I deemed it advisable to depart from the field, handing him the seven shillings he demanded, and receiving the fowl in exchange. The rest of my journey was a perpetual misery, as I walked along with an air of unconcern, holding the bird at some considerable distance from me, and not deigning to heed the guffaws of the passers-by. When I arrived at the gate, Ella, sweet woman, was already waiting for me.

"Look here, dovey," I said, "see what your ickle lovey has brought you."

Seizing the bird, and a sufficient excuse for my lateness not being forthcoming, she playfully hit me with a poker over my cranium, begging me to help with the dishes. Not being able to refuse so small a favour to anyone, leave alone Ella (she was still clutching the poker), I retired to the kitchen.

Suddenly, with a swish-swish of feminine draperies, accompanied by the thud of heavy feet, Ella strode in. I stood for some moments, lost in admiration for this wonderful woman. Her features were as beautiful as the dawn (a specially red dawn, that is); her lustrous orbs were like two glass beads stuck in a piece of clay, while her melodious voice vividly reminded one of velvet and tinkling cymbals as she rasped out:–

"So you thought your taxi killed that fowl, did you?"

Before I could dispel so absurd a notion, she concluded: "It has been dead for over a week."

The Needle Test

BILLIKINS has always read his newspaper studiously, he has taken to heart everything that they have had to tell him and almost invariably has he practised what they preached. It was by perusing a newspaper, in fact, that he managed to obtain a quite unexpected rise in his salary – though as things transpired he was jolly lucky to have retained his job.

It happened this way. Last Sunday morning Billikins was devouring with his usual intensity the contents of *The Sunday Times Farmers' Supplement* when his eye caught sight of an article which showed the reader how to determine the sex of eggs. The method was extraordinarily simple. All one had to do was to put the egg into an egg-cup and hold a needle, suspended by a piece of cotton, about an inch over and above it. If the needle swung round in a circle the egg contained a rooster, if it swung backwards and forwards it contained a hen, and if it remained stationary the contents of the egg were not fertile. The article went on to explain that those interested could test the accuracy of this method by holding a needle similarly above their own heads, when the result would be the same as in the first two instances.

"By Jove!" said Billikins, deeply, even profoundly impressed. "By Jove!"

The next morning Mr Jinks, the stern manager of the Daisy Steel Corporation, strode into the office of his junior clerks and suddenly stood still in amazement at the sight of Billikins holding a needle, attached to a piece of cotton, over the head of Miss Flipplop, the pretty typist.

"What is the meaning of this?" he demanded, in a voice that resembled nothing so much as an underground fall of rock on a large scale.

"By Jove, sir, we are carrying out a most amazing experiment," announced Billikins. "It works absolutely!" He went on to explain the method and thrust the *Farmers' Supplement* into the hands of Mr Jinks, after which he showed him how the needle swung backwards and forwards over the head of the lady typist. He demonstrated its slow circular movement over the office boy's cranium. "What do you think of it, sir?" concluded the excited Billikins eagerly.

The manager began to show interest. "Remarkable," he said, "remarkable. Now for a little lark, don't you know. Suppose I sit down here and you try the needle over my head – what?"

"Why, certainly, sir," cried the delighted Billikins.

The manager sat down in the middle of a group of clerks who had abandoned their work in order to witness the tremendous experiment. The hubbub of conversation died away as Billikins advanced to the chair and resolutely held the needle above the bald managerial head. All eyes were centred on the shining needle, and the atmosphere became tense. Seconds passed, they seemed years to Billikins. Beads of perspiration burst out on his forehead, his breath became hard, his arm tired as though he was holding an intolerable weight.

Mr Jinks bust the still, deathlike silence. "Well, what is it doing?" he chuckled.

Billikins, by this time white as a sheet, became suddenly inspired, his wrist turned sharply and the manager looked up to see the needle spinning round his head at a million revolutions a second.

"Ha, ha, ha! Now tell me what does that show?" said the manager as he rose from the chair.

"Intense masculinity, I should say, sir," gasped the exhausted Billikins, in reply.

"He, he, he!" Mr Jinks went back to his own office, chuckling with delight.

At the end of the month Billikins found that he had got a substantial rise in his salary. "What would I have got," he reflected, "if I had told him that the needle had refused to budge, and that therefore he had an infertile brain?"

The Dagger

THERE will be found, I think, one great outstanding quality in this short story – its shortness. There are several excellent reasons for making it short, and the first that suggests itself to my mind is the fact that it is so much easier, and so much less effort is required, to write briefly than at any length.

But it must not be thought for a moment that, in writing a really short, short story, I am being actuated by purely selfish motives. If such a belief be possible I must hasten to dispel it by showing that the reason I have given already fades into utter insignificance when compared with the next and mightiest reason, which concerns the welfare of the reader himself.

What right have I, what right has any man to ask his readers to strain their eyesights and nerves by following, through half the dimly lit night, and with perspiration and palpitating hearts, the varying fortunes of a hero and a heroine who on later reflection seem to have, in most cases, been thoroughly asinine throughout the entire volume? In fact, it is a very strong conviction of mine that all the people who write at length are none other than the hired agents of opticians and nerve specialists.

Is it reasonable, in these days of time-saving devices and American tourists, to expect any man to wade through a struggling sea of five or six hundred pages to discover the plot of a story when he might take a short cut and find out all about it in a few brief lines?

After all has been said, the really magnificent things of life are sent by nature in meteor-like fashion. It is a firmly established fact that Christmas only comes once a year, and the annual holiday of the vast majority of people lasts not 365 days but only 14. Exactly the same thing applies to fiction. A story should be like a flash of elemental lightning – powerful, swift and poignant; it should not be like a journey on the SAR – slow, rambling and wearisome.

If any further authority is required I would refer my reader to that well-known aphorism: "Brevity is the soul of wit."

It is, therefore, with complete assurance that I commence this really very short story:

"The blood-red dagger gleamed in the powerful rays of the electric light – "

A thought has suddenly struck me – I have already used all the space at my disposal. Brevity being my principle, brief must I be, and therefore the remainder of this short story, remarkable for its shortness, must be held over for another week. This certainly seems rather a pity, but the splendid consolation of it is that it will afford me an opportunity of drawing another magnificent cheque from the kindly Editor.

Three Phases

HE grey twilight had already given place to darkness, when, having removed the tell-tale particles of confetti which still adhered to her dress, the bride, radiantly beautiful, stepped from her compartment into the corridor. Softly she stole to where her husband was standing, too intently gazing at an object he held in his hands to notice her approach. When he raised the light-green frame to his lips and kissed it ecstatically, her curiosity was thoroughly aroused. Standing on tiptoe, she looked over her husband's shoulder, and saw that the light-green frame contained a photo of herself. She silently returned to her compartment, and far into the night was still wondering whether she was worthy of such noble, high-minded love.

That had been the beginning, but after a year or two her husband's passion had worn off – his ardour had given way to business cares, and with the gradual, almost imperceptible estrangement between them, love had grown rapidly between her and a returned explorer, around whom still clung the glamour of adventure. Yet through it all, in her inmost heart she pitied her staid, stolid husband, whose imagination never rose above his business affairs.

It was on a Friday afternoon that matters came to a climax. Long she stood looking at her lover; then, when the full realisation of what had occurred dawned upon her, she sank down to the floor of the drawing-room and knelt beside her dead husband. She felt incensed against the world in general, but particularly resented her lover's action. She felt now that she hated him with an intense hatred, for had he not killed her husband – her husband who, after all, had ever borne her a passionate affection? As her eyes lighted upon the little light-green photo-frame, which, having fallen from her husband's pocket, was lying face downwards on the carpet, she remembered that incident in the train during their honeymoon, and her cup of sorrow was full to the brim. She lifted it up and looked at it. It was the same green frame she knew so well, but gazing at her with laughing eyes – was the face of another woman!

The Dilettante

E VERY morning on my way to the office I found him standing in front of the Library, waiting for the doors to open.

His lofty, intellectual brow increased the general rigidity of his ascetic countenance, while that far-away gaze in his steel-blue eyes showed how distant from mundane matters his thoughts were.

At night, on my return, I noticed that he was always the last to leave the Library, and I observed that occasionally there was a wistful, half-regretful look on his face, while at other times his countenance bore an expression of mild complacency – even of benignity and broad philanthropy.

But in the morning there was no mistake about that strenuous eagerness which pervaded his features – which even showed through that look of intense absorption as he stood on the pavement, waiting for the Library doors to open. . .

Each day when I went to the office he was waiting on the pavement; each day when I returned the Library doors were just being locked behind him, until, having indulged in much speculation to no purpose, I determined to once and for all solve the problem as to which were the books that so irresistibly drew that intellectual giant to the Library.

He was already waiting on the pavement the following morning when I arrived, intent on finding a solution to the puzzle. As soon as the doors swung open he rushed in, while I followed some distance in his wake. Having arrived at the Reference Department, he went up to a shelf, took down a book, and with a sigh of placid contentment plunged into Chapter XXXIV of the seventeenth volume of *The Inner Secrets of Betty's Boudoir*.

Following his example, I likewise took down a volume and commenced reading.

And in the blissful days that followed I was the first to arrive on the pavement, impatiently tapping the kerb with my foot, waiting for the Library doors to open. . .

Fraternal Love

LOUDLY the man opposite me declaimed against the injustice of our social system. "It is not that I've an axe to grind," he said, "for I do not blame my brother in the least." Hereupon he commenced the story of his life.

"We were two brothers," he said, "and when the late war broke out, and the world went back to the caves and dens of savagery – when nations, with the blood-lust upon them, sprang at each other's throats, when the horizon was lurid with the flames of burning cities – then one brother responded to the call of duty; the other," he said, in tones scornful and contemptuous, "the other shirked his obligations and remained at home.

"For four years the opposing banners floated over the blood-stained fields. The swords were dripping with the best and bravest blood. The earth, filled with pain and darkness, with misery and distress, was left without a star. In the trenches the men, in addition to facing the enemy, had to battle with the obstacles of nature, and in scores they were scattered, like autumn's withered leaves, by the cavalry of the icy blast and the infantry of the snows.

"In the meantime," the man opposite me continued, his brow clouded, and anger blazing from his eyes, "the one who stayed at home speedily amassed a fortune. How he had the heart to retain it passes my comprehension, considering the fact that every day of his existence he must have met the withered hand of beggary and the bloodless lips of famine.

"Then, when the clouds of battle had rolled away, and the sword was sheathed, the one who had joined up, his duty done, returned, penniless and broken in health and spirit – and he was pushed aside by the cold hand of his brother's avarice, for, owing to their altered circumstances, the other refused to recognise him now.

"Mind you," the man concluded, "I don't blame my brother, but still – "

He looked at me curiously as I endeavoured to console him. "You see," he said, "I am the one who stayed at home. Still, I don't blame my brother for going. . . "

31

A Sad Tale

VENICE!

Well may the poet in his ecstasy have remarked, "See Venice and die!" Reader, can you picture to yourself this city, slumbering on the azure Adriatic, under the blue of the vaulted heavens, while the gentle, ozone-laden zephyrs are dreamily wafted to and fro?

What's that? You can't? You're a blamed idiot, then.

However, the question of whether or not you are able to appreciate the beauties of Venice is of little consequence really, for the scene of my story is laid in a street in Johannesburg.

Having suddenly stopped speaking to myself, I, the hero, with determination clearly written upon my ascetic features, set off in the direction of a chemist's, which establishment I was on the point of entering when, to my unbounded astonishment, Petroleum K. Jones, an old acquaintance of mine, came out of it. I held up my hand to stay his progress.

"Don't stay my progress," Jones exclaimed, petulantly.

"All right," I replied; "but what have you been doing in this shop, anyway?" Averting his gaze, my friend held up for my inspection a phial, the label on which read:

CYANIDE OF POTASSIUM.

"Heavens!" I gasped. "Is – is it as bad as all that?"

Jones bowed his head in meek submission.

"Yet consider for a moment the result of this rash action," I pursued. "You'll be chucked into your grave, with the rain soaking into the soil, your tombstone dripping with wet, and the storms of winter moaning and raging over your buried head. And – and," I concluded, "cyanide has a horrible taste."

His resolution having gradually weakened throughout this appeal, Jones at these words fully realised the error of his ways, whereupon, bursting into tears, he promised to give himself another chance.

I, however, was adamant. "What guarantee will I have," said I, "that you won't take your life after all, the moment you're out of my sight? For safety's sake, hand over the bottle to me."

Having eagerly complied with this request, the would-have-been-suicide turned and took his departure.

The while a wistful smile played over my expressive countenance, I watched my friend disappear round the corner. Then, my hand trembling slightly, I drew out the stopper and swallowed the contents of the phial. A moment later I was lying in the middle of the street, with my toes turned up, contentedly waiting for the hearse.

The Watch

WITH gentle, tear-dimmed eyes and my hands thrust deep into my trouser pockets, I stood shivering on the pavement, looking back through Time's dark avenue upon a fading past.

This, then, I reflected, was my return from the cold, hard world, whither I had gone to make known the great truths I had discovered – truths which no one had heard or wanted to hear. As the moaning night-wind swept past me, whispering solemn secrets to the listening leaves, I thought of the friends I had known and laughed with, now lying forever silent under the waving grass. I thought of death-beds stained with bitter tears, and graves in trackless deserts.

It was a cold night and I was glad that the streets were dark and deserted – glad that there was no one about to recognise or to hail me. Turning a corner, I came upon a man whose blotched and heavy face denoted the drunkard; but what especially attracted my attention was a watch-chain dangling invitingly from his waistcoat.

"After all," I pondered, "what is honesty but the by-word of fiends, and who but fools march and fight, bleed and die, beneath its tawdry flag?"

Already my hand was stealing towards the object of my desires when, hearing the sound of approaching footsteps, I slunk across the road. Only then I realised to what depths of degradation I had actually sunk, for this nocturnal wanderer was none other than the minister, whose guileless features, frank and open as the day, were thrown into vivid relief by the light of a street-lamp.

How sordid was my intention – how base and misspent had been my whole life when compared with this good man's righteousness. Yet there was no need for despondency, I determined; my case was not beyond all hope.

Thus, resolving to make one more attempt at my reclamation, I again set out upon the road of Life, with honesty and virtue, as personified in the minister, to be my guiding star.

I took a last look round.

The minister was just disappearing round the corner. So was the watch.

The Deserter

AVING drawn up the remnants of his forces in battle array, the Red leader harangued his men, exhorting them to fling off their yokes of oppression and reach out after the banner of Liberty, floating on the far horizon. "You've won, boys!" the general cried, at the conclusion of his passionate oration, every sentence of which was enthusiastically applauded by the revolutionaries in their trenches. "But, remember, don't kick the capitalist when he's down: hit him with a pick-handle."

Hardly had the thunder of applause died down when, with a curious sound, like the wailing of a tired wind, a bullet went whistling over their heads and crashed through a plate-glass window, whereupon, wishing he had been a better man and knew more hymns, a Scotsman named Van der Merwe flung away his rifle and raced off madly in the direction of home and safety.

Appalled by such flagrant desertion in the face of the foe, the general made use of language which, no doubt, in calmer moments he would regret. "Fetch him back!" he shouted at length, in a voice like tearing linoleum. Untrustworthy though many members of the commando may have been, there was one man, at all events, whose soul was not dead to all honour – one man who responded to duty's call.

Amid cheers this individual set off in pursuit, and, leaping lithely over the obstacles in the road, gradually gained upon his quarry. The general, meanwhile, had hastily climbed a lamp-post, from which point of vantage he shouted out the progress of the race. "He's only half a block behind him," he cried, "and gaining like mad. There's only ten yards separating them now! Three yards! Two feet! He's only about six inches behind the deserter –

"Damnation!" the general exclaimed as, slipping from the lamp-post, he clasped his brow in anguish: "He's five yards in front of him!"

Caste

PROFESSOR Phineas C. Finn, his brow moist and his hand trembling, was in a condition of deepest melancholy bordering on blank despair, as he gazed with unseeing eyes at the tongues of flame which leapt up, flared and subsided.

No, perhaps it is not an unheard-of or, for that matter, even an unusual occurrence for a professor of entomology to marry his housekeeper; but if, as in this instance, the household should include the professor's twenty-year-old daughter, unpleasantness is more than likely to result.

The professor realised this fact only too clearly, and therefore he sat, sorrowfully contemplating the consequences of this rash act. How was he to break this news to his daughter – his daughter who held such pronounced views of her own regarding the proper management of menials? Small wonder that he shuddered at the sound of every footstep – that he quivered and shook with chilling fear at the slightest creak of a door being opened.

He pictured to himself that look of incredulous bewilderment overspreading his daughter's features; vividly he saw her haughty countenance change from amazement to scornful disdain as the truth would begin to dawn upon her; then, finally, he beheld her when, bursting into tears, she rushed headlong from his study, her heart for ever broken, her ideals one and all shattered beyond repair!

The thought of his daughter's distress now became intolerable to the professor, yet from the truth there was no escape. Admittedly this position was untenable, but what was to be done? What could be done?

Thus ruminating on the immediate future, when his daughter's azure eyes, unused of yore to aught but laughter, would be swimming in tears, because her father had married beneath him, the professor sat forward in his armchair, gazing with unseeing eyes at the tongues of flame as they leapt up, flared and subsided, waiting for his daughter's entrance.

He waited in vain, however, for that morning she had eloped with the milk-man.

Beyond the Beyond

So I plonked down the nominal sum of ten shillings. "Put me in touch with gran'pa, please," I said to the medium.

"Hello! Is that you, gran'pa?" I asked.

"I guess that's me right enough, son" – came the response.

"And what's it like up there, gran'pa?" I queried further.

"Everything here at the back of the Illimitable," he replied, "is bright and beautiful, and our happiness is complete. Jack the Ripper and Bill Shakespeare here say the same. . . What's that?. . . Strong smell of garlic, did you say?. . . Oh, that's Julius Caesar leading the Portuguese band."

"What's death like, gran'pa?" I questioned finally. "Is the transition at all sudden?"

Hereupon my aged ancestor related the circumstances attendant on his departure to the back of the Immeasurable.

"And so, as the young fellow kept on urging me to accompany him, I at length gave way to his entreaties, but, needless to say, I still very much regret my folly. Well, although realising that it was a rashly venturesome business altogether, I nevertheless got into that motor-car of his and with great trepidation watched him crank it up. He then clambered up into the driver's seat and away we went, along the pleasant country roads, where the wayside flowers were all blossoming into rich and glorious life.

"We had travelled along in this fashion for some time, when my companion all of a sudden let go the steering-wheel and shouted, 'Look out! Jump for it!' Hardly had the warning left his lips ere the motor crashed into some obstacle – apparently a brick wall – and I was flung out on to the grass.

"I looked up at the man bending over me, and instantly recognised him as a friend of mine who some years previously had suddenly left his residence, without offering an explanation of the odour of dead bodies proceeding from his cellar. He had soon afterwards been tried, found guilty and hanged.

"'Are you in pain?' he now asked.

"I gazed at him in some amazement. I wondered if by some miracle he had cheated the gallows after all. 'But – but you are dead!' I ejaculated.

"He smiled. It was the same guileless, joyous smile which he had bestowed upon the judge on the morning of his trial.

"'So are you,' he said."

In the Beginning

ADAM had ceased to be shy, Eve not entirely; but there was a something beginning to thrill her whenever she was in Adam's presence. Still, the sensation was as nothing when compared to the fire she felt on the first occasion he touched her. The touch had been entirely unpremeditated, and the resulting sensation had come as a surprise to Adam and as a revelation to Eve. She had asked Adam to pick her a large fruit which was out of her reach, and he had grudgingly acquiesced, for the male of the species – the first bachelor known to history – had yet to be taught that chivalry should be the share of the fairer sex. And then had come the wonderful discovery.

Adam had, by accident, carelessly touched the lily of a hand belonging to Eve when he had yielded her the fruit he picked.

What a delightful leap his heart gave! What a queer pain gripped at the soul of Eve!

For a moment Adam was nonplussed, but was soon roused to action when he noticed that Eve had consumed the luscious dainty he had given her.

She looked straight at him, straight into his clean clear-sighted, flashing eyes. Adam flushed a deep crimson, and it was the first sensation of its kind that he had experienced, the first new look to adorn his face with additional beauty and attraction. He returned Eve's look with a directness that startled her. She dropped her gaze, and Adam rose unbidden, and picked another fruit. It was the dawn of chivalry – and Adam's first lesson in manners. It was a simple result of as simple a cause: Eve would be pleased by another gift and Adam by another touch.

All signs of bashfulness had fled. Adam sought only to gratify his desires by another touch. He handed Eve the fruit and she put out her hand, and almost lingeringly their fingers touched. The blood raced fiendishly fast to Eve's face, and again she averted the burning look of her mate. But she was in no haste to take wholly into her possession the natural dainty lying on Adam's palm.

The gripping of the soul Eve had first experienced when Adam first touched her became more definite and cried for something she did not understand. And Adam was by no means in a hurry to get rid of the fruit. It was Eve's pleasure to be slow in accepting his first gift – well then, it would be a joy to him continuing to feel the magic of Eve's touch. The fruit remained in his hand, and her fingers were moving up and down the strong digits.

The two were sorely perplexed by the problem confronting them – they had not the least conception of what was the matter; all they knew was, that in the touch of hand and hand, was some wonderful attainment.

Eve was the first to recover, she took the proffered fruit and quickly consumed it. Adam was spellbound. Long since he had ceased eating. He was content to gaze at the companion that man's first operation had given him. He found, as in the touch, that some satisfaction was to be got in the mere looking at Eve. Here was a new domain, unknown and unexplored. Adam had seen no other thing resembling Eve; she was unique, stood alone and was desirable, but he did not know that it was this that caused him to rivet his gaze on her. Still his eyes followed the graceful curve of her neck, and instinctively he knew that it was good; and so the whole survey of his companion was food for a great deal of thought and speculation. He was unaware that that which he was bestowing on her was admiration, as little as knew she that it was this very adoration that pleased and thrilled.

The sun was rising higher and higher, and the Euphrates was calling to them. Her cool water made music that was sweet and maddening. The scents of the aromatic trees that grew on the river's banks loaded the atmosphere with an alluring perfume. Strangely coloured birds flashed over the semi-transparent rainbow water of the river. Animals, softly furred, sped out of Adam and Eve's way as they betook themselves to the stream. There was laughter in the air, magic in the turf, the song of spring in the hearts of all creatures and something akin to exultation in the bosom of Adam. Eve was experiencing another fit of bashfulness. It was delightful, but, nevertheless, she was troubled – she could not understand why she was pleased to be in Adam's presence. At the back of her mind was still the memory of the ejectment and the curse – and before she had viewed Adam with a satisfaction never amounting to more than indifference.

But there was the river; its summons was imperative, and Adam accompanying her, likewise. There was something grim in his presence. She felt that it was right that he should be with her; her woman's soul cried for protection; she could hardly fancy herself in future going alone for a swim – hardly fancy Adam leaving her to have his plunge higher up the river and out of sight.

When she disrobed, her hands hesitated to remove entirely the fig leaves round her waist. Still the stream called, the subtle scents stirred her inmost soul, and Adam was looking at her, the first time with a wonderful light in his eyes. She noticed that he was in the same predicament as herself. He had undone the simple knot of the leafy covering that hung about him, but was waiting on her to remove it entirely. Eve felt her cheeks grow warm as he stood looking at her. And the question was answered from an unexpected source.

Eve heard a hiss, and turning about looked into the eyes of a snake. Fear gripped at her heart, but with a cry she leaped to Adam's side; and he, with outstretched arms received her in a close embrace. The snake, not unmindful of the curse, fled on the first sign of movement from Eve. And there she stood next to Adam – all naked and fair; and he did not release her from his passionate hold, being happy and as oblivious as she to their nudity.

What strange attainment was there when their bodies touched! What joy surged to their souls!

Eve gave Adam a yearning look, and he bent his face to hers, and their lips met. It was mankind's first kiss!

And Adam's lips lingered on Eve's – and Eve kept her soft round arms round his neck. They had met. The water was forgotten, as all else was forgotten, even the pain that Adam had experienced after his rib had been removed.

There on the banks of the Euphrates was but a single soul, a single person, for two people stood as one – entranced and drinking in each other's beauty.

Adam released his arm and with a caressing touch stroked the long, golden, sunbathed tresses belonging to his sweet companion, joying in the soft touch to which his being responded with a soul-satisfying vibration. And Eve nestled her comely head on the broad and comfortable breast that surged with friendly delight. She drew Adam's head to hers, and tasted again and again of the delight of the *kiss*.

How long they stood thus they did not know, but it was long. At length, when the sun was seeking his downward path, and evening came hurrying on the scene, the two betook themselves slowly to their arbour, which stood on the edge of the great forest of fruit-trees.

Stars rushed into the sky, clouds were scudding across the pale face of the moon, and the Euphrates was still making mad music – but in the arbour Eve lay in the arms of Adam.

The Gag

"HELLO! 'Sthat you, Toni? We're goin' to give Danny de works."
There was a 'click.' Then silence.
Mouth agape, I glared at the telephone. The receiver fell unheeded from my ear. My hands began to tremble and my lips twitched apoplectically.

You see, my name's Danny. I was living in Chicago – the birthplace of hot-pots, rackets and hard-boiled gangsters, who thought no more of ventilating your lungs than playing a game of ludo – and on top of all that I'm highly strung and sensitive. Or perhaps 'jumpy' is the best word.

So you can understand that when I got that brief, staccato message over the wires I wasn't in a particularly playful mood.

And to complicate matters I was alone in the house. The wife and kids had gone to sniff sea air for the week. And I was unarmed. Not that my paltry revolver would have made any difference when the tat-tat guns got busy, but somehow there's a vague feeling of security in the grip of a butt.

My first thought was that the phone wires had got tangled, and that I had received the message intended for my executioner's buddy, Toni. They say forewarned is forearmed but that was so much eye-wash in my case. Anyhow, I hurried to the window and gave the street the once-over to see if I could find any lurking crook with a machine-gun tucked away in his hip-pocket. But all I saw was a guilty-looking cat lapping up some milk from a lone bottle on a doorstep.

However, I was not deceived. Invisible though they must be I felt sure that my enemies had surrounded the house. I was being put on the spot, and it was not a pleasant sensation. Again my eyes snooped along the sidewalks and down the dark alleys and once more I saw nothing. But the vain search had no reassured effect. You see, gangsters act that way. They've been known to arrive in the laundry. And I knew quite a dozen fellows who wouldn't have minded slipping in with the bacon if they thought they had half a chance of drilling me between the ribs.

So I watched and waited. But the place remained empty. And that's an obvious sign of trouble in Chicago. To describe it in the most diluted terms, the situation didn't look healthy.

Then, quite suddenly, a man seemed to pop up in the middle of the street and walk over to my door. Under his arm he carried a large leather satchel, and with a shudder up my spine I visualised its contents.

At first I dived into the wardrobe but forsook that sanctuary when I realised it wasn't bullet-proof. No, there was no alternative, and when the bell sounded – a short, menacing ring – I decided to meet my end bravely.

I went calmly down the stairs, feeling like the hero of a two-reel drama, threw open the door, shut my eyes and bared my breast. I waited expectantly for the inevitable explosion which would lessen the population of Chicago by one man. But nothing happened. I opened my eyes. The man before me was smiling as if he had just been told a particularly weak joke.

At this moment I realised my mistake. The stranger on the doorstep was merely an innocent citizen on an equally innocent mission. I pulled him into the house and slammed the door. My next task was to keep him with me, and that was easy when I heard what he wanted.

"I represent a life-insurance firm," he said, and before he could describe his business any further I had cut him short.

"You're just the man I've been looking for," I said, pulling forward a chair. This was luck. A chance to insure myself on the brink of death. The laugh would certainly be on the insurance company when they identified my corpse on the cold slab in the morgue.

The stranger rattled papers and finally I had signed on a dozen dotted lines. I made out a cheque and my visitor rose. I went to the door and we shook.

"Glad to have been of service," he said.

He opened the door and stood on the step outside. As he reached the pavement he turned.

"Quite a clever gag, don't you think?" he remarked. "Fetches me a whole heap of clients."

"What gag?" I asked, mystified.

"It begins: 'Hello! 'Sthat you, Toni?'" he answered.

From a figure retreating hastily down the street I heard the menace: "'We're goin' to give Danny de works. . . '"

The Man-eater

I couldn't help feeling that the man was mad, somehow. Especially the way his eyes flashed when he laughed. But also I couldn't help knowing that he was sane. Only it was a terrible kind of sanity. It was that dreadful sanity of the poet who finds himself a king amongst men, because he knows those dazzling words that a child knows, and that a grown man cannot understand. I mean the way in which a poet is sane when he clasps the stars and sweeps his hand across the firmament, and talks obscenely about the way the red sun sets in blood, feeling the passion of nature, unconscious of the psycho-sexual imagery.

Anyway, it is a strange story that he told me. If it is the truth, then it is God's truth. And if it is a lie, then it is God's lie, also, for it is a lie worthy of Him who invented the universe, and who first spoke about the leviathan. Or perhaps it is all just madness, this man I met on the Town Hall steps, and his story and the café in which we sat and talked. For I know that in some things I am altogether mad.

It was early on a Sunday evening. The Salvation Army Band played between the Town Hall and the Post Office.

The band was playing red music. It is only now that the scientists in their pitiful way, adjusting their crude, steel instruments with faltering hands, are trying to establish the relationship between sound and colour – as if sound and colour were not exactly the same thing. What a hopeless lot of blundering fools these scientists are! They cut off a little bit of life – that trivial side that is material and is of no importance, anyway, because it is dead already – and with clumsy gauges and measures they try to find out what it is all about. The scientist's instrument – what could be more grotesquely inaccurate than the microscope? Then, when the scientist gets his dead results, he finds that they are all useless, and that the artist and the poet dreamt of them all thousands of years ago. This is the most pathetic situation in the universe, the puny scientist pitting his blundering instruments against the artist's dreams. Usually, the scientist is a hundred thousand years behind the poet. Sometimes, with an inspired mental leap, in which his instruments have no share, the scientist gets quite close to the poet – say within fifty thousand years of him. And all the time it is with things that don't matter to the artist. Those things which

44

to the poet really are vital matters, the scientist never even begins to understand.

As I was saying, the Salvation Army played red music. It was a hymn tune. The words spoke of love and Jesus, but the sounds were of flames and blood and murder, and of that other kind of love that people do not know when they love only Jesus. But it is a love that Jesus knew. For Jesus was an artist. Pilate understood, and for that reason he called Him a king. Pilate understood that the penniless artist, with dust on his sandals and star-dust in his heart, was a king amongst men. This is the greatest thing that can ever be said for the Jews as a nation: they once had a king who was also an artist.

"Though your sins be as scarlet,
They shall be white as snow."

The men and women of the Army sang the words when the band stopped. But they sang in a peculiar way, as though they were not altogether happy about it, as though vaguely they felt something in the music that was born of the age-old lusts and rapine of the world. It was as though they could not sing to their God in the manner that their fathers of the dawn had done; they could not sing paradisiacal words to a red tune that told exultantly of rape. So they sang that hymn as though they were afraid of its nakedness. It is only children and grown men with minds like children's who are not afraid of nakedness, whether it is in a woman or a sunrise. Only the pure in heart can face elemental things without putting a hand up to their eyes.

Red is for blood sacrifice and for hate and for love; yellow is for the sullen kiss of a dying autumn; purple is for pain, but it is an emperor's pain. And so it is with all music and all colour and all words. But there is no purpose in my going on to explain these things, because no one will understand them but a poet, and a poet needs no explanations.

Anyway, it was there, on that Sunday evening, that I met the man who told me this story. Perhaps it is a true story, as *The Odyssey* and *The Arabian Nights* are true stories, or perhaps it is merely a lie, as history is a lie. But you must understand that the man I am going to tell you about now, and the café we went into, and what happened there are all things that I have invented. For a change, I have decided to invent a story of my own. As a rule, I am indolent, and, like Shakespeare, I am content to crib my plots from lesser men, who have sweated over the medium of a good enough theme, and then have not been able to make use of it, until a man with genius came along and took their laboured contrivance away from them and infused into it the breath of a wild and a gorgeous and a gigantic life. Sometimes it is a monstrous life. But it is not the inert, pallid thing that the mechanic constructs out of hammered words. Actually, I know of only two writers who are not mechanics. God be with them both. They need it.

"Look at the fat fool with the drum," a man said to me casually; "what does he know about the God he's thumping the drum for?"

I looked at the man who spoke to me thus. He was a medium-sized man with dark eyes that had fires in them; when he laughed there was madness in his eyes. I understood then that I had very much in common with him, and although our laughter was not similar, yet we laughed about similar things. That, of course, is much. It means that in the big things of life our reactions were the same, in the manner of the men of Sodom, all of whom experienced identical emotions when they learnt that there were two angels staying in their city.

"He's a pot-bellied Philistine," I responded. "He's a slave with a dirty soul. I wouldn't even be surprised if he's a devoted husband."

You know, you can tell these things about a man. For instance, there is that Johannesburg artist who can see as clearly as I can. I spoke to him only a few days ago. He got the sack from a local newspaper because he drew the editor as he is.

"Yes," the man with the dark eyes answered, "you're right, of course. I know that man. He's not a regular member of the Army. And he is a devoted husband. You know what that means? If there is anything apt to make a clean-minded woman commit indecent assault it is to have a devoted husband."

Here Le Roi spoke only half the truth. (He told me that his name was Le Roi.) Whether they are in love or otherwise, no man and woman can live together for longer than six weeks without permanent injury to their spiritual qualities.

"The fat pig," I remarked. Why I said that I don't know.

"Do you like human beings?" my acquaintance asked.

"Not particularly," I said.

"I mean, do you like them to eat?" he explained.

"I don't know," I answered; "I have never eaten a man."

"Well, I have," Le Roi said. "And I'll never forget the taste. Your talking about a pig recalls that to mind. Human flesh, boiled with cabbage and potatoes, tastes like sweet pork. And that's how that fat drummer will taste. It would give me great satisfaction to eat part of him. Only, of course, it would make me sick. I had too much of it, that time. And you know that when you have had a surfeit of anything, the revulsion lasts for a long while. To you my slight prejudice may seem unreasonable, but nowadays nothing short of hunger could induce me to eat a human being. Like sweet pork – "

Le Roi spat on the pavement.

For a while we stood on the edge of the crowd. I had come there to study the superb technique employed by the woman whose duty it was to bring the collection up to three pounds sterling. It was a foregone conclusion that she would realise that sum. But it was thrilling to watch her moves. When there was another seventeen shillings to come, she cajoled her audience with sweet if faded phrases. At nine shillings she stormed at them. With five shillings short of the amount her voice was very low and soft; there was a note of restrained hopefulness in her utterances; there was the fever the canvasser feels with results in sight. The last half-crown took long to come. The woman turned round several times, shaking her right hand about. In her one-handed gesticulation there was an old symbolical significance that goes back to Ancient Egyptian priest-craft; but the woman did not know it and the crowd around her did not know it. Yet those are mystical elements that are common to all ages. In every religion there is something for which there is no word. And here was this woman, a carnal Christian and an unimaginative mendicant, performing that sacred gesticulative ritual that you find in the *Egyptian Book of the Dead* and amongst small boys.

The half-crown came.

A man threw it so that it splashed on to the pavement. I thought of Le Roi's spitting on to the pavement. The two actions seemed so much alike.

The woman flung back her head. She looked triumphant. With her chin up, for a moment the flabby wrinkles in her neck did not show. The crowd around the band felt with her in the consummation. She was tired, but there was a light in her eyes that came from the satisfaction of knowledge.

I glanced around me. A tall girl on the edge of the crowd encountered a man's eyes. She turned away her head, but her eyes turned also, so that they remained all the time on the eyes of that man, who for his part merely grinned and looked sheepish. Amongst the Nordic races of today those old lusts are dead, the clean lusts of our ancestors, who crossed the Rhine to plunge an iron sword into Rome's fluttering heart.

In their swords lay the victors' strength; with that thrust into Rome's soft body there went also their virility. Only the women still retain to some extent that primitive heritage of the flesh. If you are observant, and you are able to feel things as well as see them, you can detect in a nun a host of vestigial mannerisms that were born of the awakenings of puberty. I never see a nun in a tramcar without realising that the mystical is merely another term that implies eroticism.

Anyway, Le Roi was a poet. But he wrote no poetry. In fact, I learnt later on that his only attempt at serious literature was a smutty limerick he once scratched on the wall of a public convenience. The point is that he lived his poetry, for it is only the real poet who can live his work. Those of us who commit our dreams to paper and canvas are a sorry lot.

"Well," Le Roi said when we moved off, "I ate a man once. There were three of us together. I won't tell you where. It wasn't as though we were out in the wilds somewhere, or in a desert. In fact, there was an Indian greengrocer just opposite, where we bought our vegetables. Three of us stayed in that room. Of the three one happened at the time to be dead. He had died of pneumonia, and that was regrettable, as we had entertained higher hopes for him. As he was one of our band, we felt that it was an inglorious thing for him to die merely because his temperature had gone up to one hundred and five degrees. That seemed so cheap a way of dying when there were in this world things like rat-poison and delirium tremens and rope. You see, in those days we were still ambitious.

"'Let us burn him on the water,' I said. 'We'll give him a Viking's funeral. That will help us to forget the pneumonia.'

"'No,' my friend replied; 'we love him intimately. He has been more to us than a brother. For that matter, he has been more like a sister. It is in a strange way that we have loved him. Always we were one with him, like the pollen-laden wind is one with the rose it breathes on – like the ant-bear is one with the earth into which it burrows.'

"'That's true,' I said, 'we have been one with him in life. Let us be one with him in death.'

"'Let us enter with him into the most complete union of which the flesh is capable,' my friend suggested. 'Let us eat him.'

"So we pickled this man whom we loved so much that we could not allow him to die, and with the vegetables we bought from that Indian store at the corner we made stew of him every day, until there was no more left of him.

"He is dead, but he is with us still. He will always be with us. Where the two of us are gathered together in his name, there is he in the midst of us. I shall never forget him. What is more, I shall never forget the taste of him. It was like sweet pork."

I walked down the street with this strange man who had the wild light in his eye. I envied him his experience. But what I envied about him even more was that sublime confidence which alone makes it possible for a man to tell a mad story that a sane fool calls a lie.

It was getting dark. There is so much that we can understand about life when things get dark. But of the dark itself only God knows the meaning. Far off there still sounded the Army's band music. Now and again, intermittently, we still heard the throbbing of the drum. There was the pulse of life in the throb of the drum.

"Yes," Le Roi said, "he's a devoted husband, that man with the drum whom we were talking about. I know him and I also know his wife. They keep a restaurant a few streets down. The woman is interesting. She has been married to an affectionate, slobbering Philistine for two years, and yet she remains fresh. Some women are like that. When I think of her I think of dew in the lily's cup. I think of milk in a yellow goblet and red wine on the ground. Her husband is kind and meek and considerate, and during all the while that they have been married he has not once kicked her in the ribs. Whenever he leaves for work in the morning he strokes her hair and kisses her. His caresses hurt her physically because they bruise her soul. To be embraced by a man with blood like dishwater."

We went into a restaurant.

"That is the woman," Le Roi said; "but she never looks at me in the way a woman looks at a man. She knows that I understand. What she doesn't understand is that when once you have loved a man so much as to eat him you can never again love a woman."

It was a small place in which we sat, but it was cosy. There was no one else in the restaurant but the tall, slender woman who took our order for a meal. Odd bits of straw and paper were scattered about the floor, so that I knew nobody would stop me from spitting beside my chair. I liked that café. There was even something about the cash counter that made me feel I could plonk my last shilling on it like a prince.

"She's got a child, too," Le Roi went on over the soup. "A six months' old boy. And the child is exactly like his father in appearance. Which is damnable. But we can only see that the child looks like its father. The woman can see in the child, every day of her life, those thousands of little personal characteristics that go deeper than looks – all those things that her husband has also got. Imagine how she hates the child."

The woman brought in the fish. For an instant I caught her eye. I saw then that Le Roi was mistaken. There was in her eyes a terrible thing that her face did not show. The hatred she felt for her husband was nothing compared with that other thing that was in her soul. It is always frightening to see a woman with a calm face and with eyes that have looked into hell.

"Two days ago she sent away the child to its grandmother," Le Roi went on. "So she says, anyway. I don't know. It's a queer thing to do to a six months' old baby."

Once again I looked at that woman. She leant up against the counter with her left arm canted obliquely across her bosom. I have seen women stand just that way in great pictures. I suppose that is what they call an obsessional act. These habits of childhood persist to the grave, and if I told her what was the significance of her pose, only then would she understand. Obviously she was the only girl in a family of boys, and at that age when she found herself developing along different lines from her brothers the knowledge became embarrassing to her; she concealed her shy breasts with her left arm canted obliquely across her bosom.

I forget who ordered the stew.

After a few mouthfuls Le Roi dropped his knife and fork quickly. He looked at me with a white face.

"Let us go," he said hoarsely.

We left.

There is nothing more to be said, except that Le Roi reached the street a good distance ahead of me. In leaving he upset two chairs and a table that stood between himself and the door.

Rita's Marriage

RITA was going to get married. Rita was tall and thin and walked with very short steps. People noticed the way she walked and speculated about it, idly, sometimes jestingly, until they got used to her gait, when they no longer found it peculiar. But with Stephen, the poet, it was different. He knew that the reason Rita walked with short steps was to induce other people and also herself to believe in the existence of a virginity which, years ago, she had lost on the Kalk Bay sands.

Rita hated sand. Even the white sand of the Johannesburg minedumps filled her with hatred and fear, and whenever anybody took her for a motor drive along the Main Reef Road she would close her eyes, blinding herself to everything around her until she got back home. In an upside down way, this was also the blindness that came to Paul on the Damascus Road.

A man who pretended to be a poet, but was only a poseur like Oscar Wilde, said that Rita walked with abbreviated steps because her ankles were chained; he said that her body was chained to convention while her free aspirations smashed themselves ceaselessly against the bars. Of course, this was a lie. And Stephen knew that it was not even a great lie. It was an ordinary psychologist's lie. Rita's peculiarities were of the body, and the body always goes deeper than any kind of aspirations. More especially is this true of a woman's body.

What was remarkable was that in walking with abbreviated steps Rita was merely adopting a custom of her ancestresses of the dawn, who wore light chains on their ankles to preserve their maidenhood. Rita, without understanding it, was trying to wear chains after she had been deflowered.

And this was something that only Stephen could see. Only a real poet could gather, from Rita's walk, the truth about the Kalk Bay sands. After all, this is only natural. A poet is there to make words. And in making his words he has to find places that they will fit into. Any burglar can tell that the man on the corner with the red moustache is a detective. A good burglar can tell that the man with the red moustache is a detective, even when he is disguised to look like a detective. But only a poet can tell that the detective on the street corner once dreamt of plum-blossoms in a garden.

Rita was going to get married.

It was a wealthy, unimaginative young man, who had come several thousand miles from the Congo, that Rita had eventually decided to marry. Rita's mother had, of course, a share in the match, but the part she played was more of a negative character. It was not so much a matter of encouraging one particular unimaginative wealthy young man, as of discouraging others of the same kind. It was Rita's misfortune that she could attract only this one kind of man, who can never bring to a woman anything more than a warm, pasty kind of love. This is one of the things that a woman has to endure with her body if she wants to be a queen. Even the young man on the Kalk Bay sands had been wealthy and unimaginative. For a long while afterwards, perversely enough, Rita regretted his want of originality. It would have been a better seduction if the procedure had been less orthodox.

In the meantime there was the poet. He was in love with Alice, who was Rita's younger sister. It happened at a most inopportune moment, when the family was busy looking up the addresses of five hundred people whom they could invite to the wedding with a reasonable expectation of getting wedding presents. They had enough to do without having to settle with a poet who, in addition to being penniless, was probably also hungry. Still, Rita's mother did what she could. She threw a fit. She did it well, her collapse on the settee being rendered all the more spectacular by her bulk. She was prepared to go on throwing fits like that, as long as the settee held out.

Of course, the doctors who were summoned declared that a further shock of that description was liable to terminate fatally. What Rita's mother regretted was that the shock would not terminate fatally for the poet.

But although he was debarred from seeing Alice, and Alice was given a monthly allowance by her father on condition that she cut out the poet, yet all this made no difference to Stephen. He only wondered if he could not in some way approach Alice's father with a view to getting him to increase Alice's allowance. Because what Alice got from her father wasn't enough to keep both herself and Stephen.

You see, genuine poets are that way. They are stiffs and vagabonds and they are unscrupulous. It wasn't that Stephen was immoral, but he stood above immorality. All he wanted that belonged to Alice was her soul, and that, of course, was everything. Any man, if he is persistent enough, can usually succeed in getting possession of a woman's body.

And he'll keep her body until some other man, more persistent than himself, comes along and takes it away from him.

But only to the poet, who is both a king and a beggar, does God grant the sublime happiness of owning a woman's soul.

It is a divine privilege that comes but once in a lifetime, and then it is a ghostly barter, for in the exchange the poet also loses his own soul.

The preparations for the wedding went on apace. Rita's nerves were unstrung. She knew what the unimaginative young man would discover on the wedding night, and she was also sure that the young man didn't know. There was some sort of inverted dramatic irony in the situation. The classic example of dramatic irony, I suppose, is when the Court Registrar has got the tip in advance that the jury is going to find the prisoner at the bar guilty of murder, and the prisoner at the bar doesn't know it yet, but still thinks he has a chance of getting off.

The situation is one that can furnish an intelligent Court Registrar with a profound spiritual happiness, and with amusement of a divinely instructive sort, during those long moments when the jury files into their seats and the foreman rises and clears his throat. The Court Registrar, with his inside knowledge, can derive intense enjoyment from a detailed study of the rapid and devastating changes of expression that come over the face of the man who is about to be condemned to death, and still retains simple, childlike hopes that it mightn't be so, after all.

That was the position in which Rita found herself. She knew what the young man wouldn't know until after the marriage ritual. And yet, somehow, as far as she was concerned, something seemed to have gone wrong with the irony of the business. It brought Rita no happiness to possess this inside knowledge to which her wealthy and unimaginative lover had so far no access. Instead of experiencing elation through the power of knowledge, Rita was merely depressed. When they spoke about veils and orange-blossoms and bridesmaids – and presents – Rita felt still more depressed.

Actually, Rita lived through the days preceding her marriage in a state of tension known only to a pious man who has hurled a child out of a train window because of the child's nagging persistence in eating oranges.

Then, around the corner, like a sanitary cart playing havoc with a midnight romance of flowers, there lurked the poet.

It is a pity that, with the advent of water-borne sewerage, the sanitary cart, as an institution, is losing its hold on our imaginations. There is magic about what a sanitary cart stands for; there is an appeal about it that we deliberately try to ignore, turning our faces the other way, so that we can talk more fulsomely about the majesty of empire. But the sanitary cart is there. And only a great artist can recognise its presence and can tell simply of the power and poetry of the night and the mules and the buckets, of the drivers and the wheels.

The real test as to whether a man is an artist or whether he is merely sponging obscenely on the Temple of Art is to find out how he faces up to a sanitary cart.

It was the night before the wedding.

That wedding was the most fashionable affair that had taken place in Parktown for a number of years. Five hundred guests assembled in a marquee in the garden after the flummery of the church ceremony.

They ate and drank until they had guzzled and swilled themselves full up to the neck. The bridesmaids looked charming and only one of them was natural enough to have sweat running down her face. But that bridesmaid was always in trouble, somehow. Long speeches were made and various forms of abandonment were indulged in that are characteristic of animals on heat in the mating season.

The wedding was a tremendous social success.

This was only the night before the wedding, but we all know in advance what happens at that sort of marriage. It is over before the wedding morn. There is never a hitch. It is only at fairy weddings that hitches occur. The spells of the dew and the midnight trees and the warm stone with blood underneath it can weave their witchery only around the lives of elves and banshees and kobolds and princesses. The wedding of a princess's sister – who walks with short steps and wants to be a queen – comes off with the precision with which a tripe-dresser scrapes the excrement off the tripe. Pixies aren't sufficiently interested in a tripe-dresser to try and see what would happen if they make his hand shake.

Stephen was already married to Alice, and it had not been a flabby thing of organ music and over-feeding and solemnity and fleshly lust and dowries. It was a ritual of blood-marks on two brows and bleeding hands and a curse on the green leaves. It is queer that people should go to the trouble of having themselves bound by empty social vows, when even a dud poet can break them with laughter that also holds passion.

A marriage made by a priest can be broken to leave nothing behind, except, maybe, a beast pain of a torn body, like piles. A poet's marriage can never be broken as long as there is grass.

54

Alice and Stephen.

Stephen had waited at night outside her house and had kept vigils. When there was a light in her bedroom windows Stephen knew that Alice was there, awake. Sometimes she was there, asleep. Once or twice she had crept out in the night and had come to him, and Stephen, taking her hand, had led her away to the grass, where it was long and dark and the trees stood between the grass and the stars. It was a virgin love. Therefore, it was a hard, grey, flat-breasted love that had finality in it, like the sterile beauty of the Karoo, which no man can love, unless it is in complete nakedness. There is dark majesty in a sterile womb, which Isaiah understood because he was a poet.

Where seed does not germinate is eternity.

Rita's love was different. It had to be. It was soft and flabby, like an amorous jelly-fish. Like the full-green curves of the valleys around Table Mountain. A double-chinned, fat woman love. Rita and her young man – I have forgotten his name now, if I ever knew it, for I don't hate him, and after love has died we remember only the names of people we hate.

Alice and Stephen.

Close your eyes, Alice and forget. . . The stars are thorns that pierce the torn grass. A little girl's hand is on the rough bark of the fir-tree; she looks at the sap glistening between her fingers and does not understand. There is agony in a flower-garden, the pain of two who have stayed beneath the moon together for a long while, and the man, holding the maid in his arms, dreams of a deserted white wall. Only those who have lingered long past midnight in the garden and have known this pain can understand the true significance of Christ's outspread arms, and why the blood was mingled with water.

Anyway, it was the night before the wedding.

Stephen loafed about the trees before Alice's house, which was a black house, because there was no light in the window. Stephen leant up against a tree, and as it was cold, he thought of the Equator and cursed the house because it was not white.

But it was only an empty curse and meant nothing. It was the kind of curse a man puts on his landlady when he calls her a whore for stealing his blanket, or when he calls her a cow for no other reason than just because she is a cow. A curse, to have power, must be put on with a kiss. Judas knew that. A curse is useless unless it bears with it the kiss of death. It is an invocation and a challenge. Slay, God. If not him, then me, God. But slay.

That night, in the same garden where the poet kept watch, Rita walked with the man she was to marry the following day.

Stephen thought of Alice, and knew that, although she was young, yet she was the autumn's princess. Perhaps for the reason that she was Stephen's princess, for Stephen was of the autumn, when she dies in a hard, still way, slowly, and lives only by what she has in her eyes. Consequently, Stephen was supremely happy, as happy as only a man can be when he kneels in adoration before a god whom he has created with his own hands.

Rita paced about the garden, arm in arm with the young man. She was desperately eager to talk to him about her body, conveying to him certain facts about the Kalk Bay sands. She didn't quite know how.

"Sweetheart," she began, "will it. . . ."

The man put both arms around her, holding her passionately. She wasn't sure whether tenderness was the right touch. She closed her eyes. Then she bit her lips. Then Rita counted ten, and took a long breath and spoke all she could without breathing. "You know, I fell once accidentally when I was quite young on the sands at Kalk Bay, and Alice was there and she helped me to get up, and I was hurt, and you understand, don't you?"

The young man was a humorist after a heavy fashion.

"One of those frail, fallen girls," he said laughing. "The Salvation Army should have helped you up, not Alice."

"I. . . fell over a stone, accidentally," Rita explained, using unconsciously, as all women do at such moments, the sexual imagery of the Old Testament.

"You understand what happened?" Rita enquired bravely.

This kind of discussion always aroused the young man. To share with Rita in whispered words the secret intimacies of her flesh burnt his senses, like roasting raw meat on coals.

"I know, I know," he said, pressing her tightly against him and kissing her mouth and her eyes and as far down her neck as her frock allowed him. Then he released her.

"I understand," he said.

Rita looked at him swiftly. She did not speak to him again until long afterwards. She couldn't talk. There was a dryness in her throat. She could only feel that life was an ugly and pitiful affair.

You see, a queen has to make sacrifices.

For in that one swift glance Rita saw that she had lost.

56

The man believed at that moment because he was passion-flushed. Later on, in their married years, with the hot lust in him, the fact that she did not come to him physically intact would not matter. But in the chill of reaction he would taunt her with his unbelief. He would talk sneeringly and bitterly of what he believed to be the real nature of her fall on the sands.

They walked through the shadows in that part of the garden that lay nearest the street. Her lover's arms were still close about her, and in Rita's heart there was a grey thing.

Quite near them there came the clatter of a cart, of heavy wheels and mules' hoofs on the asphalt. The man tried to hide his embarrassment under a pretence of being amused. But he failed. He was that kind of man. He turned round and propelled Rita swiftly in the direction of the house. The advent of that vehicle of the night jarred him. It gave him what was actually a guilty feeling, somehow, like a little boy caught in an act of shame.

Rita hurried on with the man who would be her husband after the daybreak. Her head was erect, as a queen's should be. Her steps were even shorter than usual.

Stephen remained for a long while under the trees, thinking of the wedding. For he knew that he was the bridegroom.

Heloise's Teeth

YOU won't really understand this story unless you are drunk. A god would understand this story, all right. A god putting his hand up to his eyes.

There is no such thing as prose and poetry and literature. There are only fairy stories and verses.

What attracted the young men to Heloise were her teeth. She had beautiful teeth – very white, with queer spots in them that gleamed in the sunshine. I don't mean her artificial teeth, either. I am talking about Heloise's own teeth, which the dentist pulled out the time they didn't know what was the matter with her.

Afterwards the dentist made her a set of artificial teeth upper and lower, which she wore because she had to, but could never love. Heloise kept her own extracted teeth in a leather case.

Heloise was pretty, and the young men came to her and spoke about love, and told her that in her eyes were shadows like Boksburg Lake in the moonlight, and that in her hair was a fragrance that stirred them strangely, and that her lips held mysteries. Some of them even believed what they said about her, but Heloise knew that all the time what they were concerned about were the other and deeper mysteries about her, that were something like the spell of Circe. It made gods of men while they were still seeking, and when they had found it they were made swine.

Heloise knew this as all women know it, and as all men sometimes forget. But it is something that a poet never forgets, unless, sleeping too long, for a while he dreams away his magic. When the old Christian seers and prophets murmured of divine mysteries they did not realise how near they were getting to the human body.

It was a curious business with Heloise and her teeth. When she was being courted by a young man whose feelings were as yet undecided she watched him steadily, and then at that moment when his emotions would become either passion or nothing at all she displayed her extracted teeth.

Other women in that position make a subtle show of their legs. Or they adopt a smiling posture that reveals the curve of their breasts. Or they become suddenly still in a deadly way, as a snake hesitating to strike because he is not quite sure of his poison.

58

That was the moment when Heloise, drawing the leather case from her handbag, scattered the contents on the table-cloth. It always worked.

There was young David.

"These are my teeth. David," Heloise said. "I had a lot of pain when they were drawn."

David reached forward eagerly. He was hers.

The delightful feeling of intimacy that came to him as he handled her teeth was bewildering. After all, teeth are ever so much more near and real than thighs that have only soft shapeliness – than breasts, that have only curves.

"This one must have hurt a lot when it came out," David said.

"Yes," she replied, "but don't you think it looks ugly, a tooth like that, with two such long roots?"

"Ugly?" David repeated in amazement. "There is nothing about you that is not very beautiful. These two roots, and this hole here where your tooth was rotten – I have never seen anything lovelier in the Art Gallery."

In supreme moments even people like David talk poetry.

Without knowing it, David spoke in the language of Baudelaire, who first discovered the glory that is all in putrefaction – this startling grandeur of a king in decay. Beauty lives only when it has passed for always. Only that half smile remains eternal that will not come again. If it does come again, later on, it is no longer a half smile. It is a guffaw. It is the obscenity of a courtesan laughing about birth.

This is one reason why Byron could never be a poet: he did not know what Christ the Artist knew, that everlasting life can come only through death. Otherwise Byron could not have perpetrated the absurdity of imagining that if he were to see a girl again "after long years" he would greet her "in silence and tears." I or Keats would never have written that. It isn't poetry. It is only a romantic lie. And a romantic lie is almost as untrue as the heavy-footed rubbish turned out by that school of stable attendants who call themselves realists.

David took Heloise in his arms and kissed her. Then their arms relaxed and they looked at one another. They knew that what was between them was more than just a handful of teeth. There was Andries.

I don't know why Andries has to be introduced into this story. But that's nothing. If I did know this wouldn't be a real story; it would no longer be art, like the fifty-third chapter of Isaiah or Whistler's "Little Girl in White."

59

Anyway, there was Andries. Andries was in a sense a cripple. It was a painful matter for him to walk at all. Little boys passing him in the street were in the habit of laughing at the laborious way he dragged his left leg behind him. But in the upper part of his body was enormous strength. Only very small boys would be able to detect the sublime humour of a crippled giant. This is true humour, whose basis is incongruity. There is nothing funny about a paralytic; a totally wrecked body cannot possibly excite laughter. A man looks funny only when he is partly maimed.

G. K. Chesterton, in spite of his pretence, never understood the real subtlety of children's laughter, which is identical with a genius's laughter. What was really humorous about Andries was the contrast between his huge chest and his massive shoulders – and his dragging left leg. But the children, when they laughed, always kept at least four paces away from Andries.

People said of Andries that he was the strongest man in the world. This was possibly true. But what advantage is it, after all, to be the strongest man in the world, if you can't run? A third-rate man can call you names, and you can't run after him and catch him.

David had called Andries names, often. David was childlike in many respects. It gave him a quaint and yet thrilling pleasure to throw taunts at Andries from the opposite side of the road, in the way that the other David had impudently thrown things at Goliath. Only, Andries wasn't killed by the words David threw at him.

There were nights when David would wake up with cold sweat on his forehead: that was when he had been dreaming that the giant had seized hold of him in the darkness. It was hideous. Yet there was also something delightful in a hair-raising contemplation of the horrors of being crushed and mangled in his savage fury. When David went to bed at night he locked the door very carefully. But when he saw Andries in daylight he jeered at him.

And of late Andries had been attentive to Heloise. I don't know how far they got. Maybe they had already reached that stage where Heloise showed her teeth. It has always seemed to me singular about a woman, that she can love a number of men at the same time. Perhaps it is because I have grown to look beyond the things of love; perhaps it is that my eyes have gazed too long past a woman in searching for the goddess.

David and Heloise looked at one another in an almost frightened way.

"Sister, there is blood upon the teeth," David said, parodying a great poem. He laughed. Somehow, a parodist always comes to a bad end. Which is well.

Heloise drooped her head forward, and Andries kissed the back of her neck. It is singular how these things of the dawn persist. Inferior lovers put forward the claim that they can tell when a woman is in love with them by the light in her eyes or the colour in her cheeks or the words on her lips. This is all lies. When a civilised woman is in love with a man she shows it, poetically and unconsciously, in the way that the woman of the dawn showed it. She droops her head forward, for the man to kiss her neck. By this act, the ancient symbol of surrender, of passing under the yoke, every woman proclaims her beloved as the lord and master of her body. I am a poet. Therefore it is my business to know these things. I am pleased to think that it is only through my telling them about it that other people ever know these things.

This is a tip to every father: if you come across your daughter accidentally and she has a boy near her and her head droops forward, then you know what has happened to her. This is equally true of a schoolgirl who has just left convent, and of a woman who has been a widow three times. The old poetical things of the jungle cannot die.

When thoughtless fools say that poetry is out of date, they don't realise that the only things that are actually near to them and that have meaning for them are the things that the poet tells them. And it is so easy to tell them lies. Only, a poet never tells lies.

About two weeks after he had first found himself in love with Heloise, David went down in the lift of the building in which he worked. It was an automatic lift. On the third floor two women got out. On the second floor a man got in. But David saw none of them. His thoughts were away with Heloise's teeth.

Suddenly David discovered that the lift had come to a stop, not on the ground floor, but right down in the basement. The semi-darkness of the place annoyed him. He stepped forward to press the button. The lift wouldn't move. David laughed. Then he became frightened. It was that mad, terrifying thing that psychologists call claustrophobia. He was afraid of the confined space.

Agitatedly David turned to the man standing behind him. . .

David screamed.

A Nun's Passion

(A Xmas story)

SISTER Angelica knelt before her bed in the convent, her body trembling with a sublime love. She closed her eyes and got ready to pray. She was tired of the Ave Marias and the Misereres and the old formulas. She thought of the Mother Superior and the way she spoke about Christ and love. What did a shrivelled woman with tight lips and a cold, austere heart know about love?

Sister Angelica, her bosom pressed against the iron rail of her bed, poured out in spiritual ecstasy the fervent things of her warm body and her passionate soul.

"Oh, Christ Jesus, I love thee; I love thee only. Put thy hands on my breasts. Clasp each of my breasts with the tenderness of thy love. Come yet more near to me, Jesus. I do not fear thee.

"I was sinful once, Jesus. I loved a man. He kissed me and caressed me, and I lay in his arms, and I pressed my lips on his mouth, and there was blood on my lips after the passion with which I had kissed him. It was red blood, Christ, and it was very beautiful. But it was also very sinful, Lord. Yea, Lord, it was very sinful.

"And then he left me.

"And now I love only thee, O Jesus. I love thy body that bore all those cruel wounds for me. I wash the blood off thy body with my tears. Thy wounds are all healed now, Jesus.

"I love thy black hair. Come closer to me, Jesus. Let me put my hands on thy black hair. Let me kiss thy crimson lips. See how my mouth trembles with my love for thee. Let me know more of thy beauty, Jesus.

"So thou hast come to me, Lord. Thou hast answered my prayer and thou has come to me. Oh, the white fragrance of thy breath. Like the sweet perfume of the little night flowers. Thy presence is like a green place on the earth where two lovers have lain.

"Jesus, I feel thou art tender because thou art strong. Kiss me, Jesus, kiss me. Behold, I have kept my loveliness for thee. Put thy hand here, Jesus. Here. . . Here. . . I love thee and am not ashamed."

Afterwards, when she came out of her cell, with flushed cheeks and her brow very pale, Sister Angelica looked to the Mother Superior like a woman who had sinned.

Romance: A Sequence

Romance

N the placid fatness of the moon as it shines tonight there is still the pale insanity of ancient moons shedding primordial seeds in lines and straight dots through a funnel whose wide mouth encloses half the earth.

The full moon that lies fat on her back tonight remembers only through the folds of her thick flesh that other far-off moon that was slender as a reed and that panted lightly in swift fragrant breaths, like the air through the feathers of an arrow in flight.

The young moon ran down a white path, and the dogs were baying at her heels.

If I did not have my flesh I would run also, and I am tormented by my flesh and my back is bent under the burden of the wood-and-coal ashes from fires that burnt and burnt in nights that were whips of flame and that were scourges of blue flame.

But, behold, here is a singer. And the lute-player bears the lute, and the citharist the zither. And we will always make brave music, lo, when the heart is empty enough, lo, when the heart is a great space open on all sides, open like a poppy-bud that has flowered, and open like a virgin that has been deflowered.

Enter the bearer of the lute, preceded by an ape on a gold chain and wearing a cap of crimson velvet. Enter one with his face concealed in the dream of the lutanist, lying supine on a palanquin borne by four slaves. Enter a vision and a storm rending the ship's sails woven of strong strands of Boeotian flax. Who does not enter is a girl walking down the street with her breasts rounded like silver bells and her footsteps haunted by the sound of purple bells, and with her hair close to her, as though it is not covered.

She is the first girl you will see if you walk down the street.

Wingspread and Bedspread

Hell is an everlasting burning.

Harsh laughter rings in my ears from the coast of pearls. I have made sacrifices to the powers that carry out dewy functions and that are broader than men: I have besought them to exercise forbearance. I have prayed. I have plucked out of my heart a live vision which I have hung on their blue hooks.

Therefore will I be allowed to clothe myself in my nakedness, and in the dim coolness pouring out from the bark of old trees I will let my wound be healed – the place in my side where the spear entered in order that my last lost dream should find egress. The peaceful unguents will close up the rent in my side in the way that a book is closed.

They that have toiled in the heat of the day have lain burning in the starlit nights, when the streets have been wound up like clocks and the city has set its men and women as an alarm for the dawn. Through how many nights have you not also lain and burned? There are two separate cohorts of angels that pass invisibly through a city during the night. The angels that walk over the house-tops guard in their beds lovers whose arms are wrapped about each other and whose breathing is purple and gold and whose flanks hold the quivering of the wind on icy pools and whose spines are aflame. But the angels that walk in the streets, through the pavements and gutters, hold watch over those who lie alone in their beds, and heatedly sighing burn alone, their bodies self-consuming lightless torches.

God said to me, "Take up now thy wings and thy place in the legion of night angels and pass over the world's cities, treading the roof-tops." And so I walked through the world's cities until the dawn. And my feet were bruised from the pavements. And for my disobedience I sang not in the heavenly choirs.

A Blue Cylinder

I am sitting here waiting for her. I am sitting under a willow in the spring-time, the leafy wands of the willow bending over me in a green rain. But because I don't know for sure whether she is coming, I feel that it were better that I should be an Indian fakir, who has conquered all these feelings that surge and swirl about inside me like the many things drifting on the water at my feet: it were better that I sit under a bo-tree instead of under a willow.

What will happen if she does not come? I ask myself this question, and I know that it is only if she does not come, and that it is only if we do not meet again, that a great deal will happen. There will be the flight of a bird in a blue and grey arc through a fragment of sky. Three brown leaves will drift through the narrow part of the stream that is on its way to the sea. The wind blowing from across the cemetery will mould a new city's architecture.

But if she does come, then there will be nothing at all. There will be the confusion of documents filed into the wrong cabinets. There will be a chair and a desk under the willow-tree and there will be a white wall on the edge of the water: the wall will be there to have a calendar hung on it, marking today's date. And we will say, "We have met again. Is it indeed not gorgeous?" And I will clasp her in my arms. And around the lower part of the bole of the willow-tree there will be hung symbolical moons, full and crescent, tied to the tree with monthly strings.

She is coming. . . I hear her footsteps behind me. . . She is walking not on young grass and clayey soil, but her high heels are tap-tapping on the parquet floor of the hospital corridor.

Afternoon Ravishment

Bennet sat in Veronica's room, awaiting her return. She would not be long now.

And Veronica's bedroom told Bennet more than he had learnt from meeting Veronica at intervals, talking to her in the office or going out with her for a spot in the lounge of the hotel. Once or twice he had kissed her. Now, for the first time, he was in Veronica's bedroom. He sat on a chair next to the bed, which was covered with a green counterpane. And while he of course thought of the men who had lain on that bed with Veronica, he could not from the green counterpane learn the lusts of those men: all that the green counterpane would have been able to reveal to him were their names. On the dressing-table between the bed and the bookcase stood jars of cosmetics and a green ashtray. And there was that other small jar. It was maddening. Had a woman then no sense of propriety at all? What sort of woman was this, then, with whom he had fallen in love? And, of course, she would declare that she kept that jar there for other purposes – for her eyelashes, perhaps, or for what else? It was terrible to be a man, and subject to so many complexes. It was because he did not know enough about women, Bennet reflected.

And he saw that the room revealed Veronica's character to him in a way that her words could not do, in a way that the two occasions on which he had kissed her did not expose her inner nature and her passions to him. The green counterpane that held men's names in its texture and that squat, ugly little jar with the blue lid on the dressing-table were like the two parts of Veronica's soul. The one half of her was very honest, and the other half lied. And this was not the kind of bedroom that he was used to, or in which he could find fragrance that set his pulses throbbing with an intoxication. In Veronica's bedroom were no warmths, like of freckles on a tall white neck, like of a single wild stain on a very pale-blue chemise. In Veronica's bedroom there was none of the voluptuousness of stark honesty, breathtakingly revealed in a sinful mark. There was only that little fat cylindrical jar that was strident in its blue-lidded presence. Veronica had orange-coloured lids. And that jar had a blue lid. And the bed was covered with a green lid.

And then the breath of past strong nights crept into the bedroom where Bennet sat and waited. He was haunted by the past that was like ink-characters traced on thin white paper; written in a smooth-flowing calligraphy that was too swift to have flourishes.

Bennet heard footsteps coming down the passage. Veronica was on her way back. In a few moments her hand would be on the door-knob. Bennet jumped up from the chair. He grasped the end of the green counterpane at the top, where it was thrust in between the pillows and the bed-post. In a single sweep he tore the counterpane from the bed and flung it on the floor, where it lay, a crumpled carpet between the bed and the dressing-table. Bennet went and stood on the green counterpane. He was still standing there when Veronica entered the room.

And by that time he had already unscrewed the blue lid of the squat little cylindrical jar, and his fingers were sticky with the viscous contents. And he was looking down.

Solemn Wind

Bennet lay beside Veronica in self-loathing, in the throes of belly disgust. This is the iron key that opens the mystic lock of being put on the earth, Bennet reflected.

This is the road along which you have to pass that is narrow with self-hate. And it is this that makes a man's voice large, and it is this that you can sense in the voice of a man when he talks heartily: in his bluff tones there is this thing. And a man who has not got this wide freedom in his approach to life is somebody of whose secret practices you must be suspicious.

And what, then, of the woman? When did each woman in the world find this out? It is not the awakening of swift passion or the sullen end to acrid smoke and a slow smouldering. There is the hidden pathway closed about with tangled hedgerows, in all black and brown colours. It is a dangerous passage, noisome with use and slippery with the night. A young road winding through secret foliage and two swift dreams. All right. But what of that last degree of emptiness when the soul has fled, and witchery is turned inside out, and you say of what was worst that it is even better this way? So may a girl smile at the dew day in the consciousness of her own tarnishment. And thus is the whore's gaze bold and direct upon a man, because she is unpolluted. Thus is a harlot a virgin: she has not taken a man: she has not slept with her own self-hate.

Bennet struck a match in the darkness. The light flickered across Veronica's sleeping face, with her relaxed lips curved inwards and her blonde hair streaming over the pillow. The match burnt out again before Bennet had heard Veronica's breathing. This mirthless world, he thought. What makes city life so complicated is that the sewerage system is all underground.

Vista of Bees

"Would it not be better," he asked, "if there were no women in the world for the torment of a man's flesh and a man's heart?"

And although Veronica did not answer, there swept across and underneath her (as she sat at the table facing the man, with their brandy glasses between them) a soft coolness, like the wind of early evening that stirs for a little while from sleep because it is seeking a darker repose. At the man's words a coolness swept lightly across Veronica's bosom, and curved downwards under her green-striped jumper and her cerise-coloured blouse and her white slip, bending creamily along her skin, down her stomach and between her thighs, and in that coolness there were more colours than in her skirt and her jumper and her blouse.

"The nearer that a man gets to a woman," he continued, "the more she eludes him with her laughter and her body's stinks. And when he

67

breathes full-lunged and there is a heaviness in his shoulder-muscles and the bones in the lumbar part of his spine are first lighted like with torches, and are afterwards tamed like a mattress, then he knows that what he has sought is a stricken hollowness. And he says to himself in unfulfilled satiety, 'It is this. It is this.' And is all life then not just a searching after the purple meaning of drunkenness, and the yellow meaning of a whore?"

Veronica moved in her chair, uncrossing her knees and sitting further back, and that many-coloured coolness fluttered away from her limbs like a butterfly in the drowsiness of the summer.

"Would it not be better for a man that he should never have known a woman?" he continued. "In the pale hand of a woman there is a terrible green fire. And that terrible green fire is in her eyes also when her fingers shut lightly. And a man is mocked with memories. A niche in a back wall and passion stirring heavily like black marble. And the memory of talk in schooldays and the memory of waking nights. And eyes gaze through the hole in the back wall and red and golden sand is blown through it. And so suddenly from the dark cloud rising out of the ground in the manner and shape of a tree there descend the white rains and the white mists, and remembrance is chilled in the time of youth. What did they witness, the eyes gazing through the aperture in the back wall? And why, thereafter, with the youth's belly turned forward, with only a shaft of late sunshine slanting across the black marble, did those eyes not watch again? There is a green light in your eyes when your lids open, now, and when your slender fingers close flutteringly."

Veronica's thoughts were in parallel planes receding into a green distance.

"Perhaps you expect too much from a girl," she answered. "Perhaps you don't know that what a girl gives a man is the best she's got. It's not the girl's fault any more than that it's the man's fault. As a woman, I don't think there has been very much difference between the best kind of man I have had and the worst kind of man who has had me."

The man thought for a few moments, his face resting in his hands.

"In having had a woman," he ended solemnly, "a man has not had a flower or a poem. No, not a flower or a poem. He has had what he wanted."

Blunted Weapons

What is really going on there, in the meeting of two women? Veronica has fair hair and her face is oval and her features are trim and expressionless. But Marta's body is no less neat. And her eyes are dark and it looks as though there are no black oceans of witchery in them anymore. These two women know each other at their meeting.

Veronica's voice is high-pitched and she talks excitedly, and when her mouth opens wide and she seems as though she is going to scream with laughter it is not her mouth that Marta is thinking of. For Marta is not impressed with Veronica.

What can they have to say to each other, these two women in their friendly meeting?

When men meet they do not think of each other like that. Rather let these two women meet, therefore, not in the upstairs lounge of this hotel, but in a swamp, with the jungle mud to above their ankles, and their clothes torn from them in their passage through the thick clinging tendrils that twined about their thighs in the green-luscious equatorial rain forests. Let Veronica and Marta meet, then, with ooze-splashed bellies, and their haunches ashake in the ungainly movements of their feet through the ankle-deep heavy slime. And with Veronica's hair rent and with a small leaf to conceal the nakedness of Marta's left nipple.

Then would they get to know each other, Marta and Veronica. And in the savagery of their naked haunches they would hold out no more menace to each other, these two women. And in the dark quivering of their bellies there would be no more hatred for each other. In the putrescence of red tropical fruit and the decaying at the edge of old mud there will be the honesty of the flesh.

Instead, Veronica and Marta were sitting in the upstairs lounge of the hotel. And they drank ginger-squares and conversed together, with Veronica doing most of the talking and Marta most of the listening. And it was as though Veronica's voice bubbled with excitement. And it was as though Marta's flanks had grown chilled.

"This is the third time now that Bennet has asked me to marry him," Veronica said. "What do you think I should do about it?"

And Marta replied that it seemed best that Veronica should accept Bennet's offer of marriage. Marta said it very simply and very earnestly.

"You wait. I will yet sleep with Bennet," Marta thought to herself. "Yes," Marta promised herself in her heart's closed and burning constancy, "I will yet go to bed with Bennet. And we will lie between the sheets together. And I will sleep all night in his arms. We will lie naked together in bed, Bennet and I. And when we wake up in the morning, and I see Bennet's head on the pillow, only then will I forget Veronica, of whom I was thinking all the time when Bennet and I were in bed together, and awake."

First Served

The night flings a cloak, that is black velvet on the outside and black silk on the inside, over the earth's brain and over the dew on the elephant and over the stirrings on the grass. The night hides all songs and all sins and night-thoughts are a school of slippery kabeljou plunging and twisting in blue water. The night conceals all things. But in what shall the night itself be hidden? Wherewith will you hang a cloak around the night's self? Well, the night is hidden in a woman's handbag. The woman's flesh is the cage of the hawk and the outside of the heifer's stable, and the secret place where the night is stowed away. In the woman's flesh a million nights are fenced about. And stifled. And hushed up.

"Pieces of torn paper," Bennet said, when he had pulled open the zip-fastener of Veronica's handbag and was examining the contents.

"Give it back to me," Veronica said from across the café table. "I gave you my bag to look at, because you said you wanted to see how the zip works. I didn't say you could look inside it." She reached out for the bag but Bennet pulled it away and, sitting sideways to the table, studied the inside of the bag.

"This is lipstick," he said. "This is the only thing in your bag that is red, except for the penny stamp on this post-card. And this face-powder – whitish, creamy, ivory and pale pink – the colour of flesh and yet not quite that. And this perfume. There is only one perfume like that. Only one kind like that in the whole world. And I think it is more important than anything else in your handbag. Without this scent-sachet the crimson of the lipstick and the flesh creamy-white of the face-powder – what would they be? And what kind of perfume is this that you carry about with you in your handbag? It is an old odour. Your bag exhales primordial fascinations. But it is not a sweet smell. It is a green and unripe scent and it is also high and tainted. And it is dark.

And it brings a quick flush to the forehead of the man who opens your bag and looks inside it. The colour of this perfume that you carry in your bag is sometimes yellow and sometimes purple – ”

"Never mind all that," Veronica said. "Give me back my bag. I don't care what you think of my scent. It is good enough for me, anyhow. Lots of men like it. But give me back my bag."

"I want to see some more," Bennet answered. "What else have you got in your bag? These bits of torn paper. Parts of a torn-up letter – ”

"It's not yours, though," Veronica said. "It's somebody else's."

"And I also see something else here, in the deepest part of the inside of your bag," Bennet said. "Guess what it is."

"I don't know," Veronica said. "But don't open it so wide. If you open it so wide it is difficult for me to get it closed again properly. At another time it got opened right out like that, and you have no idea how hard it was to get the two parts to fit again properly. You must be careful with it. I have had it a long time and I still want a lot of use out of it. It has got a few wrinkles in it, but it's still all right. It's tough and can stand hard wear. . . But you must give it back to me quickly, Bennet. People are looking."

"I also saw inside it," Bennet said as he returned the bag to Veronica under the table, "money."

They sat silent.

"One thing that's queer to me," Bennet said after a while, "is how little significance we attach to the man whose crumpled letter is lying at the bottom of the bag. He means so little to us. Just little torn-up pieces."

"Maybe that's all he means to you," Veronica said.

Comings

It was because she was waiting for her lover to come, her lover who would come to her later, and who would bring a thrill to her flesh, and who would go off immediately afterwards, despising her – it was because her lover would come to her later that day, and visit her in her bedroom, that Veronica sat in irritation with Bennet in his newspaper office, after the day's work had been done.

And while Bennet talked to her of philosophy and of the day's work and of the typewriter on the edge of the office desk – the typewriter that was bent-browed from having to think so hard for several hours in the day when Bennet sat in front of the machine, writing – then Veronica sat in irritation, listening perfunctorily to the words that Bennet said, but thinking of her lover who would come to her after she had gone back to her room, and who would take her in his arms, not because he desired to press her against his heart but because only in that way could he quickly attain the end for which he had come to her bedroom.

"When I write a story that I enjoy writing," Bennet was saying, "then I take longer over it than is really necessary. I linger over passages that make my mind feel as though it is rubbed bare. And always the type-writer wants to go faster. And I try to hold back the keys. And it is a struggle that gets passionate, very often. Because the typewriter knows exactly where it wants to go. The typewriter has thought all day about it, while I have been doing other things. And when I want to relax in the enjoyment of a single phrase, that ends in an adverb, with the suf-fix –ly, and the adverb is preceded by a comma – comma, adverb –ly, stop: like that – tat-tat-tat-bang! – then the typewriter, that has been dreaming about that passage all day, and has savoured its rhythm and its lust beforehand, then the typewriter, that has felt that phrase all day in its springs and slender bars, wants to hurry on until it is all over. I want to linger awhile over that moment, but the typewriter is impatient and drags me oh so swiftly to the end, when the last couple of dozen words are rattled out, and I relax because I am emptied out, and I push the typewriter from me, since the typewriter has got nothing more to say, all its thoughts being at rest."

Veronica listened to Bennet in an irritation of the flesh. In the evening her lover would come to her in her bedroom. And he cared nothing for her. He despised her spirit as much as he despised her body. But she was easy for him to have. And he would go from her again very soon. And she would try to prolong his remaining with her. But he would hurry, hurry. And she would be left to think a long while afterwards. For her lover had done all his thinking before.

And afterwards Veronica turned to go.

"I must go," she said to Bennet.

"I suppose somebody is coming to see you tonight," Bennet said. "Is it him again?"

"Nobody is coming to see me," Veronica answered, seeking not to inflict unnecessary things on Bennet, "I want to go to bed early."

But she knew that she would go to bed only long after her lover had
gone. Only hours after her lover's departure would she get up from the
bed on which she lay with her eyes half shuttered, smoking one cigarette after the other; she would arise from her bed and remove her
upper garments, her foundation garments having been stripped from
her hours before, and she would put on her night-dress and for the first
time climb in under the bed-clothes.

For several minutes after Veronica had gone, Bennet went on sitting
back in his chair, leaning back while the smoke curved outwards from
his cigarette, dreamlessly.

Then he reached for the typewriter that was standing on the edge of
the office desk, and he drew the machine towards him, leaning forward
over the typewriter, whose round white nipples were a few inches
away from his breast. But the typewriter was cold. The typewriter had
no more thoughts left.

Bennet put on his hat and walked out of the office.

Without a Bit

Seated on a bench with frayed upholstery, a glass of beer on the little
round table in front of him, Bennet listened idly to the conversation of
the three men leaning up against the pub counter. They talked as all
men do in a dilapidated pub, whose walls are lined with sporting prints
and photographs of boxers and actresses of a generation ago.

"It's a small world." they said. "So that really was your old man, the
Slade that drove a cab in Fordsburg before the streets were asphalted."
"And then you must know Dickie's Corner." "On what side of the
plantation was your house now?. . . Wait a bit I'll tell you. . . yes, it was
that place with the red roof." "Hell, I can't believe it, us meeting here
like this. Where you been all these years?" "Fancy meeting in a bar, ha.
ha. Last place you'd expect to find us in, ha ha." "And do you remember
Phyllie?" "Do I remember? Hey, let me show you how she run when
my mother come on us from behind, when we was —— against that
back fence next to the railway-line. This is how Phyllie run. . . she
couldn't get her broeks up in time. And my old lady never said a word
to me about it. What do you think of that? She never said a word, the
old lady. She was a wonderful old lady." "Maybe your old lady chased
you and Phyllie, but what about the time your old man chased me right

through to the other end of Lovers Walk? When he caught me riding one of the cab-horses. I was trying to ride the horse bare-back. Maybe you can ride a horse bare-back, but I didn't have no reins neither." "And remember that old baker we called Olifant?" "Do I remember – you ask me do I remember – *I*? Gawd, man, wasn't it me that – "

Bennet drank his beer slowly, listening to the conversation and thinking his own thoughts, which were of that man riding the girl called Phyllie bare-back. Without a saddle and without reins. And he thought of the way Phyllie galloped off behind that back fence in the way that the man demonstrated. That man was a good mimic. Phyllie, her movements impeded by the partial descent of her underwear, had pranced and tripped off like a knee-haltered horse. Phyllie. Funny that they should have given her that name: prophetic. Or was it because they had christened her Phyllie that she had afterwards to live it out? Was everything that happened to you all part of one destiny?

And then Bennet started thinking of Marta and of Veronica. Which of the two had not had a similar thing happen to them? Had they not also in the past galloped off knee-haltered? It was a sad thing that women never related experiences like that. It was a sad thing that women were not like men. Women were not honest. It was because Phyllie would never have told anybody, not anybody at all, ever, about her constricted gallop past the back fence that dishonesty came into the world.

"Afterwards she married Joe Nibson," Bennet heard one of the three men leaning against the bar counter saying. "Remember Joe Nibson? What he seen in her I don't know." "Nor me, neither."

They were no longer talking about Phyllie.

Red Cock-crow

Marta drew her brown-striped coat close about her in the high wind. Bennet was a few minutes late. She didn't mind. He could be very late, even, if only during that while in which she awaited his coming her lover would come round the corner, from his office, and raise his hat, greeting her in passing. Her lover might even pause to say a few words to her. He might even make mention of some possible future tryst. Of late he had grown tired of her. In her room he visited her but rarely at night, and then he was always in a hurry. And he no longer told her beforehand when he would arrive. He dropped in only when he was in fleshly urgence. He knew that whenever he came she would be ready to receive him.

Marta looked at her watch. Yes, Bennet was indeed late for the appointment. She stepped into the doorway of the building to shelter from the wind. She stepped in reluctantly. Her lover might not see her now, if he should pass that way, coming out of his office.

And, of course, it was at that very moment that her lover appeared. A small trim girl with masses of black hair was leaning on his arm. And in the wind the black hair billowed about her head. And the wind blew the lower part of her floral-patterned frock about her knees, sensually very merrily, so that it looked as though the girl was walking with swaying steps through a field of fluttering poppies.

Marta's lover bent his head far forward, to hear what the girl with the blowing hair and skirt and the small trim body was saying. Consequently he did not see Marta sheltering in the doorway of the building. He did not see Marta suddenly half-incline her belly forward, opening her lips very slightly, and in an unconscious gesture bring the hand that held her handbag tight against her bosom. She allowed a sudden gust of wind to blow her coat open, from her knee to the level of her waist.

Marta was still standing like that when Bennet arrived.

A Double Night

There was a surer comfort for her in a man's cloaking her about with words that were like bed-clothes, Marta reflected. A surer comfort in the drapery of words that were like sheets and blankets lying over you in the early hours of the morning, after your lover had gone and the sheets were empty of passion and were littered with bright-hued poignancies. A dance-floor strewn with coloured papers and fragments of tinsel and torn and crumpled streamers and the bunting staled. A dance-hall with the daylight flooding in through the windows and natives with dust-pans and brooms clearing the rubbish from the trampled boards. And the white man superintending the work in an ill humour because of the empty bottles and used and filthy appliances of intercipience that the natives had collected up from the night-lawn. The man in charge of the work had not been to the dance. And he thought of all the sinful and glowing movements of the girls that had been used on the grass along with the trinkety sheaths.

75

And in his inner restlessness he hated the sight of the natives sweeping and polishing the floor. And the stench of their sweat made him want to retch.

There had been the thick allurement of the dance-hall, and there had been many girls, and all kinds of girls, and they had scattered their raw smells filtered through celanese meshes across every part of the dance-floor. And then in the powdered dust from the floor and in the heat of the hall and in lust they had gone out on to the lawn, where men had used them. They had gone out of the lighted dance-hall into the night, dripping with desire. Girls. And this was what he had to clear up as well. He had to superintend the natives in clearing up not only the litter from the floor and the lawns, but also the staled passions from the walls of the dance-hall. He had to see to it that the natives effaced from the inside of the hall the girls who had danced last night. Girls. They had been there last night and men had had them. And all that he got out of it was this restlessness inside his body. And he looked at more of the rubbish that a native brought in a dust-pan from the lawn, to fling into the ash-can. Girls. Girls, he thought. Willing receptacles for filth. Their bodies were reeking dust-bins. A girl with dark eyes and her hair done up in a perm and with a red flower stuck behind her ear. And soft laughter. And her breath perfumed. And her dress long and wide and sweeping, and glittering in the electric light. And her stockings fastened up to above her thighs with the clips of a pink suspender-belt. And powder on her face and lipstick on her mouth. And on the lawn her dress pulled up to above her stockings. And lawn-grass trim and smooth and well-kept and the girl's body rank and animal and disgusting. A stinking, dented pail that you chucked filth into. "Go and empty this bloody thing outside!" the superintendent shouted at a native, and he spat into the dust-bin.

But there was a surer comfort in this man's words, in the words that Bennet was draping around her, Marta thought.

"You are very beautiful," Bennet was saying. "Your wrists and ankles are so slender. And your eyes are dark with depth, as though you have known sorrow. As though you have known – "

Bennet hesitated for the right word.

"Filth," Marta said, simply.

The Bridge

The woman leant over the bridge and looked into the water flowing bulky-shouldered in the night's shadows. On the horizon the lights of the town gleamed a dull orange under the cold stars. The woman was unconscious of the presence of the man at her side, except that whenever he spoke his words disturbed her inward tranquillity unpleasantly; they were heavy stones flung into the black water, worrying its surface calm.

"There is grass there, by the side of the bridge," the man said again. "I'll spread out my coat there for you to lie on – and – and – "

"Yes," the woman said, "but afterwards. Not now. No, not now."

Silver spears of light on the dark water. Stabbing shafts of light, breaking in the middle and getting blunted at the points. If one of those lights could strike root a new kind of world would be born, on which strong new ages would creep about, and in the flowering of a new earth there would be perfumes that would make you sick with their swift intoxication; there would be the scent of sinful youth on your fingertips. You would be glad that God had given you a body that could bend with the moon and that could pour out yellow seasons in a rush of sadness.

"It is late, Marta," the man said. "Let us go now to the side of the bridge."

It was all right for him, Marta thought bitterly. But these thoughts did not come out of her head or out of her blood, even. They were thoughts about the man at her side that the water under the bridge sent up, and the water was flowing through her body in an elemental raping of her femaleness. To Marta it was not important that a man stood on the bridge beside her, while the rampant water was taking her in broad defilement. But to the water under her feet it was a thing of shame that in those moments a man should be there in his physical urgencies.

"It is all right for you," Marta said aloud, and in her speaking she reflected the quick-breathed passion of the water. It was too dark for the water to reflect the figure of the woman leaning over the rail of the bridge.

"Come over to the grass, Marta," the man said again, his voice husky. "It will be over soon."

"Even sooner," Marta answered.

She began unbuttoning her overcoat in a dark instinct that leant far out over the water.

Denticulated Space Bloom

Now is the time of the parade through the flat streets, and the maid is fortunate whose body has nothing to sell to the shop windows winking in the electric lights. Trumpeters walk at the head of the procession. Blaring brazen instruments set between shapely moving white pillars and open to the night scatter unripe sounds like troubled fragrances sifted through nets and fine perforations. Somebody reaches up and plucks a star quickly, to stop with it a hole in a sieve. For in the gaudy parade under the long-curved smoke of the evening the city street is become a sieve full of holes.

Peep-hole and key-hole and port-hole, and the eye of a needle and the puncture in a rubber tube. Under the pavement is the maze of sewage pipes and storm-water drains. And above the pavement there are passages and tunnels and lift-shafts and staircase entrances and dark galleries.

The young man threads his way in and out of the parade. Lo, where-with shall he be comforted? The old man who has been thrust aside and has much ado to escape being trampled under the milling feet – lo, he has already found comfort: in theology and philology, in philosophy and theosophy, in nought and in thought, in God and the rod. But the young man whose lungs are filled with a bloody air threads his way through the silver-specked flanks of the evening that is heavy with per-fume. The street is a sieve full of holes and the parade has become one single woman clad in red silk and with a sapphire at her throat, and her long smooth fingers fragrant with myrrh, and holding in her arms ex-tended in front of her bosom golden beads and many white roses, whose petals drip on to the pavement. And one by one the golden beads roll on to the pavement.

"You can come with me to my room," the woman says to the young man. "You may have me. Take me."

And so the young man lifts the roses from the woman's extended arms and flings them into the gutter. And he strikes the golden beads from her, so that they flow along the sides of the pavement like the froth that floats and flows on top of a dream.

And he dabs at his forehead because it is damp. And a million pores open in his body, from which the sweat exudes. A million holes open-ing in his body to the scented night.

"I have found that which I sought," the young man says. "When I am buried may my grave be deep. The joy of parting with life lies not in dying but in being buried. That which I sought was not what I desired. That man is truly blessed who, when he dies, has only one grave My spirit is now sorely tormented and my flesh is now sadly tantalised because in the universe there has opened up for me a million billion graves."

Out in the street again the young man met the old man. The old man wore a white rose in his lapel. Within the curve of one of the petals of the rose was caught a small golden bead that had become enclosed there when the rose was lying in the gutter, where the young man had flung it, together with all the other white roses and the many golden beads that the woman had held in her arms extended before her bosom, when she and the young man had met earlier in the evening.

"You have picked that white rose up out of the gutter, where I flung it," the young man said, and sneered.

"No. I plucked this white rose growing," the old man answered. "It was growing on a grave."

A Shorter History of South Africa

N this treatise on South African history, I am to some extent handi-
capped by the fact that I know next to nothing about my subject – a
drawback under which a number of famous writers appear to labour.
Moreover, as the one history text-book which I happen to possess goes
back only as far as 1785, I still have to rely largely on memory.

There seems to exist some doubt in the minds of historians as to
who was the first African explorer, but Henry the Navigator seems to be
very popular in that respect, while others favour his nephew, Henry of
Navarre, who flourished round about the year 1632, or perhaps it was
1362. He is now either dead or bankrupt – I don't know which, but I
know something serious happened to him.

Vasco Diaz, following in Henry's footsteps – here we wish to point
out that we do not definitely state what Henry, but the reader may take
it for granted that the one he particularly fancies is the one intended –
discovered, on December 25, some land which he called Christmas,
and spelt Natal. As an instance of the almost incredible ignorance then
prevailing, this is fairly typical. Even I would have known better than
that.

Besides the above, Vasco Diaz did quite a number of other things
which may or may not have had some effect on our country, but, that
celebrated personage being dead, we are not likely to gain much by dis-
cussing him further, either to his credit or otherwise.

Two or three centuries later, the first settlers arrived here from Europe.
As gold had not yet been discovered in South Africa, we have every
reason to believe that they were not Scotchmen. (Scotchmen, please forgive us, we simply couldn't resist the temptation.) These people, being
1820 in number, were called the 1820 Settlers. Their arrival created a
sensation which, by the way, has not died down yet.

Somewhere about this time, a new language called Dutch was invented by a gentleman whose name I forget. He is not often mentioned
nowadays, but the fact that the language still exists, and has even spread
to Holland, a country on the west coast of Europe, is sufficient proof
that he used to be fairly popular.

I fear the reader may not agree with some of the facts and figures
laid down in this history. We freely admit, however, that it does not

tally with most history books, for we highly disapprove of making use of second-hand originality, and we claim this to be entirely new information, and, as we consider our word to be just as good as anybody else's, we do not see why the reader should not find this work both interesting and instructive.

Cricket and How to Play It

A s cricket is now in full swing, we have decided to impart some information on the subject to those whose knowledge of the game is only of an elementary character. The following course of instruction, therefore, is offered for what it is worth – or even less.

In every quarter of the globe, and also in every eighth and sixteenth, this game (which dates back to the time it was first invented) is played in white boots, a white shirt and a pair of white ducks. A leather belt will also be found indispensable to prevent the loss of the said ducks and the unfavourable comment usually inspired by such an event. The alternative system, namely that of retaining one's hands in one's pockets, is not recommended, and nowadays eschewed by all first-class exponents of the game.

Having provided himself in the necessary clothes, the prospective player's next step will be to join the cricket club. This latter is a society of cricketers and not, as is usually imagined, the implement with which the ball is struck. Should the amateur cricketer desire to start a club of his own, he would be well advised to obtain a cricket set, the size of which depends upon whether he intends to play single or double wicket. Should he, for a start, decide upon the former, he will require a bat and ball and four wickets, besides a number of players. Although most professional works on the subject advocate the use of only three wickets, it is nevertheless as well to be provided with an extra one with which to enforce order.

If the founder of the club knows a thing or two, he will elect himself treasurer, thereby avoiding the useless formality of paying his subscriptions and at the same time being able to enjoy as good a game as any other member. Some years ago we personally were made trustee of a cricket fund, with such satisfactory results that all the members afterwards admitted that they could not have appointed a better man for the job. They were right, too; we have the money yet.

Everything being in readiness, the team will proceed to take the field. This latter phrase should not be accepted too literally, especially if the ground happens to be private property, in which case 'taking the field' will probably lead to complications with the owner, to the distinct disadvantage of both team and cricket set.

With the aid of the foregoing useful information, the young cricketer should be able to play fairly efficiently, and, presuming that he has acted on our advice, we shall leave him at his game until he has either become tired of it, or until he has raked in sufficient filthy lucre to keep him going until next season.

Keeping Fit

ALTHOUGH not a professor of physical culture myself, I nevertheless have an uncle who knows something about botulism, and a cousin who is acquainted with Maxwell's Law of Capillary Action; so I think that in writing an article on 'keeping fit' I am as well qualified as most writers on the subject. I have not tried any of the following exercises personally, but some of my friends who have done so and still survive state that they need no other form of exercise now, and that if they continue on my system much longer, all they will require is an undertaker.

With careful dieting, however, even the best physical culture course is comparatively useless, so that the tyro (another word for mug) who tries his hand at the system I have mapped out will be well advised to see to his diet, and, while training, to eat nothing but food. I call them the daily 'Half-dozen.'

One. – Standing erect, slowly raise one foot, and keep on raising it, after which you can put it down again and leave it where you found it. Raise the other leg in the same way, and continue lifting both feet alternately. If you particularly want to, you may, of course, raise both feet at the same time – but I will not be held responsible for the consequences.

Two. – With hands on hips, take a deep breath and swing slowly forward from the waist. I don't know where you have to swing to, but that's what it says in all the text-books, anyway. Keep on swinging in this fashion, until the foolishness of your actions dawns upon you, when you can go on to numbers –

Three, Four and Five, in which you do various stunts, such as inhaling deeply, counting ten, and exhaling counting ten backwards, until we arrive at

Six, which is the only sensible exercise of the lot. For this performance a chain and a length of rope are essential. One end of the rope having been attached to the ceiling, the chair is placed immediately beneath it. Everything is now in readiness for the performance, and, although some trouble may have been experienced in fitting up the apparatus, the result amply repays the labour involved. The performer, having mounted the chair, now secures the loose end of the rope to his neck and, counting three, gently steps off the edge of the chair. The effect is both striking and eminently satisfactory, and I would to heaven that every health crank would avail himself of the opportunity.

From a Student's Diary

December 1, 1922.

It was still dark when I awoke. The cocks were crowing cheerfully. Here and there a dog was barking. How goodly did I think their fortunes when compared with my misfortunes. It was impossible for one to sleep any longer – the heat was stifling. I had spent a very restless night. Thus, although the time was only about four o'clock, I got out of bed, dressed rapidly, opened the door quietly and went out into the still night air. Ah! The open air at last. I drew a deep breath; and, perhaps, for the first time in my life, gave thanks unto God for His great kindness in sending up the cool breeze which was blowing at the time – but not for creating me, for, to tell the truth, I wished that I was anywhere but on earth.

I hied me to the hill near our house. Having climbed it, I seated myself upon the topmost point, and decided to wait for the dawn which could not be very far off now.

At last I began to observe objects before me more plainly. The morning star gradually disappeared, and it was dawn. The dew lay thick upon the ground. I had taken a book with me to read, and as soon as it was light enough I opened it and tried to learn some Latin. Alas, it was impossible! I could not concentrate my mind on the work, and after a time, put it away.

The birds were twittering in the branches, and now and again an early labourer passed on his way to his daily toil. An hour had gone by since dawn, and the sun had not yet risen. But, lo! As I looked, a red tinge appeared on the eastern horizon. The tinge gradually deepened. A few minutes more, and out bursts Phoebus in all his majestic glory, flooding the town with light. It was a beautiful sight. Another day had begun, but woe is me! – my doom is sealed – our examinations begin today.

The Canterbury Tales

THIRTY pilgrims riding forth into the dawn!

This is the framework round which Chaucer has woven those wonderful tales, which are still as fresh as ever and reach clear to the reader's heart across five weary centuries. It is strange to think that the young squire's embroidered gown has been faded these many long years; it is strange to reflect that the "Good Wif of biside Bathe", the Nun, the Friar, the "Doctour of Phisik" and the Merchant all lived and died in those far-off days when men still thought of their religion as something worth fighting for, and – for this was long before the advent of the modern woman – when women were content to be considered merely beautiful and good; but this is the strangest thought of all, that the hand which created these humanity-breathing pilgrims lies mingled with the dust of that historic past.

What Chaucer's secret is, and how he has managed to infuse into his work that spirit of vitality, I do not pretend to know. But I do know that these people whose inmost soul he has laid bare in his gently ironic way are living men and women; they are not paragons of virtue, certainly, but with all their shames and hypocrisies, their frailties and foibles, they are essentially human and essentially lovable. We have the Nun, whose love for God's lower creatures runs to the extent of feeding her "smale houndes" with "rosted Flessh, or milk and wastel-breed" at a time when gaunt famine stalked abroad.

There is the Merchant who, according to his own account, is engaged in huge business transactions and "ful wel his wit bisette: There wiste no wight that he was in dette." Then comes the poor Parson, and we suddenly find ourselves face to face with sublimity. For we have here a man who is ardently sincere, whose prayers are not lip service and whose passionate soul is not content to deal merely in theories and abstractions, but "Christes loore and his apostles twelve He taughte; but first he folwed it hymselve."

There is, perhaps, in the poetic simplicity of the "General Prologue" nothing that can approach the haunting splendour of some of Virgil's pathetic half-lines, or that can compare with Shakespeare's thunderous magnificence. Yet ever and again we find, scattered throughout the piece, some startlingly vivid descriptive passage which is equal to anything in the literature of the world. That line, for instance, depicting a sailor on horseback – "He rood upon a rouncy, as he kouthe" – is as unforgettable as the last touch which Chaucer puts into the portrait of the Miller: "His mouth as greet was as a greet forneys."

Thus, when the "General Prologue" ends, it is with a feeling of regret that we bid farewell to these pilgrims and leave them to travel eastwards. It is a pretty scene, this last one, although it possesses a gentle sadness all its own; for it is symbolic of this life of ours, of which every day is but a further stage of our journey into the vast unknown.

Pride of the Reef

'PRIDE of the Reef' – Benoni has long enjoyed the sobriquet, but there is a feeling abroad that some mistake has been made. The other day somebody discovered that Benoni was a hot rival to Durban in the matter of soiled undergarments. This person (who, by the way, is myself) found that Benoni is not all shady avenues and ornate municipal offices, but that it contains a cesspool from which the effluvium is offensive enough to drive out all thoughts of pride. There is a front view and a back view to most things, and whilst inclined to agree with the bright young Mayor that Benoni is good to look at, as far as the front view goes, I want to say that the back view provides the most mangled scene that it has ever been my misfortune to encounter.

I refer to Benoni's 'black belt' – the native location where 10 000 souls wallow in a mire of disease, filth and corruption that almost surpasses belief. I am just a casual South African, inured to the sight of the unkempt, ill-nurtured native, and until now I have never given much thought to the advancement of anybody but myself. But I am changing my view, and I think there is a limit to what we can inflict on the native.

After viewing the conditions of this 'black belt' at Benoni, I am beginning to think differently about the various native organisations that seem to be arising in our midst. Hitherto I have regarded the right to organise as the supreme privilege of the white man, but if the inhabitants of the native location at Benoni were to rise up in arms against the conditions under which they exist you could count on me as one person who would not take up a rifle for the purpose of shooting them down. I have seen these conditions, which are enough for me.

Here is an extract from the report of the local M. O. H. issued last month: "During the year there were 119 European and 655 native deaths, a decrease of 13 European and an increase of 104 native deaths. Thirty white and 186 native infants died, representing a decrease and increase respectively of 14 and 45. The population is 15 074 Europeans and 34 372 natives." Thus it will be observed that the native mortality was 200 percent greater than that of the whites.

The M. O. H. expresses surprise at the state of affairs in view of the increased medical supervision. But why surprise? Has he not on many rainy days seen mud and slush inches deep all over the roads – there are no paths – and on dusty days fought his way through a maze of flying earth and garbage? Has he not been there in the evening when the smoke from hundreds of burning braziers gives the place the appearance of an inferno?

The M. O. H. is an admirable, conscientious man, but he has a lot to learn. What is wanted are good roads and increased sanitary supervision. A camp with a population of about 10 000 souls really requires a sanitary service of its own. An amount approaching £9 000 per annum is raked in by the Municipality from rents alone, and all the municipal tenant gets for his twelve guineas per annum are two rooms, free water from a public tap and free use, in community with some forty other families, of a public latrine. And yet he does not protest – because he has not got a vote.

It can safely be said that, owing to its isolated position, cut off as it is by the railway line, not one percent of the white population has visited the location. The oldest inhabitant does not remember seeing a councillor on the spot.

If anyone doubts the accuracy of the foregoing, let him or her give the kerk a miss on a wet Sunday morning and cover the two miles there. He or she must not look only in the shop window, attractively dressed as it is with a superintendent's model house, comfy police quarters and brass-buttoned 'boys', with the streets in the vicinity in fair condition – but go round to the back premises and see the squalor and filth. If his or her heart does not go out to the denizens of Benoni's 'black belt', then there isn't such a thing as a heart.

The writer is not a pro-Bantu, a disappointed office-seeker or a disgruntled ratepayer: simply a humanitarian who is colour blind in the cause of justice.

The Professor

I<small>T</small> was a hot day. The sunshine streamed in through the windows, so that a few of the students near the wall blinked their eyes because of the yellow glare on their white notebooks. Others in the lecture-room also half-closed their eyes, not because of the light, but just because they were sleepy and weren't thinking what the professor was saying. They were thinking of the SRC nominations. Of the heat. Of their accounts at the tea-room across the way. Of the Muizenberg beach. Of the ink-stains on the asbestos ceiling, and how they got there. Of the school-teachers who would qualify next year, and how on earth they'd all find jobs. Of childbirth. . .

All the time the professor droned on about Kant and the categorical imperative. He spoke mechanically as he had spoken for years, explaining that Kant brought about a revolution in philosophical thought by his analysis of the principles underlying human motives. The highest type of actions were those motivated by a sense of duty, and when personal inclination came into conflict with that sense of duty, then personal inclination must be sacrificed. The professor said that, whereas before man had merely been regarded as a means, now he was regarded as an end in himself. In a sense, it was Kant's teachings that had given rise to humanitarianism, and that had led to the French Revolution and the abolition of slavery. It was a new orientation –

A student wondered whether this had anything to do with what the newspapers were saying about a new orientation of political parties.

For the first time in many years the professor started thinking for himself. How absurd this whole business was, he reflected, and how futile. Also, what a lot of lies he was palming off on students. Fortunately, of the whole lot there was not a man or woman who could think independently. So it didn't matter what he told them. If he didn't tell them lies, somebody else would.

Still, it was rather funny to stand there talking about human motives, and right and wrong, and duty and honour. It was funny standing there and telling them smooth words. No man ever loved anybody but himself. No man ever performed an action for any reason other than that of self-gratification. No man ever assisted what he was pleased to term a brother in distress for any reason other than that of the feeling of smug satisfaction and superiority which it gave him.

Yet here he was standing, he, the professor, telling the students sweet and beautiful falsehoods about things like categorical imperatives, and all the time he was disguising from them the ugly truth about themselves. But was the truth really so ugly? Yes, it was. But, ugly or not, they had to face it. Swiftly the professor came to a decision.

"I have spoken about a new orientation," he said. "I find that my attitude towards you and my lectures has also undergone a new orientation. I have made up my mind that I am going to stop telling you lies."

The students looked up and gasped.

"You're a vile lot of detestable scum, the whole damn lot of you," he said. "That is the truth. You are also as mangy a collection of degraded fools, liars, poltroons, hypocrites and mental slaves as one can meet anywhere in the world. That also is truth. Now get some other soft lunatic of an idealist to tell you lies."

He walked out, swearing coarse oaths.

Afterwards, when the sensation had died down, and the professor had gone off on pension, people spoke about it and shook their heads.

"Such a clever fellow, too," they said. "It must have been his nerves."

Nerves? Perhaps. I don't know. But Nietzsche was also a man who found truth. And he ended up by dancing about, in the street, in front of a barrel-organ.

The Artist

W E cannot know how art was born. We can only guess at its origin, vaguely, and then theorise further, in the hope that our theorising may be correct. All this, of course, applies only to the fine arts. Music we can understand in a way. Literature is also not difficult to comprehend in its beginnings: for the art of the story-teller, in a somewhat sublimated form, is merely the time-old art of the efficient liar. Right through those long ages in which mankind floundered towards the light, sidetracked often, stumbling often, there was always a premium on a good lie. Today things are in no wise different. The good liar is always assured of a steady income, either as a salesman or as an author – although in this latter case the income is perhaps not so steady.

At all events, the man of the dawn who first scrawled crude figures on the wall of his cave is also the man who stands at the head of a long line that extends in unbroken fashion from the caveman's day to our own. In some manner the artist and the poet are related. I don't mean that they are similar merely in the physical sense of being useless and generally speaking pestiferous. (For the artist and the poet have this much in common, that they succeed to a marked degree in making themselves objectionable to the rest of the race.) But they also appear to have a definite spiritual kinship.

The poet and the artist are the world's dreamers. If nothing else, they have golden visions that they are sometimes able to relate in an attenuated shape to the men who cannot of themselves dream grandly.

But it is possible that the world can do without dreams.

And it is certain that the poet and the artist, that cringing and godlike brotherhood, cannot always get other men to listen to what they have to tell them. The greatest singers have probably been mute. The greatest painters have probably never set brush to paper. And we are all of us the poorer because they have remained silent. But they themselves have really been better off, for if they had indulged their dreams, the chances are that they would have gone hungry.

In the pages that follow immediately are reproductions of some of the best works of a number of famous painters. They are superb artists, for the reason that they are also poets. In sinuous lines and swells and voluptuous curves they tell of the things they have felt about the old earth, her beauty and her pain and her whisperings.

For some moments they have viewed the Vision Splendid; they have seen the dazzling hues of her raiment, and with their hands they have touched its hems.

By the Kerbside

THE other night I strolled through town in a leisurely manner. There seemed to be a certain freshness about the evening; the air held a fragrance that you don't often find about the Johannesburg streets. I noticed that there were other people, also, who obtained a profound spiritual gratification just from breathing the city air. One man even sat down on the pavement, so that he could breathe the air in better, I suppose. When I passed again, two hours later, he was still sitting there. By that time he was asleep.

I stopped near the New Law Courts. A small knot of people were standing on the corner, admiring what is undoubtedly one of the finest of Johannesburg's night effects. Radiant against a black sky the stately lines of Herbert Evans's buildings are a triumph of aesthetic grace. Our city has all too few of these architectural beauties. If we had more beautiful buildings we would be better citizens.

Curiosity led me into the H. O. D. Hall in Van der Merwe Street. Inside the hall an obscure looking gathering listened attentively to a man of about thirty-five, who was giving an exposition of Spengler's *The Decline of the West*. I ascertained that the lecturer's name is Willie Bloomberg, and that the audience, comprising the Jewish Working Man's Club, consisted exclusively of members of the artisan class.

Later that evening I met my old friend, Gerrit Heytmayer. Though I had not seen him for several years, I recognised him immediately by his erect carriage and energetic stride. He looked as youthful as ever. There is no doubt that the only natural way of preserving the figure is by scientific physical culture.

Subsequently I went to dinner, accompanied by a prominent M. P., who gave me some interesting information about an organisation that is preparing for a South African prohibition campaign on a large scale. We went into what is recognised as being one of Johannesburg's most fashionable hotels. Even outside the Transvaal this hotel has a reputation for exclusiveness. The fish-knife with which I was supplied was very brightly polished. Unfortunately, however, its flat upper edge was covered by a black, scaly layer of polish to which I drew the waiter's attention. In no way disconcerted, he calmly took the fish-knife and wiped it on my table napkin.

It is strange how a slight incident of this nature gives one the impression – perhaps unjustly – that the whole institution is run under unhygienic conditions.

Talking about hotels.

There does not seem to be very much doubt that, in order to combine first-class service and appointments with an atmosphere of exclusiveness, it is necessary for an hotel to be situated not in the city itself, but in one of Johannesburg's fashionable suburbs. From this point of view Berea seems to be ideal. Incidentally, Berea is a suburb that derives a considerable amount of prestige from the fact that the Stephanie Hotel is situated in it.

They tell me the Stephanie is a wonderful place for wedding parties. Judging by the expression on her face, the average bride seems to be the happiest creature in God's universe. If I owned a fashionable hotel I would follow Stephanie's example and encourage brides to stay at the place. Just their presence makes the world a more pleasant place to live in.

As everybody in Johannesburg knows, a new store is opening in our city this month. It is always a pleasureable feeling, this realisation that actually the trade depression of which we hear so much nowadays is insignificant compared with the one we went through immediately after the war. Of course, what is wrong with the world today is that, after the weak link in the chain of fictitious prosperity broke in the autumn of 1929, the public in general became afraid to spend. People are all holding off buying something which under normal conditions they would buy. The effect of this is obvious. By trying to cut down expenses through not making purchases that in the ordinary way we would make, we are actually lowering the purchasing power of everyone else. The present trade depression would lift in *one month* if everybody would carry on and expend his money in a normal manner. For a business firm a time of depression is ideal for advertising; for the general public this is the ideal time for making purchases, now that prices are temporarily low to tempt the buyer.

Anyway, the newly opened Paramount Stores, which will be equal in size and range to any of our present mammoth emporiums, have already got the confidence of the Johannesburg public, if only for their courage in opening business in our city at this time. If more firms followed their example and *The Touleier's* there would be less talk of unemployment.

A number of prominent businessmen have been complaining to me about the unsatisfactory results they are obtaining from foreign typewriters that are now on the South African market. They have asked me whether there is no good class of British machine that I can recommend to them. Of course there is. The Bar-lock Typewriter, which gives the best value for money of all typewriters in the world, is exclusively British. At a time like this, when canting pessimists talk gloomily of the future of Great Britain, it is comfortable to reflect that in open competition with the rest of the world British industry can still more than hold its own.

A misprint that is affording amusement of a mixed sort in Parktown social circles: "At the. . . wedding the service was a chloral one."
It would almost appear as though that was the only way of getting the bridegroom to the altar.

Only the other night I realised how intensely beautiful a spot the Zoo Lake is in the moonlight. Of course, the municipal authorities have realised this fact long ago. The amazingly low rates at which Johannesburg's municipal trams and buses convey passengers to the local beauty spots was something on which the last party of American tourists commented with marked enthusiasm.
There is a serenity about the Zoo Lake at night. The trees, vague and shadowy, stretch away softly into the darkness. When I was there last week a large number of couples had taken advantage of the moonlight and the benches. We all talk a great deal when the dark trees cast their shadows on the silver grass, and well-known objects seem indefinite about us, and the moon is full. And we mean every word we say.
This sort of thing: "You've got eyes like the still waters of a lake," the lover whispers to his mistress. "Dark eyes, pensive and mystery filled."
That is what he says, and there is no doubt that he is right. It is a way the moonlight has. The moonlight can make a lopsided coffee-pot look pensive and mystery filled.

"Your hair is golden dusky as the sunset, my dearest," the lover continues. "Let us get married soon. We shall be very happy. Then the birds will be singing always, and in our hearts the flowers will bloom. And. . . and," he murmurs brokenly, with the intense ardour that is of youth, "and when pa snuffs it I get his dough. He won't last long, now, with his lung trouble. That old man's spitting blood."

Whether it rolls forth grandly, with the tramping glory of an army in its triumph, or whispers plaintively of broken things, great music makes a direct appeal to the emotions. When the notes falter our heart throbs falter also. The other morning I spent half an hour in Mackay's music salon. What I saw there was a revelation to me. I understood, then, why it is that at bottom we are all of us music lovers. The manager told me that Mackay's is the best house in Africa for musical instruments. Judging from the variety of instruments they showed me, I should say that the manager is right.

Addison and Steele started this type of commentary on current topics at the beginning of the eighteenth century. They adopted the pen-names of *The Tatler* and *Spectator*. Today we have their lineal descendants writing as *Straatlooper*, *The Saunterer* and *The Pilgrim*. In response to the public demand for a similar series of topical notes, *The Touleier* is introducing "By the Kerbside." I therefore take this opportunity of requesting readers of *The Touleier* to suggest a suitable name for myself as the writer of this commentary. A friend of mine has suggested the name *Gutter-sheik*. I am not sure whether I should continue this friendship.

Last week I visited the Carlton Turkish Baths, in the company of a well-known man from the Corner House, who has for several weeks been undergoing electric treatment to reduce superfluous fat. . . of which he has quite a lot. This Corner House man says that a bulky appearance is a considerable advantage in a way, as it gives him a prosperous and imposing appearance, which stands him in good stead at Board meetings. On the other hand, there is no gainsaying the fact that even the best of us find it somewhat of a handicap if we are unable to ascertain easily whether our shoelaces are tied, our waistcoats being in the way.

We entered the Carlton Hotel and took the lift to the basement. We undressed in a special, luxuriously appointed cubicle. Then, clad in gaudy bathrobes, we passed into the baths. I was struck by the similarity between the modern Turkish bath and the old Roman idea. In the first place, the two rooms we first entered – in which the air was kept at a high temperature – might have been a replica of the ancient Roman sudatorium. Here, reclining on long forms, lay men of all ages. One of them greeted my fat friend from the Corner House. I learnt that a little while before he had also been excessively corpulent, but that since he had come under electric treatment he had lost a considerable amount of weight.

"I can even get into the lift these days without turning sideways," he remarked amid laughter. These boys from the Chamber of Mines will have their little jokes.

After we had passed through the various stages of bathing and electric massaging – which was administered by Professor Carey in person – we came under the hands of a Swedish masseur. He was a young giant with enormous muscles and arms and thighs that, as regards development, compared quite favourably with Professor Carey's own magnificent proportions. I was pleased that this young giant was inclined to be friendly.

When we left the baths for the dressing room I felt my body tingling with a sensation of new vigour; mentally I was exuberant. My friend and I raced up the stairs together. I would have won, too, had it not been that my friend, who is a regular visitor to the Carlton Turkish Baths, had more staying power than I.

The young lady in the office told me that on a Sunday morning it is a common occurrence for half a dozen middle-aged men to come rushing up the stairs in a body.

I think they would run even quicker if that Swedish masseur chased them.

There is good reason to believe that the trade depression is lifting. The usual Sunday night crowd that gathers round the Communist orators on the Town Hall steps has dwindled to a couple of dozen. And even they don't appear to be particularly enthusiastic. To get the public interested in them, a good idea would be for the orators to stop making speeches and merely roll about the lawn a few times. Kicking pieces out of the turf seems as good a way as any of showing their contempt for capitalist institutions.

I don't think we men are getting a square deal. Look at this Talkie Competition that Kinemas and *The Touleier* are running to find a new

Hollywood star. They want a thousand beautiful girls. Now what I want to know is why can't they give the men a chance and invite photographs from a thousand noble looking young men? A male beauty parade down Eloff Street on a Saturday would make a unique appeal to the Rand public.

Only I am afraid that some of the other men might get jealous and shoot one or two members of the Beauty Chorus.

(Readers of The Touleier *are invited to suggest an appropriate name for the writer of these notes, which will be a monthly feature of this magazine.)*

I received a large number of replies to my request that the readers of *The Touleier* should supply me with a name. Most of the suggestions were very good. The name I eventually decided to adopt is 'Al-Rashid', sent in by Miss Doreen Ogley, Smit Street, Braamfontein, to whom our prize of half a guinea is awarded.

The reference is, of course, to the Caliph Haroun Al-Rashid of *The Arabian Nights*, who scoured the streets of Old Baghdad of an evening, interesting himself in the welfare of his subjects. I can understand how Al-Rashid felt about the Caliph business. The difference between Haroun Al-Rashid and myself is that hitherto the people who have requested me to interest myself in their welfare are mostly bums and battlers.

A friend told me a story about a burglar, who in turn was a friend of his. It is a singular kind of story, and there are one or two features that would make some people doubt its accuracy.

"A few years ago," my friend said, "I was in Lourenço Marques with a man whom everybody knew to be a burglar. That is, everybody knew it, except, of course, the police. Eventually even the police became somewhat suspicious about him, for they found him driving through the town with a stick of dynamite in his pocket. There were also a set of burglar's tools and a sack of assorted silverware in the back of his car. So they took him to the police station and fined him for driving without a licence.

"Anyway, one night, when we were in the room together, I wanted to open a trunk of mine, which was locked and the key missing. With the impetuous zeal of the professional man confronted with a case, my friend took out a stick of dynamite and got to work on that trunk. We had barely got out of the room into the street when there was an explosion that shook the whole building. It shook it so much, in fact, that three-quarters of it went up into the air right away. The rest followed a few fractions of a second later. It took a little while before all the debris settled. Then, last of all, the trunk came down, right at our feet.

"The trunk was still unopened."

As I have said, to many people this story would appear somewhat incredible. Only, I know that it is true in all details, because the man who told it to me showed me the trunk, and there wasn't a scratch on it, so that you'd never think it had been dynamited, if you didn't know.

Mama turned up and papa turned up,
But no bridegroom with a ring turned up.

Only yesterday it seemed that song was at the height of its popularity. Today it is practically forgotten. It is singular, though, that a trifling circumstance such as that mentioned in the song can spoil a whole marriage. They can say what they like, but a wedding is never quite the same thing if the bridegroom isn't present (with the bride all on her own the institution of marriage is made to appear more onesided than it actually is – although we know it is onesided enough at the best of times).

Therefore, for a wedding to be really a success, it is essential to have a bridegroom. What is almost equally necessary is a wedding bouquet supplied by the Irene Florists of Cathedral Mansions.

Miss Beryl Robb's studio is situated within easy access of the railway station. She purposely chose the Tower Buildings at the corner of Plein and Joubert Streets to suit the convenience of her numerous clients from places outside the city. In many respects Miss Robb's is an ideal salon for teaching purposes. The large windows running the length of the room and the excellent floor contribute towards making this dancing academy the artistic success it undoubtedly is. A few minutes in her company made it clear to me to what extent Miss Beryl Robb has impressed her own very interesting personality on the surroundings.

It is always a pleasure to call.

For those of us who entertain secret hopes of one day becoming famous (in other words, approximately 99.9 percent of the human race), it is somewhat distressing to read of the ease with which Major Topolai achieved lasting greatness only a few weeks ago. Two men fired a number of shots at King Zog of Albania, and all that happened was –

Major Topolai, who was standing near the king, was killed on the spot. Accordingly, even before he reached the mortuary, Major Topolai was world famous, and just because he wasn't as quick as King Zog in jumping out of the way of a bullet.

This doesn't seem to be at all fair. I have been trying for years and years to become famous, and all I have got so far is rheumatism.

It is a splendid advertisement for a man to get shot, standing alongside a king. You get your name in all the papers and people talk about you for weeks afterwards. And then think of the pull it gives you to have a monarch in his own right giving evidence at your inquest.

If there is any anarchist looking for a man whom he wants to shoot standing next to a king, or even a queen or an archduke, he can always have me. He needn't pay me for my services, either. I'll do it just for the fame.

In some respects Aldous Huxley has said the last word about education. But the fact still remains that it is always preferable for a child to be placed in an environment in which it can react sympathetically towards the teacher. The most obvious principle in the general theory of education is simply that the child should be assisted in drawing on the qualities latent in him, rather than that he should be crammed from outside with a knowledge that he cannot absorb and which therefore does not become an intimate part of him. The Educational Institute of 44, Moseley Buildings, President Street, is conducted on the most modern lines, and a very earnest attempt is made to adapt the instruction to the needs of an individual scholar.

There is so much in our lives that consists of little useless things – which are also the only things that are worthwhile. Even though we do not always realise it clearly, our pleasurable emotions are bound up exclusively with dreams and flowers and pictures. Every hope is a dream, which is all the more potent and colourful because it has been dreamt in waking. Pictures are things of the sunset and the dawn light. And then there are flowers. The carnation's pink head drooping in sullen beauty. The glory of a pale rose, morning ravished, its petals heavy with the dew. . . The lily whispering of bridals. . . These are the thoughts that occurred to me the other morning in the showroom of the Grosvenor Florist in Bree Street. I entered the establishment to buy a button-hole. I remained there captivated by the fragrance of the flowers.

I don't know who the man was who first said that he had abandoned smoking because it was too effeminate. (It is a pity that this remark has become so well known, otherwise I would have had no hesitation in claiming this piece of wit as my own.) Anyway, it is a sad business – if there is anything really sad in life, which is doubtful – that so many men should be acquiring women's view and vice versa. (This is the only pun I have ever made, and I am already sorry about it.) If the manufacturers of cosmetics were able to trace all their sales, I am satisfied that a large portion of the purchasers of face cream and lipstick would be found to be men. In the same way, smoking and drinking are becoming exclusively feminine habits. In fact, nowadays no girl is considered really feminine unless, in her spare time, she smokes dagga.

It will no doubt interest readers to learn that amongst the distinguished people who have received treatment from Professor Carey are Sir Harry Lauder, the Managing Director of *The Touleier* and myself.

One of the most significant features of his Health Institute is the electric treatment administered by Professor Carey in person. A few days ago I was in a somewhat debilitated state, through over-exerting my brain – thinking out interesting topics for "By the Kerbside." For that reason I visited the Carlton Turkish Baths once more and I feel that I can now write better. No doubt unfriendly critics will contend that the benefit received from Professor Carey's treatment is not reflected in these notes. But that remark will lose its sting because I said it first.

Anyway, the scientific treatment which Professor Carey places at the disposal of his clients has an exceptionally invigorating effect on the system. It tones up the nerves and muscles, so that when you leave the institution it is with a feeling of buoyancy and exhilaration.

With a quiet affability Professor Carey conducts the visitor through the various stages of his electrical course. His profound knowledge of the human anatomy enables him to judge with unfailing accuracy the manner in which to apply the electric current, so that each client receives specialised treatment.

Professor Carey has an imposing personality. His unfailing humour stands him in good stead through the arduous responsibilities in which his professional activities involve him. After the radiant heat installation – which is probably the most elaborately conceived health apparatus that has yet been constructed – the most striking feature of the Carlton Turkish Baths is the electric bath; the visitor is almost completely immersed in water and is then massaged by Professor Carey by an altogether unique method.

Deep-chested and broad-shouldered, Professor Carey is a fine specimen of manhood. Although he is getting on towards middle age, he has an erect carriage and a general air of sprightliness which I envy him. For I am still comparatively young, and yet I am going bald on top and I also have what is termed a scholarly stoop: if I was a liquor-seller and not a writer it would be known as a criminal slouch. Professor Carey attributes his health and fitness entirely to his applying his own treatment to himself.

The fact that she is the principal of Elsie Reed's School of Ballroom Dancing, and the further circumstance of her being a SADTA, contributed towards making me expect to meet an imposing and dignified looking woman. Instead, when I called at her studio on the third floor of Nels Rust Building, I was surprised at being greeted by a girl who seems barely out of her teens. Miss Salome Blyth is graceful and slender, and there is a lissom ease about her movements that makes it clear why in every ballroom she is a conspicuous figure. The sister of Mr W. Blyth, the well-known polo player, Miss Salome Blyth gave an exhibition at the Polo Cabaret, one of the year's leading social events. One sees her dance, and immediately one thinks of another Salome, of whom the poets have sung through the ages, a dancer at whose feet lay the heart of a king.

It will interest the many patrons of the Duchess Tea-rooms to learn that the creative efforts of the new management have already met with a marked response. The Johannesburg public is quick in appreciating enterprise and initiative, and the breadth of vision displayed by the new proprietor has established the tea-rooms on a footing that enables the Duchess to compete on equal terms with any in the country.

Their orange drink bar supplies the goods.

The other day I passed through the works of Mr W. H. Hunt. I saw artificial limbs in the course of construction. I also saw limbless men, fitted with scientifically constructed legs, perform really astonishing feats.

A young man, a messenger in government service, engaged me in a walking contest. I didn't come off too badly, although I had difficulty in keeping up with this young man whose leg had been amputated above the knee. Yet he walked with a free stride and a graceful ease of movement, and if I hadn't been told about it I would never have guessed that he was not completely sound in both limbs.

I saw other things, too. For instance, there was a one-legged man who jumped on to a settee and back again on to the floor, landing lightly on both feet in such a way that no one but an expert could tell which one of his legs was artificial.

In the course of about half an hour I saw enough to realise that it is no longer a serious handicap in life to be deprived of a leg. It is a disability that cannot obtrude itself in the ordinary course, for the reason that a well-constructed artificial leg makes it possible for the wearer to perform almost any action of which a normal man is capable.

Mr W. H. Hunt conducted me through his premises in 118, Eloff Street, and in one storeroom I noticed hundreds of discarded artificial legs – crude, clumsy things which unfortunate men had worn before coming to an expert for aid. "How on earth did they ever walk with those things?" I asked.

Mr Hunt smiled slightly. "They didn't," he replied.

Mr Hunt has been engaged in the manufacturing side of the artificial limb business for the greater part of his life. In England he was for many years manager of the world's greatest artificial limb factory. He takes a profound interest in his work, speaking of it with the enthusiasm of the artist.

But what impressed me more than anything else in the course of my visit was the genuine sympathy which Mr Hunt feels for all sufferers, and the fine compassion that is in his utterances.

In common with a number of my *Touleier* confreres, I have kept cultivating the Turkish bath habit. It is a good habit. Whenever I leave Professor Carey's Health Institute it is with the buoyant assurance that life is wonderful, and that existence is very much worthwhile. I know, then, that the trade depression has genuinely lifted and that we are actually back again to the good old days prior to 1929. It is a fact that during the past two months business has brightened considerably, and it is all to the good that the rejuvenating treatment of the Carlton Turkish Baths should strengthen this feeling of optimism.

The radiant heat treatment is unique of its kind. It is like an excursion into fairyland. And when we get away, even for a few moments, from the bustling materialism of life, and enter into some sequestered spot where the world is at peace – then all of us believe, if only for a little while, in the existence of fairies.

You lie at ease in a chamber where an ingenious arrangement of mirrors and electric lights gives the impression of an infinity of gold and crimson; all your senses are pervaded by a pleasant glow. In a radiant world that seems to be blended of the real and the magical, you linger in a bliss and contentment that make outside things appear very far away. There is happiness in dreams. After a few minutes in the radiant heat chamber you feel yourself to be in a strange world of fantasy, the borderland of which is dreams.

Professor Carey is always genial. With a light jest or a quick piece of repartee he meets every situation that arises in his establishment. One feels that his engaging personality is to a very large degree responsible for that atmosphere of jovial camaraderie prevailing in the Turkish Baths. One grips his hand on departing and one feels happier for having known him.

It is the Professor's proud boast that no man or woman has ever visited Carey's Health Institute without coming back to it again. I think I know the reason why.

I wonder what the reason is that so many people nowadays have something the matter with their sight. Prominent amongst the causes contributing to eyestrain are the films; and short frocks on windy days.

At all events, large numbers of my acquaintances suffer in a greater or lesser degree from some sort of defective vision. There are also indirect results from eyestrain. Chronic headaches, for instance, can very often be banished through scientific treatment by an optometrist.

The other evening I interviewed Mr Karno in his consulting room in Von Brandis Street. With his usual modesty Mr Karno made very little mention of his extensive work in Johannesburg. He was even reluctant to talk about his exceptional London qualifications. But before leaving I obtained a surreptitious glance at a large volume of testimonials and appreciative letters Mr Karno has received in the course of his practice.

Science counts, anyway.

A question of which the biologist can give no explanation is that of the affinity existing between a man and a dog. The tame wolf and the glorified ape meet on some common ground that is not easy to understand. For thousands of years the dog has been the friend of

106

man. It is interesting to speculate on the manner in which this friendship was brought about originally. Was it the man who first made overtures to the dog, whistling to him in the language of the wilds, or did the dog first approach the man, licking his hands with a mute caress that is even more ancient than speech? I don't know.

Far back, in the prehistory of the dawn light, we find man accompanied by his dog. There is something of an epic quality about this companionship. In the irregularities of his cortex, slight convulsions in the surface of his brain, man possessed the beginnings of something that was greater than the mastodon and the dinosaur. At what stage of his development man became acquainted with the fact that he owned a force within him that no other animal could share is something that we cannot even guess at; it is enough to know that there was a time when man realised that he was the greatest thing in creation. There was a time when the dog understood that in man there was another animal like himself – but an animal whom he could love and own as his lord.

Into the furthest past where archaeological research leads us, wherever we find that man has passed by, we also discover that he had his dog with him.

"The more I see of my fellow man," said a bitter French cynic, "the more I love my dog."

Of course, an attitude such as this is not fair, either to a man or to a dog. The fact remains that at bottom all animals have the same characteristics. Only these characteristics vary within certain limits, and it so happens that the dog has qualities of courage and fidelity that have made him peculiarly suitable as a stand-by of man in his centuries-old toilings and struggling, from the kerb upwards towards the light.

The Touleier's Talkies

I N the title *Half Shot at Sunrise* there is that blending of humour and tragedy that forms the background of all genuine laughter. The wild hilarity of this comedy is rendered all the more spectacular by the contrasting associations involved in the name of the picture – a man drunk in the dawn light, a man facing a firing party with the sunrise. Thus, through the riotous scenes of two soldiers loose in Paris, the humour of *Half Shot* is of the kind that has come to be known as the great bellylaugh. It is the latest and the newest type of comedy, with the latest and newest gags and the latest and newest situations. And yet it is based on those old incongruities at which Homer and Virgil laughed, and which Shakespeare and Rabelais knew – those sidesplitting extravagances whose thunderous guffaws, reverberating down the ages, have crashed their way into the hearts of men.

On the banks of the Seine, where Baudelaire and Verlaine walked, and in the shadow of the Eiffel Tower, Bert Wheeler and Robert Woolsey wander uproariously. It is with a dim hilarity that they pursue their course; it is with an abandon that is of the gods.

Kinemas Limited are presenting this latest picture featuring Wheeler and Woolsey together with Dorothy Lee. Those of Kinemas's patrons who have seen and heard the three films, *Rio Rita*, *The Cuckoos* and *Dixiana*, will be prepared to believe everything that is claimed for *Half Shot* – except that it is better than those other Radio successes. And yet when we reflect on the matter carefully, and compare severally each one of these remarkable productions, we can only come to the conclusion that, in the rollicking grandeur of *Half Shot at Sunrise*, Radio Pictures have attained to something that they have not heretofore achieved.

Our thousands of readers who have enjoyed the humour scattered through the pages of *The Touleier* – the humour of Professor Max Drennan and of Oom Schalk Lourens and Hottentot Ruiter – will be glad of the laughs provided in *Half Shot at Sunrise*; for they do not differ in any way from the best examples of our own South African humour. In spirit they are identical. And this is as it should be. Humour is that magic thread that binds together in its dazzling fibres the hearts of all the children of men. What strikes us as funny about a Boer or a

Hottentot is equally funny when it deals with an American soldier in Paris. Humour is something that lies very close to our hearts.

Here is an example from *Half Shot*:

"After all, Gilbert, love is peace, quiet and tranquillity."

"That ain't love – that's sleep."

Here's another:

Olga: "Do you know what you are sitting on?"

Gilbert: "Well, I ought to. . . I've been sitting on it for years."

Or this one:

Gilbert: "Do you kiss soldiers, mademoiselle?"

French Girl: "That's *my* business."

Gilbert: "Well. . . how's business?"

A happy feature of *Half Shot* – and a happy feature, incidentally, that was prominent in *Rio Rita* and *The Cuckoos* – is the idea of allotting to Robert Woolsey in the love scenes a woman very much bigger than himself.

In boxing circles he would be described as taking on somebody out of his class. He appears to be in the habit of doing just that. There was Helen Kaiser in *Rio Rita*; there was Jobyna Howland in *The Cuckoos*. Yet, although this situation is as old as comedy, it loses nothing on that account. It is an obvious and hackneyed sort of fun – the laughter that is evoked by a disparity in size. But it is a harmless kind of fun, which makes its strongest appeal to those of us who, though we may be grown up in other ways, still retain, somewhere about us, that divine thing of spontaneous risibility that is present in all good children.

For the statistician the most significant fact about *Half Shot* is that two thousand dollars were expended in lipsyl, greasepaint and face-powder.

Then there is something about crime that has gripped mankind's imagination since the dawn. The story of Cain and Abel is an old-time crime thriller with a smashing climax that has remained popular through very many centuries. It is a theme whose possibilities are inexhaustible for the reason that in the primary things of life and death our curiosity will remain forever unsatisfied. Whether the hero of the piece is Cain or Wainwright, Eugene Aram or 'Flash Jack', our blood flows faster as the tale is told.

Night-birds, the great new talkie for Kinemas's circuit, is a British International picture, produced by Richard Eichberg. It deals with the depredations of a mysterious person whose identity is veiled under that name 'Flash Jack.'

Night-birds deals with a rapid sequence of exciting events, in the course of which the audience is presented with murders, night club queens, criminals and their fiancées, knife-throwings and lovemakings.

Muriel Angelus, who is regarded in authoritative quarters as the world's most perfect blonde, plays the leading feminine role in this picture. But then, it is possible in these days for almost any girl to be a perfect blonde. At all events, they can come so near to being a perfect blonde that only a woman can detect the difference at anything over two feet. Accordingly, what does distinguish Muriel Angelus from the general run of blondes is her wonderful acting. But there are certain of her admirers who contend that the Angelus curves are also wonderful – perhaps even more wonderful than her acting. At thirteen she played in *Henry VIII*. Then followed parts in *The Vagabond King*, *The Ringer*, *Infamous Ladies* and *Red Aces*. She is only nineteen. Anyway, it didn't take the B. I. P. people long to find her. Those who see her in *Night-birds* will guess the reason why.

Jack Raine is the immaculate looking gentleman carrying Muriel Angelus about. I don't know what for, except that I wouldn't mind doing it myself. Somehow, I wish I could also look immaculate. There is something I like about the sound of the word. Jack Raine takes a prominent part in *Night-birds* – although many theatregoers (male) will agree that the privilege of carrying Muriel Angelus is enough to go on with. He gave other notable performances in pictures like *The Hate Ship*, *Raise the Roof* and *Suspense*.

Every month we endeavour to supply vital information for the statistician. Here are some figures about *Night-birds*: Length, 8 761; Certificate 'A'; Regd. No. B. R. 4955.

The Recognising Blues

WAS ambling down Eloff Street, bare-footed and in my shirt-sleeves, and with the recognising blues.

I had been smoking dagga, good dagga, the real rooibaard, with heads about a foot long, and not just the stuff that most dealers supply you with, and that is not much better than grass. When you smoke good dagga you get blue in quite a number of ways. The most common way is the frightened blues, when you imagine that your heart is palpitating, and that you can't breathe, and that you are going to die. Another form that the effect of dagga takes is that you get the suspicious blues, and then you imagine that all the people around you, your best friends and your parents included, are conspiring against you, so that when your mother asks you, "How are you?" every word she says sounds very sinister, as though she knows that you have been smoking dagga, and that you are blue, and you feel that she is like a witch. The most innocent remark any person makes when you have got the suspicious blues seems to be impregnated with a whole world of underhand meaning and dreadful insinuation.

And perhaps you are right to feel this way about it. Is not the most harmless conversation between several human beings charged with the most diabolical kind of subterranean cunning, each person fortifying himself behind barbed-wire defences? Look at that painting of Daumier's, called "Conversation Piece", and you will see that the two men and the woman concerned in this little friendly chat are all three of them taking part in a cloven-hoofed rite. You can see each one has got the suspicious blues.

There is also the once-over blues and a considerable variety of other kinds of blues. But the recognising blues doesn't come very often, and then it is only after you have been smoking the best kind of rooibaard boom, with ears that long.

When you have got the recognising blues you think you know everybody you meet. And you go up and shake hands with every person that you come across, because you think you recognise him, and you are very glad to have run into him: in this respect the recognising blues is just the opposite of the suspicious blues.

A friend of mine, Charlie, who has smoked dagga for thirty years, says that he once had the recognising blues very bad when he was strolling through the centre of the town. And after he had shaken hands with lots of people who didn't know him at all, and whom he didn't know, either, but whom he *thought* he knew, because he had the recognising blues – then a very singular thing happened to my friend, Rooker Charlie. For he looked in the display window of a men's outfitters, and he saw two dummies standing there, in the window, two dummies dressed in a smart line of gents' suitings, and with the recognising blues strong on him, Charlie thought that he knew those two dummies, and he thought that the one dummy was Max Chaitz, who kept a restaurant in Cape Town, and that the other dummy was a well-known snooker-player called Pat O'Callaghan.

And my friend Rooker Charlie couldn't understand how Max Chaitz and Pat O'Callaghan should come to be standing there holding animated converse in that shop-window. He didn't know, until that moment, that Max Chaitz and Pat O'Callaghan were even acquainted. But the sight of these two men standing there talking like that shook my friend Rooker Charlie up pretty badly. So he went home to bed. But early the next morning he dashed round again to that men's outfitters, and then he saw that those two figures weren't Max Chaitz and Pat O'Callaghan at all, but two dummies stuck in the window. And he saw then that they didn't look even a bit like the two men he thought they were – especially the dummy that he thought was Max Chaitz. Because Max Chaitz is very short and fat, with a red, cross-looking sort of face that you can't mistake in a million. Whereas the dummy was tall and slender and good-looking.

That was the worst experience that my friend Rooker Charlie ever had of the recognising blues.

And when I was taking a stroll down Eloff Street, that evening, and I was bare-footed and in my shirt-sleeves, then I also had a bad attack of the recognising blues. But it was the recognising blues in a slightly different form. I would first make up a name in my brain, a name that sounded good to me, and that I thought had the right sort of rhythm. And then the first person I would see, I would think that he was the man whose name I had just thought out. And I would go up and address him by this name, and shake hands with him, and tell him how glad I was to see him.

And a name I thought up that sounded very fine to me, and impressive, with just the right kind of ring to it, was the name of Sir Lionel Ostrich de Frontignac. It was a very magnificent name.

And so I went up, bare-footed and in my shirt-sleeves, to the first man I saw in the street, after I had coined this name, and I took him by the hand, and I said, "Well met, Sir Lionel. It is many years since we last met, Sir Lionel Ostrich de Frontignac."

And the remarkable coincidence was that the man whom I addressed in this way actually *was* Sir Lionel Ostrich de Frontignac. But on account of his taking me for a bum – through my being bare-footed and in my shirt-sleeves – he wouldn't acknowledge that he really was Sir Lionel and that I had recognised him dead to rights.

"You are mistaken," Sir Lionel Ostrich de Frontignac said, moving away from me. "You have got the recognising blues."

Stephen Black

THE last time I spoke to Stephen Black was only a short while before his death. He was then in the best of health and spirits and, in spite of the large number of difficulties confronting him, he displayed a courage and an optimism that I could only marvel at.

I was then on the staff of *The Touleier*. Stephen Black's *The Sjambok* was in the last throes of its chequered life. We discussed the possibility of our building up a joint organisation for the publication of both *The Sjambok* and *The Touleier*. Stephen Black was anxious to create a means for distributing his paper after the guarantee to the Central News Agency against libel was withdrawn. He felt that much could be gained by as close as possible co-operation between the two papers.

I have since regretted that circumstances made it inadvisable for us to accept Stephen Black's proposal: lawsuits were then threatening him, in which two of our directors were reluctant to become involved.

"The real troubles I have," Stephen Black told me, "are not occasioned by these lawsuits, but just because I have an incompetent staff."

It was, of course, a notorious fact that Stephen Black would go off into spasms of fury because the men and women working for him had little talent for anything outside the monthly procedure of drawing their salaries.

People talk about Stephen Black and say that he was temperamental. This is not altogether fair. The assistants with whom Stephen Black was obliged to work and whom he was too kind-hearted to sack added considerably to the burdens imposed on him by external adversities.

There was a certain Miss Marjorie Cohen who regularly visited the Technical Press, where the old *Sjambok* was printed and where the first numbers of *The New L. S. D.* were also printed. I was in the country and Stephen Black wrote to me, requesting me to write a number of short stories for *The Sjambok*, as he expressed himself as being an admirer of my work. (Stephen Black was probably the finest literary critic this country has ever seen.)

Anyway, I arrived at *The Sjambok's* offices and was met by Miss Cohen.

She asked me to hand over the MSS to her. "You know, I also read manuscripts," she said in confiding tones.

114

"In that event I should prefer the office boy to read mine," I retorted. Subsequently I saw Stephen Black and mentioned the matter to him. I shall refrain from relating his biting references to this would-be literary critic. Soon afterwards he started talking about J. Langley Levy and I listened spellbound to hear a friend of mine saying things I had not known before about the editor of *The Sunday Times*.

I may remark that Stephen Black printed all the stories I gave him and that when I had tea with him in his office he made amends in a noble manner for the discourtesy I had received at the hands of his subordinate.

"Go and fetch another cup for Mr Malan," Stephen Black said to Miss Cohen. "Next time you give him a cracked cup there will be trouble."

There was always trouble with the futile members of *The Sjambok* staff. That is one reason why Stephen Black could not carry on.

Stephen Black also told me about another member of his staff. Some day it may be worth my while to tell the story.

The Hottentot's God: A Preface

ERE is a collection of South African stories; in the main they are related by a Hottentot named Ruiter.

This is a typical Hottentot name, in the same way as Ruiter himself is typical of his whole nation. As we read these stories, and his personality assumes definite shape and reality, we begin to entertain for Ruiter a genuine regard that eventually deepens into a warm affection. We are captivated by his childlike simplicity and his superstitious ignorance. We are also charmed by his profound insight into human motives. In a few whimsical flashes he reveals the sycophancies and frailties underlying the characters of the people with whom he comes into contact; but when he draws aside the veil it is always in a manner that is kindly. Ruiter talks about the pettifogging solicitor who swindled him, about Klaas Goosen, the master who thrashed him, about the hypocritical parson in that very pathetic story of the little step-child, and through it all his words remain untinged with bitterness or venom; through it all there remains a twinkle in his eyes, and on his aged and swarthy visage there lurks a smile. For he has lived long enough to look very deeply into life, and through the understanding that he has gathered with the years he displays an enduring tenderness towards human weaknesses; he has an abiding faith in humanity.

We begin by laughing at Ruiter's absurdities. We are amused at the queer figure he cuts at the Battle of Bronkhorstspruit, when, hiding behind the water-cart, he is disconcerted at the number of bullets passing through the spokes of the wheels. We are hugely entertained at his terror in the lonely wood after nightfall – a terror which he seeks to disguise by means of the ingenious explanation that "I always do whistle when I'm alone in the bush at night, while the moon is lingering behind the hills. I want people to hear that Ruiter isn't afraid to pass through the bush in the dark." We are convulsed with merriment at the incongruities involved in Ruiter's efforts at interpreting the Scriptures in the light of his own experience. As I said, we begin by laughing at him. But gradually Ruiter weaves about our hearts a glamour we do not quite apprehend. Insensibly we succumb to his spell, until, in the end, without realising how this orientation has been brought about, we actually feel a sort of spiritual affinity with Ruiter; we find ourselves laughing with this disreputable Hottentot, and his cunning and his brandy and his lies.

Perhaps the explanation for this change in our attitudes is not so far to seek, after all. I have said that Ruiter is a Hottentot. This is quite true. He is a Hottentot, and he is typical of all the Hottentots in the world. But when we have listened to a few of the stories he tells, and have become attracted towards him, and have grown conscious of the tremendous appeal which he makes on our imaginations, we start casting around for the secret of his fascinating qualities.

And I think that the answer is this: it is not enough to say that Ruiter is typical of the Hottentot nation; he is also typical of the human race. *Homo sum: humani nihil a me alienum puto* (I am a man: I count nothing human indifferent to me, Terence). It is that old touch that makes the whole world kin. It is that eternal human element that remains precisely the same for all times and all races and all creeds. It is this that we have in common with the European and the American, no less than with the Asiatic and the African. Ruiter is not only the primitive son of an African tribe, wandering and dusky skinned. He is also the son of Adam and the son of God. And this is the character whom the author has created as a medium for relating the stories.

So much for Ruiter. How of the stories themselves? They are told with simplicity of style and diction, and absence of elaborate plot which – with their intrinsic literary merit – make them stories that can always be read again. On the whole, I consider it a pity that O. Henry, playing like a master upon the strings of the human heart, should have subordinated his characters and their actions to the outcome of a carefully preconceived denouement. It is this 'triple-hinged surprise' which, devastatingly effective at the moment, lends an air of artificiality to all O. Henry's work. Now and again this mechanically contrived climax can do much to heighten the drama of the particular situation. But in its very power there is unreality, and exploited over a large field this form of the short story degenerates into a species of showmanship. O. Henry wrote a number of great stories. But with his undoubted genius, had he been more of the artist and less of the showman, he would have been an even greater writer.

The fourteen stories in this book are devoid of spectacular themes. In fact, some of them are stories that will yet be told as long as the moon keeps shining in the heavens, and the stars remain in their whirling courses, and the children of men still walk upon the earth. But the lasting glory of these stories is based upon the way they are told. Perhaps their most striking feature is their humour.

I shall give a few examples. Listen to this: "Floating through the air I lived through the greater part of my life with my two dead wives," Ruiter says in describing an occasion on which the Boers set about hanging him. "The thought that those women would be waiting for me was the worst part of the hanging."

Again in the same story, "The Prayer of the Hottentot's God", a young Boer is instructed by his kommandant to offer up a prayer before battle.

"'But I can't pray – I mean, I can't say a prayer aloud,' he answered. Kommandant Apie Terblanche flicked a clump of grass with his sjambok without opening his lips. Jan prayed; he was going full speed ahead before all the burghers had had time to kneel down."

Again Ruiter is arrested by a policeman for sheep-stealing. He is conveyed over a new road that has been specially made by Ndobe, a kaffir, for a funeral cortege to pass over. (Incidentally, Ruiter is fastened by a rope to the saddle of the policeman's horse.)

"Ruiter followed the horseman along the road that Ndobe had cleared. Ndobe stood at gaze. He was no longer so sure that he had made a good road. Ruiter was not borne so smoothly along it as the coffin had been. His feet were so seldom on the ground."

This is genuine humour. It is great humour. It is that humour that lies so very close to tears. Set off by a grim and tragic background, it sparkles amid the carnage of the field of battle; it flings its brilliant irradiations over the shadow of the grave. Thus Hecuba jested at Priam's infirmities while about them Troy was burning. Thus Mercutio commented on his wound that was not as deep as a well, nor as wide as a church door – Mercutio with laughter on his lips and Death's hand on his heart.

This quality I have mentioned is present in nearly all these stories. Some of them are very terrible stories, as for instance "The Coffin in the Loft." "In the Smother of the Camp-fire" is redolent of the spirit of the veld and sky, and is born of the wind that blows across the open spaces. "The Avenging Hand" is a very peculiar narrative of strange and dark happenings that only a South African will really understand. "That was All" I consider to be the greatest story in the book. But I shall not comment on it. Let the reader judge for himself. Let him also judge of the merits of this ghost story around whose conclusion there hang the fantasies of spectral things:

"We returned to the cart. I got back first. And if you should go along that road, as we did, you would feel the spider-webs cutting across your face; and, in that glade, you would find a rusty cart-lamp embedded in the sand near a forsaken grave. And if it is at night, and the lamp looks strange, you must remember that things we see in the dark are not always what they seem to be."

When we have finished this book, and the individual stories lose their clarity of outline, and grow blurred, as with the days they must, we find that in our memories there is left an echo. It is a sound that seems blended from all the sounds that we have heard reverberating through these stories; and yet in some ways it is also different; it is of more profound significance, and it reaches more deeply into our hearts, for we feel that it is pregnant with a dark and passionate meaning.

It is a low tone that, remaining unheeded amidst the noise of life and the clamour of action, is nevertheless heard in its plaintive insistence when all turmoil dies. That note is still there, vibrant in our memories, when the jolting of Schalk Lourens's wagon has cleared from the battle-field, and on Magersfontein the cattle browse again.

It is a brooding rhythm: a sombre cadence that is composed of half-notes. It is the voice of Africa.

Masters. . . and Others

A MONTH or so ago, in *The New Sjambok*, I reviewed Sarah Gertrude Millin's new book, *The Sons of Mrs Aab* (published by Chatto and Windus in 1931). I told her the truth about her stuff. A certain man informed me that when Sarah Gertrude Millin read the article she laughed. This man moves in Johannesburg's most fashionable circles and is therefore on an intimate footing with both Sarah Gertrude Millin and myself. (Try and laugh that one off, Sarah.)

I am sorry for Sarah. You see, I know that kind of laughter, which is made bitter because you know what it is that you are laughing about. I understand that there is next to no sale for her latest book. I regret that this should be the effect of my attack on her. After all, I had no intention of injuring her financially. Sarah likes money, and money means nothing to me. I would really like to see her go on and make even more out of her tripe than Edgar Wallace and the author of *Nelson Lee, Detective* make out of their writings.

I would have been satisfied if I had got the reading public to buy her books and read them sneeringly. I had not anticipated, however, that the public would go right to the other extreme of flatly declining to buy her books.

George Bernard Shaw is coming over.

Some time ago in *The New Sjambok* I invited George Bernard Shaw, on his return from Russia, to visit this country. What I wrote was: "Come over to South Africa, George, and I'll teach you a few things about Art that will enable you to return to England and write something heavier even than *Back to Methuselah*."

Many people said that Shaw would adopt a supercilious tone and pretend to ignore *The New Sjambok* – a copy of which was sent to him. But a number of his admirers said: "He is big enough to come over and find out what the trouble is." Events have proved that Bernard Shaw's admirers have not been at fault. Shaw is big enough.

After all, Bernard Shaw must be given his due. He undoubtedly is a high-grade poseur. And the Goddess of the Temple, while realising that he is not one of her own, has once or twice gone so far as to wink at him.

As literary editor of *The New L. S. D.*, it is a practice of mine never to read the works of other writers. I made an exception, however, in regard to Frank Harris's posthumous biography of Bernard Shaw. As Bernard Shaw prepared the manuscript for publication, it is difficult to ascertain how much of the book was written by the biographer and how much by the biographee. From what I know of Shaw, I should imagine that Frank Harris can consider himself extremely fortunate if Shaw split the thing fifty-fifty.

It was a nasty touch, though, introducing that story of Shaw's seduction at the age of thirty, by a music teacher. It gives the impression that the whole volume was specially got up just to give Bernard Shaw a cheap boost at the expense of a widow. Shaw, in permitting this passage to go into print, is obviously actuated by a senile weakness to convince the public that at one time a widow did fall for him on the strength of his sex.

Veld Fires: An African Omnibus (published in Johannesburg by Cape to Cairo Publications in November, 1931) is the name of a dreary looking volume containing stories and other pieces by a number of third-rate men and women who never stand a chance of getting their stuff printed elsewhere. The book has been produced in South Africa, edited by C Selwyn Stokes and B. A. Wilter, and I must congratulate the man who thought of the scheme on his astuteness in getting the support of the people who would pay anything to see their names between the covers of a book.

The most artistic part of the thing is its title. Strangely enough, "Veld Fire" is also the title of a story I wrote early last year for *The New L. S. D.* (for Vol. 1, No. 1 of 27 March, 1931). I have no objection to their making use of my title, although as an ordinary matter of courtesy they might have asked my permission.

It might interest our readers to know that practically every one of the stories appearing in *Veld Fires* was originally rejected by *The Touleier*. I say, you two dozen duds, when you submitted your tripe to *Veld Fires* did you also enclose the rejection slips you got from *The Touleier*?

Mrs Rosalind Spotswood Malan, Mr Eric Rosenthal, S. R. Yew, Grace Vivien Sprange and some other names – which I saw, glancing through the contents – were all familiar to me as a result of my occasionally glancing through the weekly list of contributions for the wastepaper basket of *The Touleier*. It was like meeting old friends, encountering this assortment of stale failures in *Veld Fires*.

But I was surprised to find that a man like C. R. Prance, whose views on literature I still respect, should have permitted himself to be inveigled into having his writings printed side by side with the dull vapourings of Napier Devitt. Also Stokes himself, formerly of *The S. A. Railways and Harbours Magazine*, is too good a man to be identified with this.

By the way, Eric Rosenthal, do you remember the time you presumptuously endeavoured to give me advice? I suppose you are sorry about it now, aren't you? You told me that what you did was to read through all the files of newspapers at the CNA and that you also spend many hours a week snooping about in the Public Library – all with a view to turning out articles for the Rand gutter press.

Poor old Rosenthal. His sole claim to literary recognition is the fact that he has a long, ungainly frame, like R. L. Stevenson's. When I see you in the street, Rosenthal, I can tell what is implied by that vacant look on your sallow countenance. You are saying to yourself, "Now I wonder what God and Herman Malan are thinking about at the moment?"

I'll tell you, Eric. We are not thinking at all, God and I. We are too wise to think. We have stopped that long ago. We only dream. . .

Taken all round, *Veld Misfires* is the funniest publication I have come across so far. When George Bernard Shaw arrives in Johannesburg, I shall draw his attention to it. Sick as he is, I bet GBS will laugh.

A week later, and I have read *The Loving Hand*, a collection of poems by Stella Blakemore. This little volume, together with *Groen Grassies* (both published privately), are the only books of verse I have read in five years. *The Loving Hand* is well got up and has only nineteen pages of short verses with simple words that are easy to read. This circumstance and one poem, "If You Should Go By", constitute the sole merit of the publication. The rest of the stuff, with the exception of the black margin round the title page, is so much tripe.

But that one poem, "If You Should Go By", is good. I wouldn't even be ashamed to carry it round town and tell people that I wrote it. You see, I am big enough to do these things. If Sarah Gertrude Millin tried it, they would laugh at her.

This is what Stella Blakemore writes:

> If you should go by
> Would I call?

No, I would stand,
Speaking not at all,
Up away at my window high.

Good on you, Stella. You stick up at that window high and you won't go far wrong. And if a chap comes along at night and asks you to jump down into his arms, Stella, just don't take any notice of him. Tell him to go away in case he wakes the neighbours.

Of course, what is wrong with English poetry today is that, since the appearance of *The Blue Princess*, English as a medium of poetic expression is finally played out. For this reason I am going to write all my poetry in Latin. My stuff is so good that I feel I want to make it hard for people to read.

Art is a divine way of getting God's words mixed up. But it must be a divine way. Otherwise it is nothing. This is what Beauty Bell knew and what Roy Campbell doesn't know – Roy Campbell who wastes his time on the high seas in writing what he calls satire. Every so often Roy Campbell gets a job aboard a fishing boat and writes his rhymes while the rest of the crew are handling mainsails.

I would also advise the captain of the next boat Roy Campbell works on to boot this young man up the hatchway as soon as he tries to borrow a fountain pen off the bosun. We don't want any more of Roy Campbell's sterile wit; even Professor Max Drennan is better at it when he writes Witwatersrand University prose. Only Max Drennan's work has this merit about it: that he doesn't realise how funny it is until I point it out to him. Then he tries to change it. It's all right, Max Drennan, I know how you feel. I feel that way myself, sometimes. I feel that if Africa won't listen to me I shall make a new continent. Only, Africa listens.

Last week I was shown a book, *Amongst the Nudists* by F. and M. Merrill. This book was handed to me in *The New L. S. D.* offices by a Johannesburg purveyor of pornography. On subsequent enquiry I learnt that this highly suggestive publication is circulating freely throughout the Union of South Africa.

As far as I can gather, *Among the Nudists* is a propaganda work specially got up by Germany's nudist sects of moral perverts for the purpose of enticing South African men and women to their haunts of vice. This book is profusely illustrated with real photos of men and

123

women disporting themselves in various attitudes of abandon – and all of them without a stitch of clothes on.

I cannot understand how a decent man glancing at these depraved photographs of debauched females can feel anything but loathing at the thought that there can be women – apparently occupying a fairly good social status – who are so utterly devoid of modesty and self-respect. It seems that, as long as they have what they consider to be presentable figures, it doesn't matter to these women as to which lecherous Zulu is gloating over their naked bodies.

With revolting detail these authors relate their experiences in parading about stark naked before men and women in a similar state of undress. At the best of times, with plenty of clothes on, a woman's figure is clumsily built and ungainly. Schopenhauer knew that long ago. Stripped of her gauds and wearing apparel, the average naked woman is a pitiful spectacle that makes me forget all I ever knew about fairies.

If a man who peddles filthy postcards gets six months for a first offence, it strikes me as most unfair that fashionable bookshops are permitted, without police molestation, to sell the flagrant pieces of debaucheries that are contained between the covers of *Among the Nudists*. I genuinely feel that no young girl can look through the pages of this book without losing a great deal of her virgin charm and modesty. To circulate a book of this description is the vilest form of crimen injuria. It is a form of indecent assault that is all the more criminal because its effects are more insidious than the effects of physical ravishment.

This book may be excellent for the purposes of a boarding school headmistress with debauched lesbian proclivities, who makes a practice of contaminating with lewd caresses the younger and prettier girls in her school. But a filthy book with filthier illustrations should find no place on the shelves of South Africa's better class booksellers.

What are the police going to do about it? Especially that part that deals with the naked Chinaman, Mr Wang, who assumes salacious postures in front of naked, giggling white women.

The other day I was talking to a man. Quite casually he mentioned the Hottentot Ruiter stories of my editor, Aegidius Jean Blignaut, which appeared in this publication. "They are wonderful stories," he said. I agreed with him. I knew right away that this man was not one of the literary critics who get their pay from one or another of South Africa's big newspaper syndicates. I knew also that he was not one of this country's third-rate novelists who refrain – on account of personal jealousy – from acclaiming genius in another.

When the Hottentot Ruiter stories first appeared they received from the critics little more than the lukewarm praise accorded to Roy Campbell. It is the old business of a prophet in his own land. The same thing happened to Chatterton and Keats, and even O. Henry was dead a good while before people started saying that he was a streets better artist than Jack London, that sadly overpraised typewriter mechanic.

I assert dogmatically – and they can take me to court if they like – that Sarah Gertrude Millin and Guy Gardner and Max Drennan and the rest of the plodding bunch of scribblers have been afraid of acquainting the South African reading public with the true merits of Blignaut's stories for only one reason: they'd have to chuck writing and take to manual work if they did.

Take Sarah Gertrude Millin, for instance. She has read at least a dozen of the Ruiter stories. All she could say was, "Oh yes, I like them." And it was with an effort, too, that she said it. It's all right, Sarah, you needn't be jealous. Aegidius Jean Blignaut is not going to compete with you. He is not going to do you out of a job. Pauline Smith is there for that purpose.

Aegidius Jean Blignaut wrote those stories for the only reason that an artist does anything at all. He wrote them because he liked doing it. That is why his stories will live, and people will laugh and sigh and wonder over them long after your *Men on a Voyage* has been forgotten. As it is, I believe that I am the only person today, apart from Mrs Millin and Advocate P. Millin, who still remembers that there was a book called *Men on a Voyage*.

I know that the Hottentot Ruiter series will go well in England and America. These stories will be acknowledged immediately as masterpieces. Even in South Africa Aegidius Jean Blignaut is not altogether without an audience. And I am a hell of an audience.

When Roy Campbell cracked up William Plomer in *Voorslag* he did it in a surreptitious fashion, concealing his identity in case the mob should laugh, when the mob found out that he was advertising a friend. Well, I am writing my opinion of Aegidius Jean Blignaut's work, and I am doing it openly, in the proud knowledge that in drawing public attention to Aegidius Jean Blignaut's work I am advancing the interests of South African culture.

I sometimes feel sorry that I was not alive in the time of Queen Elizabeth. Shakespeare's art would have been different if he had come under my influence. With his effective command of the English language, his ability to get down to business and turn out a neat job, his dexterity at signing his name to other people's ideas on the impudent pretext that he improved them – all these things would have made a wonderful dramatist of William Shakespeare, if only he had known as much about the theory of art as a Bechuana wood-carver knows, or as much as a Fordsburg procuress knows.

If Shakespeare was more of an artist he would not be so great a figure in the world's literature. But he would be a finer Bard of Avon.

Shakespeare could never have written what Elizabeth Barrett Browning wrote, that poem about "Love me for naught." He would not have known what it meant. In every syllable of Shakespeare's majestic pentameters there breathes the marketplace spirit of barter. Shakespeare could not understand the idea of anything for nothing. And that is what all art is and what all religion is and what all love is – doing things "for naught."

You can't compose a line like "The multitudinous seas incarnadine" for nothing.

There is Othello. He loves Desdemona. He ends up by strangling her. That is all right. There is an eternal grandeur and magnificence in the thought of strangling the woman whom he loves. We can all feel that there is an intense beauty in the act. But the thing remains lovely only as long as we don't know why he does it. But Shakespeare ruins the dreadful sweetness and nobility of Othello's fatal midnight antics with the handkerchief by making the Moor shamble about the stage in the ludicrous guise of a jealous husband. This is a devastating commentary on the pettiness of William Shakespeare's soul. He had all the material for creating a beautiful story. He had the energy to sit down and write it all up, scene after scene. Then, at the end, when he could have pulled off a shattering climax born of the splendid madness of poetry and of wine, he confessed that he was not a poet, after all.

So Shakespeare made Othello murder Desdemona because he thought she was carrying on with another man. Oh, Shakespeare. You had hold of something beautiful. You degraded it into a sordid squabble in a bedroom in Stratford-upon-Avon. I can see the soiled counterpane on your second-best bed. I can hear Anne Hathaway's strident voice declaring that the butcher didn't have his arm round her. And there is that flat hideousness in her tone of a woman rendered irritable by continual child-bearing. I even know what kind of underwear she has got on.

How much finer it would have been had Othello strangled Desdemona for no reason in particular – merely because he loved her, or simply because he wanted to, or just for fun. *Othello* is the tragedy of a man who is bigger than his creator. I feel that Othello could have murdered Desdemona for nothing.

Shakespeare couldn't even have bought Anne Hathaway a new pair of shoes for nothing.

Two Unauthorised Biographies

THE other day I called on Mr Teddie Garratt on the second floor of the Central City Buildings, where he has his offices, studios and music saloons. I recognised him immediately from the photos of his which I had seen at various times in the press. Although his time was fully occupied, and at that very moment a number of people were waiting to interview him, he nevertheless waved me smiling to a seat. I knew then that his smile has contributed as largely to his personal popularity as his short-cut method of teaching popular music and syncopation has won for him the position he occupies in musical circles.

Mr Garratt is a naturally modest man, and evinces a marked reluctance to discuss his triumphs. Consequently, I had to piece together the story of his career from various newspapers, and from information kindly supplied by his secretary and manager.

It was in Montreal that Mr Garratt first became enraptured by that strange spell that music holds, but it was not until after he had devoted eight years to the study of classical music at the Montreal Conservatoire that his interests became bound up with syncopation and modern jazz. By virtue of this early training there is to all Mr Garratt's work a sound basis. Immediately Mr Garratt's services were in demand with some of the world's most famous dance orchestras. In New York, Chicago, Detroit and in London, through Norway, Sweden, Denmark, France and Germany his name is still familiar with lovers of popular music. Incidentally, he is proficient in German and French, being able to teach in both languages.

Teddie Garratt took up jazz in its infancy in 1913, when this type of music was still known as ragtime. He was one of the first South African pianists to broadcast in the days when wireless was still very much of a novelty. Many of us can remember his tour of this country only a few years ago.

In 1925 Teddie Garratt founded his Johannesburg school. Subsequently his marked success in this direction obtained for him the exclusive South African representation of the famous Billy Mayerl Postal Courses in Piano Syncopation and Standard Pianoforte Playing. Today the Teddie Garratt Schools of Piano Syncopation extend from Rhodesia to the Cape; each branch representative has received personal training from Mr Garratt, and the selection in every case involves careful discrimination.

Mr Teddie Garratt, approached by the Columbia Company, recorded on two pianos his original syncopated paraphrase of "Sarie Marais", as well as a pot-pourri of Afrikaans Liedjies, which he himself compiled and arranged. The test has been accepted and will arrive shortly. Thus he is in the unique position of being the only South African syncopated pianist and teacher of piano syncopation whose records have as yet been accepted for issue. Mr Garratt also makes a speciality of arranging and reharmonising amateur compositions, a number of which have been in this way regularly accepted for publication by overseas publishers. Of late Mr Garratt has himself undertaken the publication of compositions. Mr Garratt has also associated himself as business manager with the Silverstring Studios, which teach the ukelele, banjo, guitar, etc.

Before I left I prevailed on Mr Garratt to play a few of his own compositions. He played a reverie, something that was redolent of the moonlight, or orange trees and the fragrance of roses blooming in a half-forgotten garden; there were soft notes that whispered of the old things of earth; there were gentle, wistful notes, like the night wind in the grass. As an artist in words, I felt that I was one with this man, who was an artist in sounds. I knew what he was trying to say, and that he would never say it, for as soon as we have said all that we know and feel, our work is no longer art.

Then, abruptly, Teddie Garratt played one of his own marches There was the tramp of an army in the rhythm of the music. His fingers swept across the keys like the white flash of swords leaping from their scabbards. I felt the iron tragedy of war, the grandeur of conflict, the crimson-bannered panoply of an army in its triumph.

Above all else, Teddie Garratt is an artist.

Mr Aegidius Jean Blignaut, editor of *The New L. S. D.* – when I am off duty I don't call him Aegidius: I call him plain Jean – asked me to travel down to Durban to interview Major Giles, popularly known as Durban's Own Hitler. I may mention that I travelled first class, my expenses having been paid by *The New L. S. D.* I like to mention the circumstance of my having travelled first class, because it enables me to feel like a Corner House magnate. Usually I travel second class in the Transvaal, Orange Free State and Natal, and third class in the Cape Province.

Once I travelled first class from Doornfontein to Jeppe. It was only a short distance of two miles, but I enjoyed both miles.

I found Major Giles at his home in Hullion Hall, Grey Street, Durban. I was at a bit of a disadvantage in talking to Durban's Hitler owing to my having broken my false teeth in trying to eat a railway sandwich. (If Minister of Railways Charley Malan had had the forethought to advertise the SAR in *The New L. S. D.*, I would not have got in this dirty slap at our railways.)

Major Giles is a fine, impressive looking man. He made no secret of his ambitions. And with a little resolution and the right sort of encouragement I see no reason why he should not pull it off as well as Hitler has done. But there is an overwhelming difference between a Mussolini and a Hitler. Major Giles told me that Natal's strong racialism makes it difficult for him to bring about real unity amongst the element he leads. That is just the point. Hitler would be appalled by these difficulties. Mussolini would not only triumph over the problem of racialism: he would actually exploit it, using it as a lever to attain his ends.

But I liked Major Giles.

"Do you think you could rule this country?" I lisped – remember that ham sandwich.

"Certainly," he replied.

There was something fine about the assurance with which he said it. A dictator must be an egoist. Alexander the Great, Julius Caesar, Napoleon Bonaparte, Ovamboland Chief Impumbu – these men were all egoists. It is not necessary for a leader to have confidence in his followers. The mob is nothing. What a leader does require – and this is something infinitely more difficult – is confidence in himself.

And I think Major Giles has that confidence.

He has achieved much in starting this Unarmed Citizen's Force. He has achieved much more in residing in a comfortable flat in Hullion Hall. If he is guided by some person with soul force – with real creative power – who can make him dream big enough, Major Giles may yet succeed in ruling the country.

Some people laugh at Major Giles. Well, I laugh at Sarah Gertrude Millin. I laugh at all the millions of smug, self-satisfied people in the world. I laugh at the railway steward who sold me that ham sandwich.

But I don't laugh at Major Giles.

The Urge of the Primordial

Scene 1

SCENE: *The combined office and boardroom of the Society for Elevating the African. There is a door on the right, a table with writing materials, registers and minute-books, and about half a dozen chairs. On the wall there is a bannerette with the inscription 'Education and Civilisation for All.'*

Professor Holzgene and James Kellaway, missionary, are seated at the table, while De Carle occupies a chair a little distance off.

DE CARLE: Well, I must be going now. This Francis Chamberlain Clements of yours may be all you claim for him, but I can't stay to see.

HOLZGENE: I'm sure you'd be glad to make his acquaintance. And so would he.

DE CARLE: I don't know so much; I simply can't reconcile myself to the idea of having to shake hands with a nigger. My whole soul revolts against it.

KELLAWAY: So did mine until my eyes were opened, praised be the Lord. Now –

DE CARLE: Now you fling your arms about his neck and call him brother.

KELLAWAY (*not seeing the sarcasm, his eyes gleaming with a fanatic light*): Yes, thanks be to –

DE CARLE: Anyway, I think I'd sooner be a free savage than go about with a thin veneer of pseudo-civilisation.

HOLZGENE: I used to think the same.

KELLAWAY: So did I.

HOLZGENE: Even now I find the restrictions of civilisation hateful. You can almost hear the chains clank. But we have definitely raised Clements from the primordial stage of development in which we found him. He is now as highly developed as any of us. And his civilisation has stood the test for more than a decade. He has made speeches and been howled down and had bottles flung at him. Yet through it all he has remained calm and dignified and a gentleman.

DE CARLE: That so?

HOLZGENE: We have entertained him at banquets, and when some of the spoons were missing and they blamed him for it, he was far more grieved than angry.

DE CARLE: But why do you display all this interest in the niggers?

HOLZGENE: Are we not here for the express purpose of exploiting the native? Is our civilisation in this country not based upon his toil?

DE CARLE: Then what do you want to educate him for? If you educate him, Jim Fish, instead of going about his work with his wonted docility, will haul out a Communist pamphlet and start arguing about Karl Marx's Theory of Value, and that is undesirable. While we have the nigger down it is our duty to keep him down, and if necessary, let us hit him with a pick-handle.

KELLAWAY: Oh, but that is not right. That is not Christian. As the Good Book says –

DE CARLE: It is a question of racial dominance.

HOLZGENE (*excitedly*): If there is such a thing as racial dominance, I don't want it. It has been achieved by the blood and sweat of slaves.

DE CARLE (*with feigned interest*): How's that?

HOLZGENE: Western supremacy, I suppose, was established by the Battle of Actium. And who won it?

DE CARLE (*suppressing a yawn*): Who, indeed?

HOLZGENE: Read *La Victoire* of Pierre Mille. He tells you there. He says Actium was won by the galley-slaves, rowing in chains in the holds, amid the stench of bilge-water and the smell of blood, amid the vermin and the lashes. They won it. And as far as I know, the only intimation they ever received of their victory was when they arrived at Alexandria, and the crowds strewed roses over the decks of the galleys, and a few rose petals fell down beneath upon bare and bleeding shoulders.

KELLAWAY: Roses, did you say? Ah, roses! Roses have thorns, like the thorns in the crown of Christ. . . The martyrdom of Man!

DE CARLE: Very interesting. But I really must go now.

HOLZGENE: No, it's not interesting. The whole damn thing is steeped in shame and it's sickening. And I think the less we hear about racial dominance, the better – the better for both the victors and the vanquished.

DE CARLE: Quite. I am now going home to read old Pierre Mille. I want to find out who won the Battle of Blood River.

He leaves.

HOLZGENE: It's about time Clements showed up, isn't it?

KELLAWAY: Yes. Don't you think Clements is wonderful? Don't you think that, in spite of all that De Carle says about it, he's splendid? Isn't he a tribute to our educational work?

HOLZGENE: It shows –

A knock is heard at the door.

Enter Francis Chamberlain Clements. He is a big, full-blooded Zulu, elegantly dressed and with an American education. They all shake hands.

KELLAWAY: Take a seat, brother, take a seat.

HOLZGENE: You look rather worried. What's wrong? Have you been kicked off the pavement again?

CLEMENTS: I have just been thinking of the grave difficulties confronting us.

HOLZGENE (*sententiously*): Oh yes, but prejudice, after all, is only based on ignorance, you know, and we are overcoming it. We are overcoming it.

CLEMENTS: It's not that so much. Look at my own case. Even amongst friends my position is invidious. I have heard some people state that the negro is the equal of the white man. I have heard others prove in the same dogmatic way that he is superior.

HOLZGENE: Well, what of that?

CLEMENTS: Don't you see? The unconscious prejudice remains. The stigma is still there. The negro is regarded as something peculiar, something to be studied, like the amoeba under the microscope. It should not be a question of tolerating a man in spite of the fact that he is a negro. It should be a matter of not caring in the slightest degree what his colour is.

KELLAWAY (*not comprehending*): Yes, I see. However, let's start work.

They get round the table, open the books and proceed to business.

Scene 2

SCENE: *The front veranda of Professor Holzgene's residence. Professor Holzgene and John Kellaway are reclining in deckchairs.*

HOLZGENE: What time did you say Clements would be here for dinner?

KELLAWAY: Half past six.

HOLZGENE (*consulting his watch*): Oh well, he won't be much longer now. You know, Kel, whenever I grow despondent about our work – as I sometimes do – I just think of Clements and it really makes me feel ashamed of myself. To think what insults and indignities he has endured, to think what supreme tests he has been put through – and every time he has triumphed.

KELLAWAY: It's Christian, that's what it is.

HOLZGENE: Yes, I suppose you're right. Nevertheless, it makes me wonder what a white man, a civilised white man, would have done under similar circumstances, and I don't mind telling you that I doubt very much as to whether that white man would have risen to the same heights of sublimity as Clements has done.

KELLAWAY: Hark! I heard the gate bang. That must be Clements.

HOLZGENE: So like him, isn't it? Always punctual.

Enter De Carle, wildly excited.

DE CARLE (*to Holzgene*): That's what I have been telling you all along. Ever since the first missionaries landed on these shores, our relations with the natives have been jeopardised by a gang of Bible-thumping crooks. Do you hear me? By a lot of reptiles who haven't got blood in their veins, but a mixture of microbes and dish-water.

HOLZGENE: For heaven's sake try to keep calm. What's all this trouble about?

KELLAWAY: Why hasn't Clements come yet, do you know?

DE CARLE: Ha, ha. That's rich, that's really exquisite. Why hasn't Clements come? I'll tell you why he hasn't come. He's in gaol.

HOLZGENE ⎤: What!
KELLAWAY ⎦

DE CARLE: He was walking down Eloff Street this afternoon –

HOLZGENE ⎤: Yes, yes. Get a move on!
KELLAWAY ⎦

DE CARLE: – when somebody called him a M'Shangaan. Now, a European wouldn't resent that word very much, but of course a nigger's mind flows along –

HOLZGENE: Oh, leave that out. Quick, what happened?

DE CARLE: Well, he dashed home, took off his clothes, dressed himself in a blanket and went back brandishing a knobkerrie. He shouted out that no Zulu would allow himself to be called a M'Shangaan. He then assaulted a policeman and got gaoled.

134

KELLAWAY: Well I never. I don't – I don't suppose Clements is a
    M'Shangaan, is he?
*Holzgene says nothing. He sits bent forward, his face buried in his
hands, and*
    The curtain falls.

Mara

A Play in One Act

Prologue

SCENE: *The Johannesburg Town Hall. Mayor, Citizens, Herman Malan, Bishop.*

MAYOR: Ladies and gentlemen, here this day in the City Hall of Johannesburg, we are assembled to honour Africa's greatest poet. As the Greek of old decked singers with garlands and cypress and myrtle, we in Johannesburg have gathered to bestow on Herman Malan a small token of our esteem and admiration. We lay at his feet the homage of a continent.

MALAN: Lay it down softly, Mr Mayor. Don't let it fall on my sore toe.

BISHOP: Let us pray.

Act One, Scene 1

SCENE: *Peter's bedroom. Peter and Estella.*

ESTELLA: So that's all you wanted me for. You brought me up here for this. And you said that you loved me. . .

PETER: Oh, Estella. Oh, I am sorry, Estella. I didn't mean to. . .

ESTELLA: Go away from me. Let me go at once. Take your hands off me. I won't have you touch me. No, no, never again. To think of all the things you have talked to me about. You said you were different. You spoke to me about flowers and shadows and the moon's feet on the grass. Do you remember that, about the moon's pale feet?

PETER: Don't hurt me, Estella. I know I am low and worthless. I know I am a swine, Estella. I won't ask you to forgive me, either. It's hopeless now.

ESTELLA: Forgive you? Of course, I'll forgive you. I'll forgive you for being a man, just like thousands and thousands of other men. I believe now what the other girls told me at the Jeppe Girls' High School, that all men are alike and that that's all they want from a woman. And they said that was all that a mathematics master from King Edward VII School was hanging around one of our young teachers for. They said all men were like that. And I didn't believe it – then. And when I met you I thought that at last – Oh, Peter, how could you do that to me? No, no, it's no use. You mustn't try to put your arms round me again. You know that you must never do that again. . . I am going away now and you know that it is for always.

PETER: I know I have lost you, Estella. You are beautiful and I have soiled you with my. . . (*Sits down on bed*)

ESTELLA: You've insulted me, Peter. But that's nothing. You've treated me as a street-girl. I thought you loved me, but it was only. . . something else. Still, all that is nothing. What hurts me so terribly is that it is you who have done all these things to me. The insults are nothing. A girl can't grow to womanhood without encountering ugly things like this. When I was eleven an old man with a beard tried to do a vile thing to me in a café, a bioscope café. I told you what he did, Peter. To think that you –

PETER: Yes, yes. Go on saying these terrible things to me, Estella. They hurt me and I deserve to be hurt. I am only surprised that I can still feel shame.

ESTELLA: To think that you whom I trusted, Peter, you whom I loved – to think that you should copy this old man with the beard. You. You. You. I suppose that you'll turn round later on and say that I corrupted you. You'll say it was what I told you of the dirty old man in the bioscope café that gave you the idea.

PETER: That's not true, Estella. But of course it makes no difference. It's because I'm yellow, inside. I am yellow. I have got a filthy soul.

ESTELLA: I won't hate you for it though, Peter. You made me believe in dreams, and those things you said about the moon were fine things. Do you remember what you said about that little girl in Joubert Park, with all those red spots on her frock? You said she had slept in the arms of a wounded angel. And I know now what you meant. All the things you told me have lost their innocence. That thing about the little girl and the angel isn't a fairy tale any longer. It's an ordinary dirty story. Oh, you've broken everything. I suppose you thought you would like to be a wounded angel in my arms.

PETER (*rising from bed*): You mustn't go on like that, Estella. And if you don't love me any more I want you to hate me. Now you just despise me. Wait just another five minutes, Estella. We might be able to mend the smashed things. I couldn't do it myself. But you could help me. You can take away my shame and it will never, never, never happen again. Oh please, Estella.

Music outside of a Salvation Army brass band marching past.

ESTELLA: Can't you understand, Peter? I loved you. You had magic for me. I thought you were pure and good. I thought you loved me. How can you love me when you don't even respect me? Your magic has gone, Peter. I can even laugh at you. I can laugh at you as at a silly little boy. I thought nothing could ever destroy the lovely thing we had. I thought not even God could destroy it. But you destroyed it, Peter. And so easily. You must be lots greater than God, Peter. I suppose your friend the bioscope café man with the beard is also greater than God.

PETER: Oh, Estella, Estella, my little Estella. Oh, my darling Estella, oh, why did I do this to our love?

ESTELLA: Stop that now. Don't try to lure me with the old words. Their power has gone. And it's of no use getting between me and the door. Oh, my heart, my heart. Oh, Peter, why did you desecrate our love?

She exits.

PETER: Goodbye, Estella. . .

Act One, Scene 2

SCENE: *The same evening. Mary and Peter.*

MARY: What's wrong with you, Peter?

PETER: Nothing.

MARY: There is something wrong with you. Talk to me, Peter.

PETER: I am all right.

MARY: You have been crying, my little brother. You are crying now. You must tell me what is wrong. Only I can comfort you. . .

PETER: I can't tell you. I won't tell you. Oh, I can never tell you.

MARY: You needn't tell me. I know. You think it's something evil, this that happened to Estella –

PETER: Don't, don't. You don't know anything about this –

MARY: Oh yes, I do know. And you needn't pretend to laugh. My darling Peter. My little boy. Fancy, I was eight years old before you were born. I know every bit of you. And yet you are afraid that I should know this little thing about you and Estella. But I know it already. I knew it long ago.

PETER: Oh Mary, I am a terrible swine. I told Estella so too – about myself.

MARY: You see, I do know. Estella wouldn't give you love.

PETER: Love, love? Wouldn't give me love? You desecrate the word when you talk of love like that. . . Estella also said it was desecration. Love!

MARY: It is Estella who was not worthy of love.

PETER: Do you know what happened? But I can't tell you. Estella wanted to love me and I made it vile. She loved me and I – oh, I am mean and filthy.

MARY: It is Estella who was filthy.

PETER: Stop talking like that. You mustn't say such things. You mustn't insult her – her, Estella.

MARY: What I have said about her is nothing compared with – with –

PETER: Yes?

MARY: With what she has done to my brother. You wanted to give her love and she was ashamed of it. She preferred the cold rags of her virginity to the warmth and beauty of your love. No, no, I was wrong. She was not ashamed of love. It is love who was ashamed of her.

PETER: Mary, you mustn't talk in this mad, terrible way. Do you know what I wanted to. . .

MARY: Of course I know. You wanted to give her yourself. And you are lovely.

PETER: You're disgusting.

MARY: Don't turn your face like that when I talk to you, Peter. You musn't be bashful any longer with your sister. It has lasted much too long. When you were a little baby boy you weren't bashful. It was all love, then. It was only afterwards that you started getting shy. That made our love ugly. We both started getting shy and our love grew tarnished. It got ugly through fear.

PETER: There seems to be an awful meaning in what you are saying, Mary. I don't know. I can't explain it, I –

MARY: It is because you are afraid to explain it, Peter. It is simple enough. All true things are simple. All the beautiful things are simple. But it is my fault as well as yours that you are afraid. I remember when you were growing up and you started growing different – I

139

could see that you were ashamed. And I couldn't bring myself to tell you that I knew and that it made you even more wonderful than you were before. It is just because that made love so wonderful, so very wonderful. It was so grand and so terrible that we couldn't face it. We were afraid of the splendour of love.

PETER: But, Mary, is that really love? You know, Estella made me feel that I was being disgusting. When she said those things to me I felt I could die. She was so pure and lovely. And there was I: I forgot her sweet soul and her soft smile; I only wanted something dirty. That was what she made me feel.

MARY: Don't you see, Peter? Estella made you feel that what you wanted was something dirty. You wanted her, all, all of her. And she made you feel that what you wanted was unworthy of you. She is right. She is unworthy –

PETER: Don't say all that again, Mary. It can't be true. No, no, it mustn't be true. She said I was treating her like a street-girl.

MARY: If she feels about love like a street-girl, surely that's her fault – not yours. But it is true. What you wanted to give her was clean and strong. But she was afraid because it was naked. She had fastened a blue ribbon around love. And she was trying to make you believe that love was only that blue ribbon. For her, love is only a blue ribbon. That is because she is so little – so terribly little and unworthy. She has got a sort of cheap and ugly virginity. She has got nothing else. Inside she is smutty and nasty and degraded. That's why she hangs on to this tawdry body thing of hers. She knows that when that is gone she will have nothing left. She is afraid of seeing herself as she really is. That is what Christ said about the Pharisees. And to save herself from knowing her own emptiness, she hurts you. And she'll go on hurting you. And it is always so easy for a petty, cowardly woman to hurt a man. A man is so big and gentle. Any little cocky pygmy, if she is mean enough, can hurt a giant. Nobody can ever get hurt by strength. You can only get hurt by meanness. Look at David and Goliath.

PETER: I don't agree with you about Estella being small, Mary. But it's true what you said about David and Goliath. Ever since I was a child I have disliked David. I always knew that David could never have killed Goliath if Goliath hadn't let him. Goliath was afraid to hurt David, and so he got killed. I know what an old game it is. All through history the world has killed its giants and it is always the inferior, unimaginative people who have done the killing, people like parsons and purity league women.

MARY: A giant is simple and good-natured. It is because he is big that it is easy for him to get hurt. There is so much of him for the smug men and women to hurt. Look what the respectable scribes did to Jesus, and look what Estella did. . .

PETER: They are all like that, Mary. It seems to me they are all like that.

MARY: They are not all like that, Peter. I admit that most women are like that. But about one in every million is different. Perhaps only one in every ten million, or one in every hundred million, is different. But that one is enough. And it is because of these lonely women here and there, sad women who have not flinched before sorrow, sweet women with clear, brave eyes, that love has not died altogether in the world.

PETER: But are there still women like that, Mary?

MARY: I am one of them, Peter. Then there was Mary Godwin, who went away with Shelley and did not even bother to laugh when all England pretended to despise her. Think of that. Twelve million tenth-rate weaklings, who possessed nothing but their numbers and a degrading smugness, had the interfering impudence to sneer at a girl who had found the love of a poet. They knew that Mary Godwin was rich and that they were beggars. And they envied her the riches. Because they were jealous of her, they hated her. The mob always hates the man or woman of whom it is jealous. Then there was Byron's sister, Augusta.

PETER: Do you really mean this about Byron's sister, Mary?

MARY: She loved her brother and she was not afraid of that love. She was greater than Byron, really. They say that afterwards Byron regretted what he considered to be his sin. But Augusta never regretted it. That was the flaw in Byron – that he regretted what he had done. Genius does not regret.

PETER: But they said, you know – they said that it was incest.

MARY: Of course they said it was incest, Peter. Incest is a word that has been invented by unclean men who have defiled love. When the puny Davids can't understand a giant's love, because it is too large for them, they call it silly names.

PETER: But it sounds so terrible, Mary. Incest –

MARY: Incest has a deep, florid sound, like murder, or like heaven. After all, if it really is love, what does the rest matter? If it truly is love, then you must love the body as well. It is hypocritical to pretend otherwise. It is sin to imagine that because people are closely related they can love each other's minds only. If it is love at all it must be everything. To try to forget about the body is immoral.

PETER: But I have grown to believe, because of what people told me, that it is a terrible thing, incest.

MARY: People only talk like that when they are not worthy of incest. As Estella talked when she was not worthy of you. It is only when you are big – oh, very big, that you can love somebody closely akin to you without being afraid. Every man and every woman, except the few I have mentioned, is terrified by this kind of love. And it is wrong and sinful that it should be so.

PETER: Yes, I can see that. After all, closely related ought to mean somebody who is close to you in other ways also. Somebody who actually is near. Closer than anybody else.

MARY: It ought to be a love that is closer than arms are to the body to embrace. Closer than the warm breath is to the parted lips of passion. Closer than the heart is to the pain by which it is touched.

PETER: That is beautiful, Mary. Only I know how close my heart is to the pain inside it.

MARY: And I am still closer to you than that pain, Peter. For I know what the pain is and can soothe it. I can come between you and that pain. It makes me very happy to know that I can comfort my brother's pain. Thousands of years ago the barbarians north of the Rhine had a beautiful marriage custom. The women of the tribe took all the clothes from the bride. They even took away her armlets and her necklace. Then the men and the women and the children of the tribe gathered together and the new bride threaded her way through the midst of them, and naked with her head back she walked forth to meet her husband. And they all knew why the wedding was, and they sang of the bride's body, and they knew that she brought her husband everything, because she brought nothing in her hands. They knew what a splendid thing creation is. And I know what a splendid thing creation is. For I am creation. Creation is of the earth, Peter. Poets and their songs, painters and their pictures, drunkards and their dreams – all these fine things are of the earth. It is to the earth that these big ones come, when their hearts are wearied with a sorrow they cannot understand, and there is dust on their feet, and their eyes are mournful with having gazed too long on the old shadows. For it is only shadows that are blinding. . . Oh, they all come back to the earth. And I am the earth, Peter. Oh, I could never be jealous of God. God can keep his heaven. It is God who is jealous of the earth. God knows that His heaven must pass away and that the earth – only the earth – is eternal.

PETER: But if, Mary. . . supposing we. . . you know what I mean. Won't we feel sorry about it afterwards?

MARY: I know that I shall never be sorry. But even if I thought I would be sorry it would not deter me. If sorrow does come to me afterwards, what does it matter? I am not afraid of sorrow. Sorrow is not less beautiful than joy. My sorrow is as precious to me as my happiness. I would be equally reluctant to part with the least bit of either.

PETER: I feel that what you have said is what Christina Rossetti meant when she said that thing about dreaming in the twilight.

MARY: I have seen a portrait of Christina Rossetti. She has got a fine face. A beautiful, stormy face. And she has a radiant expression. Something like the way Mary Magdalen would have looked if Pilate had accepted Jesus Christ's plea of 'Not Guilty.'

PETER: Christ is fine. Christ invented love for love's sake. Before Christ there had been love for the world's sake – love so as to get children, and so on. But it was Christ who said you ought to seek love for no reason at all except that it is love. But it wasn't love in the way you mean, Mary. I think Christ would have thought your way evil.

MARY: No, he wouldn't. He said resist not evil. When Christ said we had to love one another he meant every word of it. And he knew that a thing is evil only when you make it evil by resisting it. If I said to you, "No, Peter, my brother, you must not love me, because that would be incest," then it really would be incest. We make an evil of something which was innocent. By trying to resist a thing we betray ourselves into committing sin.

PETER: Christ was the world's first Don Juan. All the tenderness and the sweetness of the world's great love stories come direct from Jesus. People knew before Christ that flowers and trees and rain were beautiful. But it was Christ who gave them their meaning. White flowers growing on a hedge in the evening. They were only sad with fading light. They were only wakeful with memories of peace and perfumes. It was Christ who gave them their soul. The haunting thing of beauty is the ghost of love. And Christ made love. Jesus gave love an air – a flourish.

143

MARY: You spoke about trees, Peter, and about the evening. It is curious about trees. Sometimes, when I am alone, I think of a clump of trees standing all on their own on the veld, somewhere. When I think of those trees, tall and alone and strange in the dusk, there is something about the feeling I get that makes me want to cry. It is something tragic about love that I can't understand. And it seems to me that one day, when I am dying, in my last hour I will remember those trees and in the moment of death I will realise that I am never going to understand the meaning of those trees.

PETER: I know that about trees, Mary. I know of other people who also experience that strange sort of emotion. And I think that's how you feel when you die. A lonely clump of trees on the veld at sunset is a symbol of the moment of dying.

MARY: Do you know, Peter, that what we have been saying now are grand things. Big, creative things. I know that the earth grows sad when we get so very near to her. For she knows it is sadness that makes things. In the beginning there was nothing. Then sadness came. And sadness made life.

PETER: You are very beautiful, Mary.

MARY: You have put the beauty there, Peter.

PETER: Your eyes are wonderful tonight, Mary.

MARY: I know, Peter.

PETER: If I put my hand on your bosom my fingers would feel dark things.

MARY: Come closer to me, Peter – closer – closer. . .

Street-woman

A Play in One Act

Cast
Polly
Bernard
Detective-Sergeant Nick Johnson
Detective-Sergeant Andries Norgarb

*The scene of the whole action of the play is laid in the room of Polly,
a prostitute. A bed; a table and two chairs; wardrobe; dressing-
table; washstand, etc.*
The door opens. Polly enters.
POLLY: Come on in – quick. I don't wan' the landlady to know how
many men I get. Blasted old Nosey Parker. That's all she is.
Enter Bernard.
BERNARD (*starts taking off his overcoat*): That's all right. She didn't
see me. Funny thing about all you prostitutes. Brazen as you like out
in the street. But going past the landlady's door on tiptoe. What is your
landlady? A retired whore, I suppose?
POLLY: I don't know so much about the retired part. And she's not
really so particular about us getting men in the rooms. Only, she
won't allow us to do no cooking.
BERNARD (*hanging his overcoat over chair; sits down and lights a
cigarette*): Real old Joburg dosshouse. (*Looks around room*) The old-
fashioned kind, I mean. The same furniture, smell and all that. Gives
me a homesick feeling. Lucas's Café. And Rosalind House. And
Anderson's Buildings. They're all gone, now – replaced by these
modern flats. My earliest recollections of Joburg are of rooms just
like this one. And there was Railway Chambers –
POLLY (*takes off her coat and seats herself on bed*): Never mind all that
talk. Come on. Let's get it over. I said two quid for a short time I got
to get back into the street for more men. It's early yet. You said you'd
be quick. You can't stick here all night for just a couple of leaves.
BERNARD (*takes out his wallet and flings a handful of notes on the
table*): That's okay. I am loaded.

145

POLLY (*jumps up from the bed and grabs the money*): God! You're carrying. . . heavy. Look here, I don't want no trouble. And I don't want no queer business, neither. You don't want me to hit you with a strap, likely? Or to give you the lift? I don't want none of that, see? I never yet come any of that funny stuff in my life. I may be a whore. But thank God I am a respectable whore. I don't pull none of that immoral Frenchy sort of business.

BERNARD: Don't worry, sister. Take it easy. I don't want you. I want a place to sleep. I just got back from Durban, and I couldn't get accommodation. You know, the housing shortage. So I walked about the pavements a bit, and when I saw you standing in that shop entrance in Troye Street, I thought I would let you pick me up so I could get a place to sleep. I'm tired. (*Stretching himself and yawning*) On the train all day.

POLLY (*seats herself at table opposite him*): That's a new one. But you don't expect me to swallow a tale like that, do you? And you loaded with all that dough. Where's your luggage?

BERNARD: Booked in at the station. (*Takes out his wallet and produces cloakroom receipt*) There's the cloakroom ticket. Now do you believe me?

POLLY: Well, maybe it's true and maybe it ain't. But why don't you go to a hotel? And ain't you got no friends here that would put you up for the night?

BERNARD: I tried a couple of hotels, but I got tired of walking around. And I have been away from Joburg so long that I can't remember just offhand what friends I have still got left here, or where they are likely to be staying. You know how people move about in this city.

POLLY: Well, it seems all right. But I can't just somehow *feel* that you're on the level. Sure you ain't lying to me?

BERNARD: Would it make any difference if I was lying to you? I've paid you enough, haven't I – for you to allow me to stay for the night? Or do you feel that it isn't regular – that I pay you and don't have you?

POLLY: If you have me or don't have me, I won't even know the difference, I don't think. I haven't had no feelings like that for years. And it ain't the first time that a man has come up here with me, and him paying me, and wanting to take me and all, and then he finds that he's too played out and he *can't* take me, and he curses me up and down, as if it's my bloody fault that he's no good any more, and he goes out still swearing. *That* ain't what's wrong with you, perhaps, is it?

146

BERNARD: Maybe it is. I don't know. I'm not interested. Mind if I start getting undressed? (*Unbuttons his jacket and begins to loosen his tie*)

POLLY: Do what you like. I've already said as you can stay the night. But there's something mighty queer about you all the –

BERNARD: Oh, just a minute. (*Readjusting his tie*) There's something I forgot. What about your – you know – the man you keep? The man that lives on you? Where's *he* going to sleep tonight, if I've got his bed?

POLLY: Don't make me laugh. A ponce? I've had my share of ponces And if ever a man comes and tries to ponce on me again, I'll shoot him. That's what. A pimp is the lousiest kind of mongrel that there is – lower than a snake's backside – and I only wish I *did* have a ponce again, just for the pleasure of turning him over to the johns, so he can get time and lashes. *And* lashes, the low-down mongrel. A pimp? Every pimp should be first raped and then get lashes with the cat-of-nine-tails, and then he should get shot.

BERNARD: Oh, well, if there's no pimp to come and wake us in the early hours of the morning, to pull your money off you, and then to take my place in bed. I suppose we can turn in. I'm tired. By the way, why are you so dead set against pimps? A pimp has got to live, too, I suppose. And you say you have got like that only recently. Does that mean that in the past a pimp was good enough for you? Did your last pimp let you down, or what? What happened?

POLLY: That was Alec. The first time I seen him. . . him coming up to me in that pub just around the corner from where I picked you up in Bree Street. . . and him saying as it was true love and in the same breath asking me did I have a ponce. And because I was soft-hearted I said all right. And I got no feelings for him, any more than what I got feelings for you or almost any sort of man. And it is only because I am lonely, and I know he's lonely and my last ponce has turned me up. . . and so he comes and lives with me. And I never got *that* amount of feeling for him. And all the time he's as jealous as hell. And he says I've got feelings for the other men that I haven't got for him. And yet when I want to come to bed earlier than twelve o'clock because I'm not feeling too clever, he chucks me out again, and says, "The night is young. Get out while the going is good." And every pound I get he goes and spends on trollops. And I'm not in love with him, but I fancy him, if you understand, and I feel sorry for him. I can't tell you what it is. And all the time he takes all my money off

147

me and wastes it on other molls. And one night he doesn't come home as usual to take my money off me and to sleep with me. And I lie awake all night thinking of him, and of his pointed patent-leather shoes, and I hate him and feel sorry for him, and I think he's filth, and I can't get to sleep waiting for him to come up the stairs. And he never come up them stairs again. I never again heard his footsteps on that landing. I know every man that comes up them stairs, just by his footsteps, after I hear them once or twice. And I would know Alec's footsteps from out of a million other men –

BERNARD: But if, as you say, you never loved him, what difference would it make to you, hearing his footsteps or not hearing them? I mean to say, if this Alec meant so little to you. . .

POLLY: I don't say I didn't love him. Otherwise I wouldn't have allowed him to ponce on me, of course. But I don't have no respect for him, or for any man as ever ponced on me. And the only man I could ever fall in love with – *really* love, I mean – is the man I could look up to, and have respect for.

BERNARD: And then what happened to old Alec? But cut it short. I want to get to bed.

POLLY: He buggered off to Cape Town with some trollops. And afterwards I heard as he got pinched for living on the proceeds. And at first –

BERNARD: Proceeds? What do you mean, proceeds?

POLLY: Proceeds of prostitution, stupid.

BERNARD: Perhaps I am not as stupid as you think. But go on.

POLLY: And at first I was glad, and afterwards I got around to feeling sorry for him again, when I heard he got lashes in Roeland Street Gaol. I could picture them lashes cutting into his back and him yelling to beat the band. Because he never had no guts. And that was part of the feelings I had for him, if you understand what I mean. I was sorry for him because he was white-livered and a squealer and with no guts. But afterwards I got over that, also, and I say that a ponce stinks, and a man that lives on a woman selling herself on the streets is the lowest kind of rat that there is. The only way to make a man out of a ponce is to turn him over to the johns.

BERNARD: Look, on second thoughts, I don't think I'll sleep here, after all. I've just remembered something.

POLLY: Afraid I'd steal the rest of the money out of your wallet when you're asleep?

BERNARD: The few pounds that's left in my wallet you can have. That's nothing. But I'll be honest with you: you've been straight with me. The ticket for my luggage that's in the cloakroom. How do I know you don't take it off me and collect the dough in my suitcase in the morning?

POLLY: Say, mister. . . I also just suddenly thought of something.

BERNARD (*sharply*): What?

POLLY: You must be the guy that pulled that bank job in Durban. Just about two days ago. Everybody's talking about it. The newspapers is full of it. (*Advances towards him, pointing her finger at him*)

BERNARD (*gets up and reaches for his overcoat slumped over the back of the chair*): Well, if I am – what about it? Are you going to holler for the police? Don't forget I've got a gun on me. Not that I would use it on you, of course. It's not necessary. Just one squeak from you and I'll lay you out cold. Get back to that bed.

POLLY (*slowly retreating*): Say, mister, what's your name?

BERNARD: They call me Bernard.

POLLY: No, that ain't the name that was in the papers. But there was three of you in it. And a bank teller got shot dead. So you're a killer! A killer!

BERNARD: I'm not saying I am, and I'm not saying I'm not. But you make one move to shelf me to the police and you'll be a dead whore.

POLLY: You think I'm afraid of you, don't you? Well, I'm not, see? And look, Bernard – I don't know if it really is your name, or if it ain't – I would never shelf a killer to the johns. I got too much respect for a killer. At least, a killer isn't a ponce. At least, a killer doesn't hide behind a woman's skirts. A killer knows what he wants in the world, and he goes out and gets it. And if he ends up with a lot of lead in his belly, or a rope around his neck, he still tried to give them a run for their money. Can't you see I'm on your side, Bernard? I'm your *sort*. I got no time for rats, neither. Or for squealers. Nearly every man in my life has been a dirty rat. Bleating his guts out over what a hard life he's had, and how he's never had a chance. Men!. . . I know them all. And the worst kind isn't the sort that just wants to have me, and after he's had me he pays me and buggers off. I'm saying nothing about that kind of man.

BERNARD: Yes, I think I know what you mean by the other sort.

POLLY: And you'd be surprised to know how many. And they come in here ashamed because they're going with a whore, and because

149

they can't do without a whore, and the bleats they put up – all about how –

BERNARD: You say you won't shelf me to the police?

POLLY: Shelf a killer! Never!

BERNARD (*slowly*): Yes, I think I believe you. But remember what I said. Any monkey business and I'll do for you.

POLLY: Oh, in case you'd like to know, my name is Polly.

BERNARD: Glad to meet you, Polly. And, you know, here's something queer. If you hadn't guessed about the Durban affair, I'm sure I would have told you on my own. That just shows you. A person can't keep a thing like that to himself, all bottled up inside him. He's got to talk. Talk. Talk. He's just got to. You've got no idea what I've gone through. I've just had to tell somebody.

POLLY: Say, how did you come to get mixed up in that bank job, anyway? Do you always go in for the big stuff? How many stretches have you done?

BERNARD: This is the first time I've been in a killing. Honest it is. You think I'm kidding you?

POLLY: Well, no. I don't think you're kidding. I mean, how many times in a lifetime do you think you can get away with shooting a bank clerk? And I also think that if you wasn't new to the game you wouldn't have let on to me so quick about it being you that the johns is after.

BERNARD: Well, I honestly don't know how it all came about. And, if you must know, I'm all gone in. I can't stand it. I just want to break down and cry like a kid. And I know I've made a hell of a blue, somewhere along the line, letting you in on the whole works so easily, just because you made me feel that you – that you *understood*, somehow. That shows I must be all in. I must have been mad to have admitted all I have done. But I just couldn't help it. I was all in pieces. You got no idea. And there was something about you that made me feel I could trust you.

POLLY (*going up to him and putting her hand against his cheek*): But of course you can trust me, Bernard. And it's a very good thing you come along here. Maybe you got *led* here –

BERNARD: Don't make me laugh. Fancy a man getting *led* into a brothel.

POLLY: What I mean is. . . maybe I'm the only woman in the whole of Johannesburg that was waiting for a chance to be able to be a friend to a real killer. Or maybe that ain't so, neither. Maybe there's thousands of people in Johannesburg, right now, tonight, that feel exactly the same way what I do, and that would be proud to have a chance to hide a real killer from the police.

BERNARD: You may even be right, at that, Polly. We all know Joburg is a hell of a queer place.

POLLY: Well, if I can feel like that about you, so can thousands of other women, I'm sure. Women as have had the same kind of experiences with men that haven't been men at all.

BERNARD: But the trouble is, I'm not a real killer, Polly. You see, it's the first time I've been in this kind of a jam.

POLLY: But the police are after you, aren't they? I mean, aren't the johns looking for you? According to the papers they are looking for you for murder and bank robbery –

BERNARD: Don't say that word again. I can't stand it. Murder! It all happened so quickly, I just can't believe it. And there we were filling the pillowcases with notes and the bank teller was lying on his face, with the blood flowing all over the floor, and his legs still twitching. It all looked just like a dream. And I thought I'd never make it to the getaway car. We split the dough three ways and they dumped me at Maritzburg. And I got on the train, and every person that came into the compartment I thought was a detective. And when I was lifting the suitcase on to the counter in the cloakroom somebody bumped against me, and I thought it was a john putting his hand on my shoulder. And I was scared to walk about the streets here in Johannesburg, although it was night. And I was scared to go and book in at an hotel. And then I thought: I'd pick up a prostitute and use her room as a hideout. And that's the whole story. I've blabbed it all out to you in ten minutes after we were alone here together. That's the kind of killer I am. All I've still got to do is to tell you what an unhappy childhood I've had, and how when I grew up people never understood me because I was too sensitive – God, how sick I get of all this slobber –

POLLY: That's all right. Your nerves is just conked in. Let me get you some brandy. I got a bottle in the wardrobe.

She gets up and fetches a bottle and two glasses from the wardrobe. She fills a carafe with water from the jug on the washstand and puts it on the table.

BERNARD: Do you know what? I never thought of drink. Can you beat that? Of course, I've got to have brandy. Lots of it. But I was actually so scared that, although I walked past dozens of pubs tonight, it never occurred to me that a couple of drinks would put me right. – Hold hard. Not so much water with mine. Well, here's down the hatch. Have another? Good. Let me pour them. Ah, that's better. – You know, it was only after I had picked you up, and you took my arm, and we started walking towards this building – it was only then that I started feeling less scared. I didn't have the blue funks so much, with you holding my arm. I felt, right away, when you took my arm, that I belonged with humanity again. I felt that I was in life again. That's something about you, Polly. Something you've got that other women haven't got. You're the kind of woman that makes a man feel he is something in the world – even if he is a skunk. You get me? – Well, here's down the hatch again. What kind of brandy is it? It's good stuff, anyway. Another drink for you too? That's fine. We'll make a night of it, after all. – There's something protective about you, you know, Polly. Something independent. You don't make a man feel that you are a drooping sort of a lily that he has got to revive. You make a man feel, instead, that you can look after *him*. And that's what a man wants off a woman when he's in trouble. He wants a woman to be nice to him. The other kind of woman is all right to show off in front of, and to act romantic in front of, and to tell lies to, and all that. But when a man is licked, like I am licked tonight, and like I've been licked before in my life, then you are the only kind of woman that can do him any good. I could never feel romantic about you, Polly. But who the hell wants romance, when he's on the lam, with the johns after him for a killing? – Another drink for you? No?. . . Okay. I'll have this one on my own. Here she goes. – You're not one of those doll-like creatures that a man is afraid of exposing his weakness to, Polly. But you're a real woman. And I say, Give me the real woman, the kind of woman a man can come to when he is in trouble. They can keep the other kind. But how's it you're not talking, Polly? Or drinking? You haven't said a word for I don't know how long.

POLLY: It looks like you're right. I'm the kind of woman that a man hangs on to when things go wrong with him, and that he drops in the shit when he's on his feet again and a trollop with a pretty face comes along. Like what happened with Alec. And I can see now that all you men are the same. And I thought that you were different. I am all right for a man to ponce on when he's buggered to the world. But when he's on top he won't give me as much as a look.

BERNARD: Don't get hard, now, Polly. You're the kind of woman that helps a man. A man can come to you just as he is, just as a plain human being. He has no need to put on an act when he's with you. He hasn't got to pretend, when he's with you, that he's a knight in shining armour. He comes to you just as he is, and he says, "This is me. Take me just like I am."

POLLY: Yes, and with his clothes undone. So that's the kind of man what you are also. And because you're supposed to carry a gun, I thought as you was different. I looked up to you. I didn't think you was just another weak sod. I didn't think you was just another Alec Just another rat hiding behind a woman's skirts – behind the skirts of the kind of woman that I am, and making out you're no end of a hero to the kind of woman that won't let you come crawling to her when your mozzle is out. What I say is –

BERNARD: I say! Shht! Listen! Footsteps. . .

POLLY: Don't worry about them footsteps. I heard them long ago. I can tell any one of my customers just by his footsteps. Before he's halfway up the stairs, I can tell just who he is. And he's going to knock on my door in a couple of secs. He's Marmaduke, just a bank clerk, coming round for a late bit. But his luck's out. Seems to me this is a bad time for bank clerks. . .

BERNARD: For God's sake don't remind me of that. And don't make jokes about it.

POLLY: Keep your hair on. What's walked over your grave all of a sudden?

BERNARD: No, nothing. Only, it shook me when you started reminding me of. . . of that other bank clerk. You're sure it's not a policeman coming up?

There's a knock at the door.

POLLY: No, it's only Marmaduke. I know the way he knocks, too. (*Goes up to the door, which she opens a few inches*) Sorry, Marmaduke old boy, I got a full date for tonight. You didn't see me on the corner? No, I been in here with this horse. It's a all-night. Come round tomorrow night if you don't get fixed up. Ta-ta!

She returns to the table and takes up her glass, Bernard having in the meantime poured out and swallowed another drink quickly.

BERNARD: There's something about you that makes a man feel he's all right, no matter how low he is.

POLLY (*fiercely*): That's what you said before, and that's what I don't want, see? I want a man that feels, because he's got me, he's got to *be* a man. And what's more, I'm the kind of woman as is no good to men. You see that, Bernard? I'm no bloody good to you. The only kind of woman that can help a man up is the woman that makes it damn hard for him. And that says to him, "You got to pull your socks up and you got to put your guts into it, and you got to look after me like I'm a doll. Otherwise you can't have me." And I thought you was a gunman. And I could of taken a fancy to you – like I did. And if the johns had come in and took you away I could of cared for you. I could of felt for you in a big way. And I thought you was that kind of man. The kind of man that I could respect. So that if the police *did* come –

Footsteps off.

BERNARD: For God's sake! There's more footsteps –

POLLY: Don't worry. I heard them footsteps also. That's Pinkie. They say he's a stockbroker. But I dunno. He goes round to Mabel Smith, two doors from here. Not that I haven't had him also, one or two nights. They never tells us their real names, of course. So we gives them our own sorts of monickers. And *he's* Pinkie. Hear that? He's knocking at Mabel Smith's door. I know his footsteps. *And* his knock. Very queer knock. (*Rapping on table*) Tap-tap – tap-tap-tap – tap, like that.

BERNARD: Edge that. It works on my nerves. Let's have another drink.

POLLY: All right, Mr Gangster. We'll have another drink. God, how I wish you was a real gangster, though. Like I thought you was when I first found out you was in that Durban job. (*Laughing shrilly*) Oh, Bernard – you know those two blokes that done the job with you? It just struck me all of a heap. What are *them* two doing tonight, do you think? Also hiding behind some woman's skirt, likely? (*Reaching across table and slapping him playfully*)

BERNARD: From what I know of them, I wouldn't be surprised. I suppose they are also busy tonight telling some woman or other a hard-luck story. Feeling sorry for themselves for having a pillow-case full of dough. . . (*They both laugh*)

POLLY: Damn it all. I dunno if it's the brandy. But there's *still* something about you. Bugger me, but I *still* feel you got something. Yes, Bernard, my boy. You got something. You got something that them rats like Alec haven't got. I dunno what it is right now. You seem just as big a squealer as any of them rats that ever ponced on me.

You seem just as yellow to me, somehow. But there's something – God – I dunno. It must be the brandy, I think. Because you seem just the sort of bum and bleater that's sorry for himself. But all the same, there's something about you what's different. Perhaps you aren't different. Perhaps it's just that you shot a man, and that that's the thing about you that *looks* different. But, blast it all, Bernard, I dunno –

BERNARD: No, I'm just like the rest of them. In fact, I'm lousier. I had more opportunities than they had. And here's a funny thing, too. And it's just come over me now. I've had queer changes of feeling all night. First I was a cowardly, cringing thing, out in the streets, afraid of its own shadow. Then, when I met you, and you put your arm in mine, and we started walking along towards this building, all my guts came back again in a strange sort of way that I can't explain, so that when we came in at this door here, I felt that I really was somebody. Do you remember what I was like when I came in, and I spoke airily about old Joburg buildings, and smells, and things like that, as though I didn't have a care in the world – leave alone worrying about getting a rope around my neck?

POLLY: Remember? Of course, I remember. And when I found out afterwards as that you *was* scared of the rope – hell, how I looked up to you then. I thought as how you was the one man I had waited all my life to find. And if you *did* get the rope, I thought as it would be nothing at all. We all got to die. And I thought that if you did get to go through the trapdoor, it would be knowing that there was one woman in the world that respected you –

BERNARD: Good Lord! You must be mad! I can see, now. You're stone mad, or you're drunk. Yes, of course, you're drunk. And I feel I'm getting drunk, too. Have you got nothing else to think about, except a man getting hanged? Why? I might even get away with it. It wasn't premeditated. And we are all three of us equally guilty, all three of us who took part in it. And I'm sure they won't hang three men for the death of one bank clerk. Not three men, anyway.

POLLY: Maybe I'm drunk, and maybe I'm mad. But look at it like this. We all got to die, haven't we? .

BERNARD: Well, yes, of course.

POLLY: Every man and every woman and every child that is born into the world. Each one of us has got to die, sooner or later, ain't we?

BERNARD: Yes, but I don't want to die now. And I don't want to die *knowing* that I'm going to die. It was all right for that bank clerk. It came to him so suddenly, he never knew that his hour had come. But with me – think what it means: a fugitive skulking around like I am now, and then a trial and only months later, after my last appeal has been turned down, and everything – only then will I die. And I'll know it all beforehand, on black and white, to the very minute when I'm going to die. We never did anything like that to the bank clerk.

POLLY: But what I mean is, if you got to go, whichever way you got to go, why don't you go like a man? That's all I'm saying to you. And I can look up to any man that, when the game goes crook, takes it like a man. Instead of coming round to a woman, squealing for her to be sorry for you. Okay, they might get you tomorrow. They might get you the next day. Or next month. Or they might not even get you at all. We know how slow a flatfoot is to get on a trail. But what does it matter what happens tomorrow? Think as how you got *tonight*. Do you get me, Bernard? You got *tonight* – right here with me. Ain't that something? And that is how I feel about you, Bernard. How I *could* feel about you. And it's a feeling I ain't got for any other man in the world. I feel that, if you was took, it could be with a gun in your hand. And not feeling sorry for yourself. And not wanting the woman as what took a fancy to you sudden-like to feel sorry for you, neither.

BERNARD: Do you mean all that, Polly? All that you've been saying now?

POLLY (*goes up to him and kisses him*): I mean that more than what I meant anything before in my life. Even though I am a whore.

BERNARD: I am very grateful to you, Polly. You helped me get my manhood back. I see what you're getting at, and I see that you are right. And I want you to promise me one thing. Promise me that you'll never feel sorry for me. You can feel as sorry as you like for all the ponces and Alecs in the world. But you must never feel sorry for me. Promise.

POLLY: Course I promise.

BERNARD: It's wonderful to feel a man again. I'd sooner be dead than go about snivelling again, like I've been doing ever since that killing. Life isn't worth anything if you're all trembling and white-livered inside. My God! I'll still give them a run for their money! Just you see if I don't. What's happened to me? I've got all my guts back, all at once. It must be something to do with having shot a man. No, it can't be that, either. And it isn't the brandy. So it must be you,

Polly. It's you that did this thing to me, suddenly making me no longer afraid to face whatever I have to face. Making me feel that if I have to go down, I want to go down like a ship with its colours nailed to the mast. Courage! What a wonderful thing that is. And that's all I want. . . I want to live and die like a man. And imagine that you have done this to me, Polly. You, a harlot that I despised. You, a whore, making a man of me, like this, suddenly. It must be that you were always meant for me. It must be that you were always meant to be my woman. And life was like that, that we never met until now. And now when we meet, I am a murderer running away from the police, and you are a whore selling yourself on the streets. And I feel that you are my first and last love. And this is the way we meet. We meet, just to part. But what if we had never met? And isn't it funny, our meeting like this, after we have both been sullied by the world? Oh, there's so much I want to tell you. All about my past life. And how I got to be mixed up with criminals. And I don't see you as a street-woman, now. I see you only as somebody very beautiful. And here, in this room, over a bottle of brandy, I came across you, Polly, almost when it was too late.

POLLY: Better late than never is what I says.

BERNARD: And all your life is this really what you wanted? All your life did you know that you would one day meet a man, and that the meeting would be like this?

POLLY: I didn't know, of course, Bernard. But I did have – well, I did have – *hopes* –

BERNARD: And that is all I ever dreamt about – about what I could get from a woman. Funny, isn't it? Just this. I mean, like we are now. Like the way we feel about each other.

POLLY (*putting her two hands around his throat*): You aren't afraid of the rope now, are you, Bernard? How does it feel now, the rope? They says as it gets you behind the left ear when the trapdoor drops. Well, if that *does* happen to you, remember that it's only my fingers. How does it feel, the knot pressing under your ear? Like this?

BERNARD: It feels fine. God, it feels fine. Press tighter. I want more of it. And say, Polly, I'll give you the ticket for my suitcase at the station. Maybe you can use that dough. A pillowcase full.

POLLY: Do you know what, Bernard?

BERNARD: No. What?

POLLY: There's more footsteps.

157

BERNARD: Oh, footsteps? Where? Coming up the staircase, I suppose? I can't hear a thing. I can only feel the blood ringing in my ears from your fingers around my neck. And if those should be the last sensations of which I would ever be aware – well, it would be lovely. . .

POLLY: But them footsteps. I know whose they are.

BERNARD: Footsteps – eh? Footsteps on the stairs? Alec, I suppose. Yes, I suppose it's Alec. Or perhaps it's another one of your customers.

POLLY: It's two customers.

BERNARD: Two! Don't say it's –

POLLY: Yes, it's a couple of johns from Marshall Square. Detective-Sergeant Johnson and Detective-Sergeant Norgarb.

BERNARD: What! (*Breaking out of her grasp*) What! Those two bastards? Quick! Hide me. Can't you hide me in that wardrobe? What about the window? Hell, they got me! They got me! (*Dashing in direction of window*)

Loud banging at door. Cries of: "Open! Open in the name of the law! Open or we'll smash the door down!"

POLLY: Bernard! Use your brains, man. It's too late to duck out. Sit down and pour yourself another drink. Look as if you're my ponce. Come on, quick now! (*Bernard seats himself hurriedly*) The door is open in any case. You got no chance to scale out of here. (*Goes to door which she opens a few inches*) Sorry, I can't let you boys in tonight. Oh, it's you Nick Johnson, and it's you, Andries Norgarb. You can't come in tonight. I got someone. Make it some other night.

The door is forced open and Detective-Sergeants Nick Johnson and Andries Norgarb enter.

JOHNSON: Who's that?

POLLY: Just a friend. I known him a couple of months. But he ain't poncing on me. He's working down town. Drops in on me now and again.

JOHNSON: Well, he looks a lot like the bloke we're after. What do you think, Norgarb? Answers to the description of the man that had the gun, doesn't he? (*Draws his revolver in a single swift moment*) Stick 'em up. You frisk him, Norgarb. (*To Bernard*) Don't suppose you know what we want you for, do you?

BERNARD: No, of course not. What's all this about?

JOHNSON: Never been to Durban, I suppose? Or in the Standard Bank, I suppose? Or ever carried a gun, I suppose? Make one move and I'll drill you. Come on, lift those hands higher.

BERNARD: I still don't know what you're talking about.

POLLY: He's been sleeping with me here for the last two months. If you think as –

JOHNSON: Come on, Norgarb. Frisk him. He looks like the description we got of one of the killers.

NORGARB (*steps forward, then calls out in surprise*): Well! Well! If it isn't Gentleman George!

JOHNSON: Do you know him?

NORGARB: Know him? Of course, I know him. Gentleman George! You was poncing on Big Mavis for years in Fordsie, wasn't you? So you back at your old games, eh? You can drop that gun, Johnson. He's not a killer, he's a ponce. Once a ponce, always a ponce. I put him away for three years when I was on the Mayfair branch of the Immorality Staff. And he got lashes, too. Let him drop his trousers and show you the marks. He's still got the marks. We're wasting our time here. Let's get going.

JOHNSON: But he answers the description of one of the killers. Better search him for a gun. Or a ticket. Or a account. Or a letter with a Durban postmark on. Something to pin it on him – to connect him with Durban.

NORGARB: Garn, don't waste time. Once a ponce, always a ponce. Gentleman George! Him and his dude ways. Don't I know him? Say, what happened to Big Mavis after you got put away, George?

BERNARD: I have said that I don't know what you are talking about. It seems to me: once a policeman, always a policeman –

NORGARB: None of your lip, see? (*Punches Bernard on the jaw; Bernard staggers back*) But we got no time to waste on the likes of you now. We're looking for a killer, this time – not for a ponce. . . I'd like to take another smack at you. (*Bernard dodges the blow*)

JOHNSON: Okay. Don't let us waste more time. We got to get going. (*To Polly*) Seen any killers around here tonight, sister?

POLLY: If I did, I'd be sure to tell it to a john.

JOHNSON: Tell you what, sister, the minute you get tired of him poncing on you, turn him in to us cops. We'll get him a stretch and lashes. Turn him in like what Big Mavis done. I can stand for a killer. And I'll go all out to get him hanged. But there's nothing gives me more satisfaction than to see a ponce getting six of the best across the arse. Bah! Gentleman George! Don't hit him again, man. We got no time. We got to try all the rooms on this floor. But I think just for luck I'll look through the pockets of this coat. There may just be a gun in it. (*Moves in direction of Bernard's coat, hung over chair; Norgarb intercepts him*)

NORGARB: Don't be a goat, man. I know he's got all sorts of things in his pocket. But not a gun. Not him. Let's hit the trail after the killer. You know we got no time to waste –

JOHNSON: Okay, let's get cracking.

Exeunt Norgarb and Johnson.

BERNARD: Well, thanks very much, Polly. That was a close shave, wasn't it? They nearly had me. Hell, I thought it was the rope. Still, as they say, once a policeman, always a policeman. Thank God, there's still a drink left in the bottle. . . Say, what's wrong?

POLLY: Gentleman George!

BERNARD: Well, what of it?

POLLY: So it's true. Another one of these bloody ponces! So that's why you got all these taking-in ways. Gentleman George! And that was what you meant, wanting to tell me all about yourself and all about your past life, and I dunno what else. And about the opportunities what you had, and what others didn't have. Gentleman George! And Big Mavis – what turned you in. And the lashes across your back-side – for poncing. So it's all true. And here was I having respect for you, and thinking you was a killer. And you're just another blasted ponce. . .

BERNARD: Well, you saved me, Polly, and I'm grateful. Do you mean, now, that you didn't want to save me? Good Lord, what's gone wrong with you all at once? Hell, that was a close shave. They just about had me, then.

POLLY: Of course, I didn't want to save you. It just happened quick, like that, because I'm always used to sticking up for a man when the johns is after him. But I thought you was a man. I thought you was a killer, and all sorts of things. . . Just a minute ago. And now it turns out what you are only – Gentleman George. And say, what did they call her 'Big Mavis' for? What part of her was big? And I thought you was a man. . . Do you know what, Bernard? It's struck me now again, all of a heap. You're not a ponce. You're not Gentleman George. You're Bernard. You're a man. You're a killer. And I'm going to make a man of you, if it means –

BERNARD: Hey! Hey! What's all this about? Of course, I'm a man – but what the hell –

160

POLLY: Of course, I'll save you. I think too much of you to let the johns get away with the idea as you're a bloody ponce. You're a man, and I'll still make a man of you, even though you got lashes for Big Mavis. (*Dashes to the door, which she flings open*) Norgarb! Johnson! Norgarb! Johnson! The Durban killer is here in my room! Norgarb! Johnson! The Durban bank-robbery killer –

Bernard rushes to the door and closes with her, trying to get his hand before her mouth.

At the same moment Norgarb and Johnson return. Scuffle, at the end of which Bernard is handcuffed.

Johnson picks up Bernard's coat from the back of the chair and produces the revolver from the pocket.

JOHNSON: That's all we need. You come along with us. And I must warn you that anything you say may be taken down in writing and used at your trial in evidence against you.

POLLY: You see, he's not a ponce. He's a killer. No matter how many lashes he's got across his backside, he's a killer.

NORGARB: Well, I'm damned. And I took him for a ponce.

JOHNSON: But he was – wasn't he?

POLLY: He ain't a ponce no more, he ain't. He's a man. I got respect for him now, what I wouldn't have for a yellow rat ponce. And I see you got respect for him also. You got respect for a killer. Ain't you? Come on, I'm asking the both of you. You got respect for a killer. Ain't you? Ain't you?

JOHNSON: Let's get going.

BERNARD: Okay, I'm coming. . . There's no need to shove me.

Footsteps off.

NORGARB: Sounds like somebody coming up the stairs. Pretty late for a customer.

POLLY (*dashing for door*): Oh, Alec! Alec! Oh, Alec, you've come back to me. You been away from me all this while. Out of a million men I would know your footsteps. Alec! Alec! Come to me. . .

Curtain.

161

Johannesburg Christmas Eve

EVEN in those days – when Johannesburg wasn't much more than about forty years old – there was already a noticeable decline in the popularity of that particular way of celebrating Christmas Eve. It was the same way that, a week later, Old Year's Night would also be celebrated.

With the years it had grown into a sort of Joburg institution that on two nights of the year boys and girls – young men and women, and some of them not too young – would parade up and down Eloff Street and Pritchard Street with many-coloured paper switches tied on to wooden handles. And they would hit out at each other, left and right, boys and girls, paper plumes shaken in young white faces.

If you were eighteen or nineteen, and you were out on Eloff Street on Christmas Eve with a pal, say, why, it was wonderful to be alive. In those days, that is. For Johannesburg was still busy growing out of a mining camp, like it will to the end of all time still be growing out of a mining camp. And the institution of Johannesburg Christmas Eve, followed a week later by Old Year's Night (celebrated Johannesburg style, also), had about it a naive quality due to the fact that it wasn't copied from anything. The ritual of men and women – *young*, for preference – walking about the streets trying to pick each other up at that time of the year was something that had sprung naturally from the soil of the African Highveld, with the end of December and the beginning of January holding in the calendared arms the hottest days and nights of the year.

Already, however, the newspapers were beginning to question the propriety of Johannesburg's way of doing things. For one thing, the newspapers began to hint, it wasn't a civilised way to carry on. In other words, it wasn't the way people in Europe acted. And it made no difference that people in Europe darned well couldn't act that way at Christmas time – not with snow on the ground, they couldn't. Not with the weathercock pointing east for weeks on end, you couldn't – the weathercock on the church that you can see from the third-storey window of the building at the top of Shaftesbury Avenue where it intersects New Oxford Street. Because the Johannesburg press was one hundred percent English, staffed by Fleet Street journalists who were not only unsuccessful at their trade (otherwise they wouldn't have left Fleet Street) but were homesick on top of it, it was only natural that the Johannesburg press should not view with too kindly an eye any indigenous custom. A Johannesburg Christmas was quite different from the kind of Christmas that Johannesburg newspapermen had been privileged to know 'at home.' And it made no difference to them that, to anybody born in South Africa, their 'home' was a little foreign island in the North Sea, six thousand miles away from a country with its capital in Pretoria and its shores lapped by the waters of the South Atlantic and Indian Oceans.

On their own, the Johannesburg newspapers would probably not have prevailed against popular sentiment. Through all the history of the Witwatersrand, from the time when the first man since the Phoenicians discovered gold on a bleak inland ridge in 1886, the Johannesburg newspapers, owned by the Chamber of Mines, have not exerted much influence on public opinion. What constitutes the Rand's public opinion is, of course, the Rand's army of miners. At least one man in three who opens the Johannesburg morning paper, on his way to work, is a miner. And because the paper that he opens is owned by his boss, the Chamber of Mines, it is only natural that, apart from the sports news, there is nothing *in* that blasted paper that the Johannesburg miner pays much attention to. Not that he isn't gullible. If he is an English-speaking miner, for instance, and the morning paper carries a banner headline attacking the Afrikaans-speaking miner, then he is with that article in the paper, boots and all. And the Chamber of Mines press can always play on his feelings in respect of getting him to join up in a war, and all that sort of thing. But matters like war and peace and politics are only a very unimportant part of life, after all. What his employer's press will never convince the Rand miner about is that he is getting a square deal from his employer. For that is something inherent in the very nature of the master-and-man relationship. No man, unless he's a moron, can be made to believe that his boss has given him an even break – ever. Not even if that boss is an exalted being who created cosmos in a six-day week, working union hours. Inside you you just *know* how your boss is exploiting you and how little he thinks of you *really*.

That is the tragedy of the English press on the Witwatersrand. To the largest single section of its readers it is suspect, except for the racing results and the diatribes against the Boer section of the population. On its own, the Johannesburg press would never have succeeded in getting the institution of a Johannesburg Christmas Eve abolished. But more power-ful influences than the press got to work. It wasn't doing the owners of night clubs any good, having the entire population of Johannesburg parading the streets with coloured plumes and packets of confetti. The dance-halls and night clubs and restaurants run by Cypriots and Levan-tines were empty on Christmas Eve. Nobody bothered to patronise the theatres and cinemas on Christmas Eve. To walk about the streets and find romance by means of a paper tickler that cost you sixpence wasn't a form of relaxation that the vested entertainment interests could be expected to regard with any sort of approval. The leading spirits in Johannesburg's entertainment world could just as well have stayed where they were, in different parts of the Middle East, if Johannes-burg's citizens didn't come and spend their money in night joints.

What the daily press would never have achieved, the Greek club pro-prietors pulled off in a couple of years. And they didn't use the subtleties of propaganda. They didn't follow the line adopted by the newspapers – which was to suggest that it was a *low* thing to parade in the streets, laughing and waving plumes. They knew, the entertainment bosses, that nothing could be anywhere as low as their own cabaret turns. So they took different action. They went straight to the representatives of the people. In a few years enough municipal by-laws were passed to make Johannesburg about as dead on Christmas Eve as on a Sunday night.

All over the world you can talk to a city councillor in a way that he understands. Whether it is in Kandia or in Johannesburg. And it's quite cheap, too.

On that Christmas Eve Johannesburg was only about forty years old.

And Gideon van Blerk and Robert Murray were only about half that age.

And the black-haired owners of bejewelled dives were only begin-ning to get to work on the city councillors. So the fun was still good and the fun was still free. So, if you were as poor as an advertising man trying to sell space the honest way, you could still enjoy yourself that night. If you were as poor as a medical student, with only half a crown in your pocket, you could still have a good time, as long as you were white.

"Gosh, I didn't know there were so many people in Joburg," Gideon van Blerk said to Robert Murray, who worked with him in the same office in Rissik Street. "I wonder where they all come from."

164

"From overseas, likely," Murray said. "At least, the most of them, I should say. I mean, look, my father came from overseas, even though my mother is a – a South African woman."

Before Murray could say any more the two of them got caught up in a laughing crowd of young fellows and girls. There was laughter and shouting and the swish-swish of plumes. Hurried words and an excited squeal and a melee that resolved itself when the confusion was at its thickest. There was an inextricable pattern of plumes and faces, of jackets and trousers and shoes and dresses. It was all in one moment. By the next moment that crowd had sorted itself out into its component elements. All that was left were a dozen young men and women, each separate and each lonely under the electric lights of the city and under the stars. But in the next moment they would mingle again, body and jacket and wide-swung skirt and dark hair and shoe. They came apart and they blended. For all the fuss they made of it, Christmas Eve was actually no different from any other part of the year. . .

All the same, Gideon van Blerk had noticed Robert Murray's hesitation in speaking of his own mother. There was something for you, now, Gideon van Blerk thought, eyeing a number of sailors who, with arms linked, were trying to encircle a group of girls, with their male escorts and all.

"Sailors," Robert Murray called out. "Those girls have got chaps. But what difference does that make to a sailor? Hell, you know I'd rather go to sea than work in a blasted office. But what do you think of that for cheek, man? There's those two sailors running off with them two girls and the rest of them sailors is keeping their chaps away – throwing their arms around them. I wish I was a sailor and I could have so much cheek." Robert Murray laughed loudly.

But again that other thought came into Gideon van Blerk's mind. He thought of the way that Robert Murray had said that his mother was a South African woman – and of the way that he had hesitated when he said it. Well, from the way Robert Murray had said 'South African' it was quite clear what he meant, of course. He meant that his mother was an Afrikaner woman, a Boer woman. He meant that his mother was a white woman, and that she had an Afrikaner surname, that was either Hollands Dutch or Huguenot French – a name like Bonthuys or Van der Merwe or Du Plessis or Malan – and that she had grown up in a household in which the father, mother and children had spoken not English but Afrikaans. And because of the way that Robert Murray had hesitated, Gideon van Blerk was able to guess at his inner thoughts. He knew that, much though Robert respected his mother, he would have been happier if he could have thought of her in another way. If he could have thought of her as English, as he could think of his father as English. (Well, perhaps Robert's father wasn't English, quite, but it was near enough not to matter, really. Because, in spite of his name, Robert Murray's father wasn't exactly Scotch. For one thing, he was born in Liverpool. And you couldn't call a man a Scotsman just because he was born in Liverpool, and his surname was Murray.)

The part of the pavement in Rissik Street in which Gideon van Blerk and Robert Murray at that moment found themselves was again suddenly overrun by a shouting throng. Laughter. Blouses. Striped ties. Coloured socks. Suspender belts holding up silk stockings – nylons would not be invented for another ten years. And that interlude was so exciting that, by the time the plume-swishing crowd had once more departed (splitting up into units of urgent solitariness), Gideon van Blerk had forgotten. That wave of thinking had been broken into by myriads of flashing lights. He had forgotten that what he had felt disturbed about was the fact that he himself was an Afrikaner. That both his father and his mother were white South Africans whose home language was not English but Afrikaans. He had forgotten that, when Robert Murray had spoken with some irresolution about his mother being an Afrikaans-speaking South African woman, it was as though a slur was being cast on him, Gideon van Blerk, also.

But the night was young. As Johannesburg was also young. Only forty, or so. And there would be a lot more people in Johannesburg in twenty years time. Only those people would not be parading the streets at Christmas. They would be in the theatres and cinemas and night clubs. Or they would be sitting at home in stuffy dining rooms, with the windows wide open because of the heat, the end of December being midsummer in Johannesburg. Sitting in hot dining rooms and gasping for air would be the nearest Johannesburg people would get to being like overseas, where people sat at Christmas time in front of fires.

"Did you see the way she smiled?" Robert Murray asked of Gideon van Blerk.

"Yes, nice isn't she?" Gideon van Blerk answered.

"Well, I don't *know*," Robert Murray said. "Shall we run after her?"

"But what about that kid she's got with her?" Gideon van Blerk asked. "That kid whose hand she's holding. What about that kid, I mean?"

Robert Murray looked at his half-section in surprise.

"Only her small sister, I suppose," he said. "But that doesn't make any difference, does it? We don't want to pick her up for *that*, do we? I mean, you can see she's a respectable girl."

"Oh yes, she's respectable enough," Gideon van Blerk assented. "I was only thinking about that kid."

But Robert Murray was the more realistic of the two. He had never had anything to do with a girl. And he knew that Gideon van Blerk hadn't, either. And there was something that told him that the girl with the dark hair, whom they were already starting to follow, was not going to furnish either of them with that sort of experience. At least, she certainly wasn't going to, tonight. So what difference did it make that she had a kid sister along with her, anyway?

The girl with the dark hair knew that those two young men were following her. She knew they would be following her before they knew it themselves, even. For she was eighteen. Afterwards, when they spoke to her, she would tell them that her name was Pauline. She was truthful, that way. Meanwhile, as she turned into President Street, her heart was beating very fast. Her fingers closed tighter on the hand of her kid sister. And she did not know which of those two men, tall, slender, each in his own way good-looking, she fancied. She also did not know whether she should run. Some youths passed her, swishing green and orange plumes into her face. "Why didn't you hit them back, Pauline?" the kid sister, aged about twelve, enquired. Pauline did not answer.

"Let's walk a bit faster," Pauline said next, to her kid sister. "Let's turn into Rissik Street. Let's run."

She felt her knees going weak, suddenly. And there was an urgency in her breathing of which she wasn't aware, right at first. And her fingers, clutching her kid sister's hand, seemed damp, all at once. And she felt that it was her kid sister that she had to depend on now – now, in that wild moment when one of the young men called to her. For Gideon and Robert had caught up with her and her kid sister by then. And after the two young men had spoken, Robert Murray and Gideon van Blerk, each in turn, and she had been able to distinguish between their voices, clearly, Pauline knew which of the two young men it was that had thrilled her, making her run away. When Gideon van Blerk spoke she

167

knew that it was from him and not from his pal, Robert Murray, that she had run away.

And when Gideon van Blerk went on speaking, and said should they go and have tea, her beating pulses told her that she should have run faster. And ever more she felt the need for the protection that she got from the tightly clenched hand of her kid sister, aged twelve, who knew nothing of what was going on on that mad forty-year-old pavement, that had seen many meetings just like that, in the light of the new electric bulbs hung by town council employees beneath the ancient stars.

They went into a café, Pauline and Gideon and Robert and Pauline's kid sister, and they talked a little and they were silent over long intervals. And Pauline poured the tea. And one of the young men said she poured it so good she ought to be a waitress. And Pauline's kid sister said indignantly that Pauline wasn't a waitress, but worked for an insurance company. And you could see from the quick way in which Pauline's kid sister spoke that Pauline might easily have *been* a waitress, but that through some fortunate circumstance she had been spared that kind of job.

And then they went on talking. And then they were silent again. And then they all laughed when they found out that they didn't know each other's names, even. And so they started telling each other their names. And Pauline said that, of course, she knew they wouldn't tell the truth, Gideon and Robert, because she had never known young men to give their real names, when they just picked up girls.

Gideon van Blerk and Robert Murray felt very proud of themselves, then, thinking that they had succeeded in picking up a girl, which was something other young men of their acquaintance prided themselves on being able to do. And it didn't strike them, either, that they hadn't pulled off anything very marvellous, seeing that between the two of them they had succeeded in picking up only one girl. For you couldn't count the kid sister. You couldn't be interested in a girl of twelve when you were twenty. It was only when you were about sixty that you started taking notice of a girl of twelve. And then it was always very scandalous when it got into the newspapers and the police courts. Magistrates – even senior magistrates – seem to have a constitutional inability to understand that elderly gentlemen are the natural prey of twelve-year-old girls who want money for sweets and the cinema and ice-cream.

But because Gideon van Blerk and Robert Murray were only twenty, they looked on Pauline's kid sister as nothing more than a kid sister. And they even thought she was a bit of a nuisance. Nor were they interested to learn her name. Even when she shouted it out, for their information, they displayed little more than polite interest.

When Pauline told them her own name, however, they were both suitably impressed. Gideon van Blerk even went so far as to say that he had a kind of feeling that that was her name. He couldn't explain it, he said, but all along, somehow, something told him that that was her name. He couldn't say *why*, exactly. He supposed it was just that the name, Pauline, suited her. But all the *time*, he said, he had had the funny feeling that her name was either Pauline, or Vera, or something like that.

And after Pauline had been truthful enough to tell the two young men her name, they, in their turn, were equally honest. Except that Gideon was perhaps not quite as straightforward as he might have been. For he pronounced it Giddyun, the English way. Though he was an Afrikaner and a white man, and belonged to the numerically larger section of white South Africans, it was strange how deep-seated was the sense of racial inferiority that Gideon van Blerk had in regard to his fellow citizens, who were white, like he was, but were English-speaking; who were co-heirs with him in the white man's overlordship in the southern part of Africa, but who spoke English while his own language was a form of Dutch.

It was quite late by the time they had left the tea-room and found themselves back in the streets again – Pauline and her two escorts and her kid sister. And in some queer way they felt subdued, now, the girl with the dark hair and the two boys that walked beside her. They had, after all, come out in search of high adventure, and what had happened had been that meeting that had taken them into the tea-room. And if you asked each one of them, singly and apart, if they had wanted any other sort of termination to this evening of high adventure, they would each have said, no, it was just right. They had got all they wanted out of that Christmas Eve. They had wanted no more, just for that night. They had gone out in the streets, searching. And they had got what they had hoped to find.

And yet they weren't laughing about it. They walked now with no gaiety of step. Their paper plumes hung down like plumes of mourning, trailing in the dust as they walked. And yet they had found all that they had come out into the streets to find.

"Could you bring along a girlfriend of yours, next time, for one of us, Pauline?" Gideon van Blerk asked. He did not say for which one.

"Yes, I've got a girlfriend, May," Pauline said. "She hasn't got a steady chap. Yes, I'll bring her."

"When?" Robert Murray asked. "Soon?"

"Well, when you like, of course," Pauline said. "I mean, that's if you want to – if you *want* us to meet again."

Some instinct made her start acting coy, then. In spite of herself, she started getting difficult. And she was being pushed that way. She didn't want to be like that at all. It must have been because the boy from whom she had run away had said she must bring along another girl. And he didn't say which one of the two wanted her. A rough sort of tone came into that boy's voice, sometimes, when he spoke. She knew now that he was the one she had hurried away from. She knew that she would never want to hurry away from the other young man like that, holding her kid sister's hand tight as she fled. And Gideon hadn't said if it was for him or for his pal that he wanted her to bring along with her, next time, her friend, May.

"I don't think it's me you want to see at all," Pauline said. "It's my girlfriend. Otherwise, why were you so quick to ask if she's got a steady chap?"

"But we don't even know her," Robert Murray explained, trying to sound as reasonable as possible. "And it wasn't me that asked. It was Gideon, anyway."

"Yes, that's true," Pauline admitted. "It was Gideon, wasn't it?"

They were standing on the steps of the Town Hall, now, where it was mostly shadows. The crowds were thinning. And some of the voices sounded hoarse. A drunk man staggered past them, calling out "Merry Christmas." He went on a little further. Then he turned round and proceeded slowly to retrace his steps in their direction. But he didn't come all the way. Something distracted his attention. It took him a little while to realise that it was one of the plinths recently erected on that part of the Town Hall steps. He lurched up against the plinth, found that it offered support to his shoulders, and thereafter contented himself with staring at the little group conversing in the shadows.

"Yes, it *was* Gideon that said it, wasn't it?" Pauline repeated.

"But you surely don't want two fellows all to yourself," Gideon answered, trying to make a joke about it, but not succeeding, altogether.

170

"Are you so hard to satisfy, Pauline? Isn't one enough for you? I don't mean what you mean, ha, ha."

"Oh, so that's the kind of remark you pass to me," Pauline said. "Just because you picked me up, you think I'm cheap, I suppose. And so you think that's how you can talk to me, in front of my kid sister and all – And just because I let you speak to me only because it was Christmas Eve and I wanted to be nice – "

"Oh, please stop all this now," Robert Murray interrupted her. "You been nice. I tell you you *been* nice, Pauline. And Gideon didn't mean a thing about what he said as how you need two men. He was only larking."

"He wouldn't talk that way to May, I'm sure," Pauline said. "He's got too much respect for May, of course. He can't wait to say will I bring her along next time. That's all he thinks of. . . May. All he can talk of, too. . . May. That's how all men are, it looks like to me."

Even though Gideon took pains to assure Pauline that he didn't know May, and had never seen May, and if he passed her right in the street he still wouldn't even know that it *was* May, it seemed only to make matters worse. Because Pauline said that that was, of course, just what he wanted. To come across May in the street, right there and then. Pauline also asked why he didn't go to her. Why did he waste his time talking there on the Town Hall steps, when he could *be* with May, seeing that it was Christmas Eve and all.

The drunk man disengaged his shoulders from the embrace of the plinth's stonework. He lurched forward; then took a step to one side; then advanced with an air of fierce resolution. "Merry *Christmas*," he announced to the girl and the two young fellows and the kid sister. He went on past them. He went on quite a distance before he again turned round. The words Pauline was speaking floated across to him on the night air. He pondered Pauline's utterances for a few moments, carefully. Then something seemed to strike him. "Loversh – loversh *quarrel*," the drunk man called out.

They all laughed. Pauline and Gideon and Robert. And the kid sister.

It was getting really late, now.

The pubs had closed. Litter had begun to collect on the pavements. Empty cigarette packets. And orange peels. Plumes lay in the gutter. And the revellers were different from those who paraded the streets earlier in the evening. And they were fewer. There was a certain kind of earnestness, too, in the way they set about having fun. The police were more vigilant, now. There were several free fights.

As often as not, when they intervened in a street brawl, the police – going in couples, now – would arrest the participants. But since even the policemen knew that it was Christmas Eve, they seldom bothered to take their prisoners all the way to the station, but released them in some deserted alley-way, with a good-natured cuff on the ear, as likely as not.

"Two white men fighting in the street," a police sergeant said to a young constable from the backveld, many years his junior. "I dunno what Joburg is coming to." Then he addressed the two prisoners that he and the young constable were escorting handcuffed away from the scene of the brawl: "Aren't you ashamed of yourselves – two young fellows fighting like that in the street? Not that there's much damage done to either of you, as far as I can see."

"He started on me first," one of the revellers declared.

"Maybe I called him a bloody son-of-a —— first," the other prisoner explained. "But he hit first. Yes, he hit first. And look at my eye."

"That's not the point," the sergeant said, sternly. "You got no right to fight. And no matter who started first, neither. Well, I don't want you to get disgraced, seeing how you're young men, and all. And when we get a bit further away from here me and this constable will be letting you go. But don't let it happen again, mind. I got a couple of high-spirited lads of my own, about your age. And I don't want to get you disgraced, see? It's not for *your* sakes I'm doing it, neither, going to let you go, just now. It's for your fathers' and mothers' sakes, understand? But that's my trouble – always too blasted good-hearted."

The two young gladiators thanked the police sergeant profusely.

They came to a dark corner and the constable proceeded to remove the handcuffs.

The sergeant continued with his homily.

"What gets me beat," he said, "is what you want to go and do a thing like this *for* – two young white men hitting each other up in the street. Good Lord, I was brought up in Joburg. And I've had my skylarking along with the best of them. But what we'd do, see, when we was young 'uns, and we wanted a bit of fun, well, we'd go and lather up some coons. We'd go and pick ourselves a couple of kaffirs and we'd chase them for miles. And then we'd slosh the living daylights out of them. And there's no harm done. See what I mean? Now, look what you're

172

doing. A couple of decent young white men, beating each other up in the street."

"But there weren't any kaffirs, sergeant," the prisoner with the black eye declared, gaining confidence to speak up for himself now that he was no longer handcuffed. "We couldn't find a nigger anywhere to chase. We even went to look by the back door of the pass office."

The sergeant looked thoughtful.

"Oh," he said, scratching his chin. "Did you go and try the cemetery? There's always an odd nigger or so hanging about the cemetery."

"Too far," the other young man observed.

"Yeah, that's the trouble with you young men, today," the sergeant said. "No enterprise. That's your trouble. Now, when I was a youngster – "

"But it's different today, sergeant," the young man with the black eye interjected. "You never see a kaffir anywhere near the centre of town when it's Christmas Eve time. The kaffirs nowadays all *know* when it's Christmas time. And so they lie low in the locations. And they won't move *out* of the locations until it's all over. It's not like it was in the old days, when the niggers would still be ignorant, and they would come into town, not knowing it was Christmas. Well, I suppose it was all right, in the times you're talking about, sergeant. But it's all changed since. The niggers know when it's Christmas, now, and so they keep clear of town."

The other young man went on to say that the kaffirs had got so cunning that they even knew when it was Communion, nowadays. "When I used to go to catechism classes," he explained, "just before I got confirmed – well, it didn't happen once but lots of times that a couple of us young fellows would get together, walking home from catechism, and we'd say let's go and stoush some niggers. And we wouldn't see as much as one nigger on the streets all the way home. The niggers had got wise that we were having Bible classes at night because we had to go and get confirmed. And so they didn't move out during catechism time."

The sergeant was impressed. "Well, can you beat that?" he said. "It just shows how spoilt these kaffirs is getting. It's through their getting educated. That's what I always say. A kaffir with school learning is a useless kaffir. So they don't only lie low at Christmas, but at confirmation time, also, hey? Well, I'm damned. Education is going to be the ruin of these kaffirs, yet."

173

The newly released prisoners once more thanked the sergeant and constable, and withdrew into the shadows. In leaving, one of the young men extended his hand diffidently. "My name is Pringle," the young man said.

"And mine is Cripps," the sergeant boomed. "Police Sergeant Cripps. Kind-hearted Cripps, they call me. But that don't mean to say you got to take liberties with me, understand? And don't think you'll get off so easy next time."

"There won't *be* a next time," the young man assured him solemnly.

The sergeant followed their retreating figures with an appraising eye.

"Nice, clean-looking couple of youngsters," he remarked. "Wish I was their age again, and knowing what I know now, that is. That's one thing I envy now about you, Viljoen. That you're still young. Well, anyway, still young enough."

It was the constable's turn to look thoughtful.

"Well, it's this way, sergeant," Constable Viljoen said, "you know, *I've* been *thinking* about things, lately – "

"Then you mustn't," the sergeant broke in, with a good-humoured laugh. "Come on, let's get back into town. Maybe there's some more disturbances of the peace going on in Eloff Street. But if you take my tip, you won't do any thinking. Not while you're in uniform, that is. And after a while you'll find that you'll always be in uniform. Even when you're off duty and you're in the swimming baths, even – when you're doing the breast stroke in a one-piece striped bathing costume, you'll still have a helmet on. And if you know what's good for you you won't think. I've seen more than one young chap go wrong in the force from trying to think. Even when he seemed to have the makings of a policeman in him, he's smashed himself up from getting ideas. You can take it from me that any idea is a wrong idea."

They walked on for some little while in silence.

"I'm not arguing with you," Constable Viljoen said at length, "but it's this way, sergeant. You know, of course, that I come from the farm. I was brought up on a farm and I went to school on a farm. I don't know much about a town."

"But most of the recruits we get today comes from the farm," Sergeant Cripps replied, trying (not altogether successfully) to keep a note of condescension from creeping into his voice. "And I say you recruits from the backveld are an asset. That's what I say. You got the right stuff in you. One day you Dutch-speaking chaps from the farms will be in the high positions in the force, and the likes of me will have to call you sir. Not that I think it will happen in my time, mind. And not that I don't think there's a lot to be said for overseas experience, like what all us Britishers in the force has got. But I've noticed that a lot of you Dutch-speaking young fellows from the farms have got your heads screwed on right."

There was another silence, a somewhat more uncomfortable one, this time. Immediately Sergeant Cripps understood the reason for it. It was because he had spoken of Viljoen as a Dutchman. Sergeant Cripps knew that a Boer resented that name. It had come to be invested with a suggestion of contumely, the word Dutchman. The Dutch-speaking South African didn't want to be termed a Dutchman, Sergeant Cripps remembered. And even though he spoke Dutch – or something so near to Dutch that you just about couldn't tell the difference – he didn't want his language to be *called* Dutch. There was a thing for you, now Sergeant Cripps thought. He had gone and insulted this young Viljoen and he hadn't meant to. And he hadn't *meant* to, what with its being Christmas Eve and all.

"See here," he said suddenly, "you mustn't get funny ideas in your head just because I said you're a Dutchman. I know you call yourself an Afrikander, now, don't you? That's right, an Afrikander, hey?"

"Afrikaner," Constable Viljoen corrected him.

"But what's the odds?" Sergeant Cripps continued. "I mean, what *is* the bloody difference? I am married to one of your Afrikander women myself. And a finer wife than what she's been to me I'd like to meet anywhere. But it's only that we Britishers always think of you as Dutchmen, and we talk of you as Dutchmen. I mean, bugger it, it's too blasted *hard* to have to think all the time that you call yourselves Afrikanders. And what's wrong in being called a Dutchman, anyway? I mean, look at you. You're matriculated and all, aren't you? I mean, you've got *education*. And you're white."

And in the way he said it, it seemed as though the fact of Constable Viljoen having passed the matriculation examination was an affront to himself, Sergeant Cripps, personally.

"Yes, I've thought of it, too," Viljoen acknowledged. "I've also wondered why I get so upset when somebody calls me a Dutchman. Like I wouldn't be upset if he called me a Frenchman, say. Or a German, maybe. Or an Englishman, even. It's being called a Dutchman that makes an Afrikaner all hot under the collar. I've thought that maybe it's because for so many years – *hundreds* of years, even – Englishmen have called Afrikaners Dutchmen in that superior way that an Englishman has got of talking to somebody belonging to a different nation, even though the Englishman doesn't mean anything *by* it, when he talks that way – and I've thought that – "

"Just what I've been telling you, Viljoen, old boy. You mustn't think. It's not healthy in the force, to think."

They rounded the corner of the Town Hall, coming up the steps from the direction of the Market Street tramlines. And that was how they came across that drunk man. That same drunk man, yes, who had extended seasonal compliments to Pauline and Gideon and Robert Murray and Pauline's kid sister. The drunk man had again lurched over to the plinth. The plinth had been started as a memorial to the first Mayor of Johannesburg, but a couple of months before a dispute had arisen in the council chamber as to whether it should be a memorial to the very first Mayor of Johannesburg, who had been appointed by President Kruger's government in Republican times, or whether it should commemorate the first Mayor since British occupation. Actually, of course, the British majority in the city council had not imagined that there could ever have been a Mayor in Johannesburg in Republican times, and when it looked as though that memorial was after all going to be erected to a Boer official under Paul Kruger, work on the memorial was immediately suspended. Ten years were to pass before the City Engineering Department did anything more about the plinth. Then they put an electric light on top of it, so that courting couples couldn't hold hands in the shadows.

"That man looks tight enough for us to pinch, sergeant," Constable Viljoen said.

"We won't, though," Sergeant Cripps announced, authoritatively. "You don't know who he is, of course, do you? Well, let me tell you, he was once Deputy-mayor of this city. What do you think of that? Hardly believe it, hey? Well, that's what he was. Deputy-mayor. Only he took to drink. Funny place he's picked for getting soused. Seeing they're going to erect a statoo to a Mayor there. Funny if it turned out it was a statoo for *him*."

The sergeant laughed. He had come to Johannesburg as a child – which didn't, of course, prevent him from still regarding himself as a Britisher. And he had developed an affection for Johannesburg. Many people did.

"There's a place for you, now," Sergeant Cripps added. "I bet you won't find the likes anywhere. Deputy-mayor one day – next day. . . Well, not next *day* exactly, it took a bit longer than that. . . a hobo. Yes, sir, a down-and-out bum. He's been picked up, too, more than once, by some rookie that's new to the town, but of course we never charge him. We just give the rookie a choking off – tell him that his prisoner was once Joburg's second citizen – and we scratch around for some black coffee for the ex-Deputy-mayor. Yes, he would have been Mayor, next year. Only he took to drink."

Constable Viljoen looked thoughtfully at the figure hunched up against the plinth. Constable Viljoen was attending a course of lectures on Psychology at the Tech; he had heard that a knowledge of this subject would stand him in good stead in his profession.

"But I wonder what made him take to drink," Constable Viljoen said after a pause. "There must have been some reason for it. What they call in psychology a frustration. I mean, if it was his ambition to be Mayor – as it must have been, otherwise he wouldn't have got as far as Deputy-mayor, would he, now? – then why did he take to drink when he was so near the top? There must have been a deep-seated psychological reason – "

Sergeant Cripps shut his left eye ponderously.

"The deep-seated reason," Sergeant Cripps said, "was that he was too fond of lifting his elbow. Don't you take too much notice of that tripe they teach you at night school, young fellow. It gives you wrong ideas – sets you off thinking. And that ain't healthy."

But Constable Viljoen didn't take that good advice. He was already too far gone, maybe.

"What will your mother think of you coming home so late?" Robert Murray asked of Pauline. He asked that question after they had got off a tram and had walked along an asphalt road between two minedumps. They were now drawing abreast of a row of houses of a type – not unprepossessing after its fashion – that was at that time being erected by the Chamber of Mines to accommodate the better class of mining official. A bluegum plantation partially screened the houses from the minedumps.

Pauline and her two male escorts and her kid sister had come to a stop in front of the larger of the houses in the row.

"I'll just say that I picked up two chaps in the street and that they came with me as far as the house, and then went off," Pauline said. "That will be all right, won't it?"

Robert Murray didn't understand that she was joking.

"But won't your people perhaps think it's funny?" he asked. "I mean, it must be a good bit past eleven."

It was only when Pauline and her kid sister and Gideon van Blerk laughed that Robert Murray felt that he was being slow-witted, again. That was his trouble, he knew. He always said to himself that he could laugh as good as any. And as quick, too. There was that time the woman selling oranges in front of his school in Op de Bergen Street had her basket upset. And he started laughing about it before anybody. And he was still laughing about it when the schoolmaster was caning him. Or, at least, up to the moment when the schoolmaster told him to bend over, and he heard the swish of the long rattan cane through the air. Well, there was an example, now, of his having a sense of humour. Not that he had had anything to do with upsetting the woman's oranges, of course. He would never have thought of doing that. When he came on the scene the oranges were already rolling over the gutter, and kaffirs were coming past and picking them up and running off with them. The boys who actually threw the basket over were never caught, of course. So he got caned for standing there, laughing. Needless to say, that was the funniest part of it. And he would have explained all that to the headmaster before he caned him. Only, he couldn't. He was laughing too much.

So now, when Pauline and Gideon, and even Pauline's kid sister were standing there, laughing in the lights of the house and the shadows of the bluegums, Robert Murray knew, very well, that it wasn't that he hadn't got as keen a sense of humour as any of them. It was only that they didn't laugh at the same things, it would seem. But the same sort of situation had repeated itself so often that he began to accept it that he was perhaps slow-witted. Seeing that it had been said to him on such numbers of occasions. And so he had come to believe that maybe he *was* slow-witted. But he wouldn't accept it that he didn't have a sense of humour. There were the six cuts he had got across his backside from the schoolmaster at the school in Op de Bergen Street that *proved* he had a sense of humour.

All right, let them laugh, Robert Murray said to himself, then. All right, he was slow-witted. . . He could take that. But when it came to a sense of humour. He only wished he had known them – Pauline and

178

Gideon and Pauline's kid sister – when he was still at the Op de Bergen school. He could have shown them, next day, if he had a sense of humour, or not. The day after the woman's basket of oranges was upset. He could have shown them just by taking down his pants, and they could have *seen* that he had a sense of humour. Those six cuts looked a real treat, then.

Pauline had stopped laughing, suddenly.

Robert Murray knew what was coming. He also knew he hadn't the power to stop what was coming. He would have to endure it all. He would have to listen to everything Pauline had to say, and act as though it was something quite new to him. And it hurt more than the six cuts.

"You know," Robert Murray heard her saying, "you know, I don't think you've got a sense of humour. And you *really* imagine my walking into the house, with my little sister alongside of me, and me saying to my mother, 'Well, why I'm so late is because I picked up two chaps'? I mean, can you *imagine* that, Robert?"

Robert Murray felt so miserable, then, that he said to himself that he *could* imagine it. He could imagine it easily, he said to himself, that Pauline was just a slut. It was just because she said he hadn't a sense of humour that he felt that way about her. After all, many a man has felt a woman is a trollop for saying less than that about him.

It turned out, however, that Pauline would not have to tell the truth. Nor that she would have to tell much of a lie, either. It appeared that she and her kid sister had been taken into town by their Uncle George. And their Uncle George had parked his car near the railway station. And it was at a pub near the railway station that their Uncle George had met a buddy that he had last seen in France during the 1914–18 War. So after Pauline and her kid sister had waited – for periods that got longer, each time – outside pubs for their Uncle George and his 1914–18 buddy, they decided to go home. They meant to take the bus home, and not the tram. And it was on their way to the bus stop that they had met Gideon and Robert.

Consequently, it was as simple as anything. Pauline and her kid sister could say that they had to come home, because of the way that Uncle George had carried on. They should never have gone out with him in the first place, they would say. (Which was true enough.) And there would be no need for them to mention that anybody had brought them home. It looked as though the only person likely to catch it in the neck would be Uncle George. And, as likely as not, he in turn would put all the blame on to his 1914–18 buddy. In one way and another, a lot of odium gets fastened on to wars.

And that was how they parted – the four that had picked each other up. And for quite a long while afterwards Pauline's kid sister clung to the illusion that the pick-up would never have taken place if *she* hadn't been there. Years afterwards, when she was meeting boys on her own, Pauline's kid sister still imagined that it was because *she* was there that those two young men made such a dead set at Pauline.

They also arranged that they would meet again, next day at three in the afternoon, and that Pauline would bring her girlfriend, May, along, so as to make it company.

It was the moment of parting. Both young men sprang forward to open the front gate. And they sprang forward, also, the next moment – not because they wanted to, so much, as that they regarded it as some sort of a ritual – to kiss Pauline. Pauline, wiser than they, knew what was coming. Before it had entered their minds, maybe, she had got hold of that thought.

In her reaction Pauline proved that she had not been caught off her guard. She evaded Gideon van Blerk skilfully – so skilfully that all he remembered were her half-parted lips, that he had missed kissing, and her dark hair trailing behind her past the gate and into the night. She could have evaded Robert Murray as easily. But she didn't. She allowed Robert Murray to catch her in his arms and to push his mouth against hers. The next moment she had slipped out of his embrace and was darting up the garden path.

Robert Murray had kissed her awkwardly, betraying his lack of experience. But his effort was none the worse, for all that.

"Remember, Zoo Lake – three o'clock," Gideon van Blerk called out.

For a moment he wondered if he hadn't called too loudly. He wondered if her parents hadn't heard, perhaps. And then he realised that he hadn't shouted loudly enough. He hadn't shouted so that the whole world could hear. And that, after all, was what he wanted. He wanted the whole world to know.

But did he? Somehow, he wasn't quite sure. No, he wasn't sure. And something inside himself told him, right then, that Pauline sensed that he wasn't sure. That was why she allowed Robert Murray to kiss her, Gideon said to himself. Why she wouldn't let him, Gideon, kiss her. It was the moment of their parting, and Gideon van Blerk's senses were more than ordinarily acute, then. For a little while he saw certain truths, sharply defined. Afterwards he would doubt their validity, however.

Anyway, he would shout, now, so that the whole world *could* know how he felt about Pauline.

But it was too late.

She had arrived at the front door. It was quite a long path, up the garden. There was a sudden splash of light as the front door opened. The next instant the splash of light, that had revealed, confusedly, a hat rack in a passage and a red chandelier and a girl with dark hair speeding forward slenderly like an arrow, had vanished. Gideon van Blerk and Robert Murray were left alone at a garden gate, in the shadows of the bluegum plantation. And they moved off. They moved off after the anticlimax of the front door opening again in a second splash of light, this time to admit Pauline's kid sister.

It was a pity that Pauline's kid sister did not have more respect for the intrinsics of high romance. Otherwise, the least she could have done would have been to have gone in at the back door.

Round about that time a dark figure crept, if not out of a back door then out of a back yard. The dark figure had gone courting. The dark figure. an African from a kraal in the Waterberg, had not been in Johannesburg very long. His name was Mletshwa Kusane. That was his name in the kraal in the Waterberg. In Johannesburg he was known as Jim Fish. That name stood on his pass, too. With Mletshwa Kusane, alias Jim Fish. walking into the street through a backyard gate at Christmas Eve, the first black man enters this story. And since it's the season of goodwill, Jim Fish comes into the story skulking a little.

In those days a black man didn't mind what sort of 'working name' he adopted. He was not coming to Johannesburg to stay, anyway. At least, that was what he hoped. And while he stayed in the city, saving up money as fast as he could to take back to the farm with him, he didn't particularly care what name his employer chose to bestow on him, provided that his employer handed over his wages with due regularity on pay day.

Jim Fish had found work in a baker's shop in a part of the town known as the Mai-Mai. He lived in a shack behind the bakery, the proprietor of which in this way received back as rent a not inconsiderable part of his employees' emoluments. Since his employees were also his tenants, the owner of the bakehouse did not have to employ a rent-collector.

Afterwards, when Johannesburg took on more of the external characteristics of a city, the owner of the bakery was to find that this arrangement did not pay him quite so well, anymore. For the City Council
began introducing all sorts of finicky by-laws relating to hygiene. In no
time they brought in a regulation making it illegal for the owner of a
bakery to accommodate his native services on the bakery premises.
The result was that, at a time when business wasn't too good, the owner
of the bakery found himself with a municipal health inspector on his
pay-roll. Afterwards it was two health inspectors. And they came round
every month for their rake-off like clockwork. Because of this increase
in his overheads the bakery proprietor had been reluctantly compelled
to cancel an advertisement that he had been running in a religious
magazine for a long time. It was purely a goodwill advertisement, bread
being a staple commodity that didn't require advertising. But on the
following Sunday the baker – who was also a sidesman – had to listen
to a sermon on the evils of avarice. He knew the parson meant him, of
course. Because he had cancelled the ad that for years had been the
church magazine's mainstay. But there were moments, in the course of
the sermon, when the baker could not, in his sinful mind, help associ-
ating words like 'cupidity', 'selfishness' and 'money-grubbing' with
those two municipal health inspectors.

Jim Fish's main work at the bakery consisted of helping his black
colleagues – there were quite a number of them – to carry in the sacks
of meal and to clean the mixers of yesterday's dough. (The mixers *were*
cleaned, quite often, in spite of what quite a lot of bread-consuming
citizens might have thought, going by the taste.) He had also to carry the
pans to the oven, and to help stoke the fires, and to help pull out the
baked loaves with long wooden scoops. Because Jim Fish was black,
that was about as far as his duties went. The white men on the night
shift were there in a supervisory capacity.

There had been one or two nights, however, when Jim Fish and his
black-skinned colleagues had, through the machinery breaking down,
to perform certain additional duties that brought them into somewhat
more intimate contact with the ancient rites of bread-making. On those
occasions that particular bakery's proud boast that its products were,
from start to finish, untouched by human hand, was only literally correct, in the sense that it excluded human feet. Strict adherents of the
school of thought that places the coloured races outside of the pale of

humanity as such would in this situation find themselves in something of a dilemma. For it would not be human hands *or* feet, but just the feet of the niggers that kneaded the dough, in long wooden troughs, at those times when the electric power at the bakery failed.

The white supervisors would be in a state of nerves, all right, on the night when there was mechanical trouble. They would be all strung up – hysterical and panicky, almost, like ballet-dancers.

"Hey, you, go and wash that coal off your feet before you get into that trough," the night foreman would shout at a nigger. And at another nigger the foreman would shout, "Hey, you black sausage – don't you bloody well sweat so much, right into the kneading trough and all."

For it is characteristic of any person whose ancestors have lived in Africa for any length of time that he *does* sweat a lot. Whether he's a nigger, or a white Dutch-speaking Afrikaner, or a white English-speaking Jingo from Natal, if his forebears have resided in Africa for a couple of generations he sweats at the least provocation. Readers of Herodotus will recall that that great historian and geographer said the same thing about the Nubians of his time.

Because he was a simple soul, Jim Fish was, taken all in all, happy in his work. If he were asked by an American newspaper correspondent or by an earnest enquirer delegated to the task by a UNO committee (UNO being in those days as much of an anachronism as nylons), Jim Fish would probably have confessed that he was deserving of one shilling and sixpence extra on a night when the bread-making machinery did not function as it should. The one shilling and sixpence would be to cover all that extra work he had in treading, Jim Fish would explain, marking time, left right, left right, to explain. And also to recompense him for all that trouble he took in cleaning himself, washing his legs and feet and toes in hot water. No, not when he got *into* the kneading trough. He never worried much about *that*, Jim Fish would declare, truthfully. It was when he had to get the sticky white dough off him afterwards. There was a job for you, now.

The real trouble about his job at the bakery, Jim Fish, alias Mletshwa Kusane, would confide to the correspondent of an American newspaper was the fact that it was nearly all night work. He didn't mind the pay so much. That was all right. Even after he had paid his rent and he had bought mealie-meal and goat's meat and such odds and ends of clothing as he needed, he was still able to save quite a bit, each month. This was a lot more than most white wage or salary earners were able to do, incidentally. All that happened to white people who worked for a boss was that they got deeper into debt, every month. Jim Fish would admit that he was saving, here in the city of Johannesburg. But he needed every penny that he could scrape together. All the money he saved in Johannesburg had to go in lobola, when he got back to the kraal. Lobola was the money he had to pay some girl's father, so that he could get that girl as his wife. It wasn't any particular girl that Jim Fish was thinking about, of course. Practically any girl belonging to his tribe would do. As long as she could bear him children, and work for him, planting mealies and hoeing in the bean-fields, and bringing him a clay pot full of beer when he called – him lying in the sun in front of the hut, and following the sun around. And maybe afterwards, if he came to Johannesburg again, and worked for the bakery for another season, he would even be able to buy a second wife, having enough money for another lobola. And then his children would be able to work for him, too, the children of his first and second wife – and the children of his third wife, too, if he went to Johannesburg that often to make money to save up for a lobola. And who he would also have to work for him would be quite incidental children, that weren't his own, even, but that one or other of his wives begot by some other nigger man while he himself was in Johannesburg, working in the bakery.

That was a laugh on that other nigger man, all right.

It wouldn't be too pleasant for that other nigger man, carrying on with Mletshwa's wives, and all that, in Mletshwa's absence, when what would happen out of it would be that that nigger man's children, by Mletshwa's wife, would end up by working for Mletshwa: tending his cattle for him, if they were boys; planting beans and kaffir-corn for him, if they were girls.

And if it turned out that the child that Mletshwa's wife conceived while Mletshwa was working in Johannesburg wasn't the child of another nigger man at all, but was the child of the white missionary at the Leboma mission station, then it would be a laugh on the white missionary, right enough. For that child would be lighter of skin than its brothers and sisters. Instead of its having a complexion like boot-polish, the missionary's child by Mletshwa's wife would be dark lemon in colour, with its hair less peperkorrel than the average negro's, and in the cast of its features there would be a couple of European traits. Consequently, that child would receive special privileges at the mission school and would be educated to be a school-teacher, or maybe even

184

higher than a school-teacher, so that Mletshwa would be good for at least a pound a month from that child, whose education had cost him nothing. No wonder, therefore, that many a missionary walks about with an embittered look.

Late one night Mletshwa Kusane, alias Jim Fish, came away from the bakery with a deep sense of inner satisfaction. He felt he was somebody, and no mistake. For the mixing machine had broken down again. And this time he had been set to tread the dough in a confectionery trough. Not the dough for the plebeian quartern loaves and twist loaves and standard brown loaves. But he had walked up and down, left right, left right, in a trough that had chilled eggs, even, mixed with the flour and water and yeast. Left, right, left right, he was kneading, with his feet – brown on top and pinkish between the toes – the dough for slab cake and cream cakes and (with a few sultanas thrown in) for wedding cakes. The night foreman had noticed that, last time there was trouble with the mechanised equipment, Jim Fish had seemed to sweat somewhat less than the other niggers. And that was how Mletshwa got promoted to the confectionery trough. What the night foreman didn't notice was the effect that this unexpected promotion had on Mletshwa. Because he had been picked out for the unique honour of treading the dough in the confectionery container, Mletshwa suddenly started thinking that he was a king. A great king, he thought he was. And he started chanting in the Sechuana tongue a song that he had made up about himself, in the same way that any primitive African makes up a song about himself when he finds that, by chance, he is standing first in a line of pick-and-shovel labourers digging a ditch, or if it's a gang of railway labourers moving a piece of track, and he happens to be walking in front.

And so that night, having been selected to tread the dough in the confectionery trough because he sweated less than other niggers, Mletshwa really let himself go. He felt no end proud of himself.

"Who is he, who is he, who is he?" Mletshwa chanted, going left right, left right, in double quick time,

Who is he chosen by the Great White Man
To walk fast in the fine meal with the broken eggs in it?
Who is he but Mletshwa? –
Who is he but Mletshwa Kusane whose kraal is by the Molopo?

185

Who is he, the Mighty Trampling Elephant, elephant among ele-
    phants,
He with his feet washed clean with carbolic soap?
Who is the Mighty Elephant with his feet washed clean
With the thick white bubbles coming out of
The red carbolic soap – the White Man's red carbolic soap?
Who is he but Mletshwa Kusane whose kraal is by the Molopo?

Who is he that treads heavier than the rhinoceros –
The rhinoceros with his feet washed in the water from the White
    Man's faucet?
Who is he that treads with his feet washed cleaner than the White
    Man's feet?
Treading out white flour and yellow, stinking eggs and yeast
That is the beautiful food of the White Man?
Who is he but Mletshwa –
Who is he but Mletshwa Kusane whose kraal is by the Molopo?

Inspired to unwonted exertions by his singing, Mletshwa was making a first-class job of treading that dough. When the night foreman
looked again, Mletshwa was leaping up and down in the tub. One hand
was raised up to the level of his shoulder, balancing an imaginary
assegai. His other arm supported an equally imaginary raw-hide shield.
What were not fictitious were the pieces of dough clinging to his working pants and shirt and even to one side of his neck. The night foreman
was not a little surprised to see a nigger performing a Zulu war-dance
in a kneading trough at that time of the night. Especially when those
white splashes of dough could have passed as war-paint.

"None of that, Jim Fish," the night foreman called out – impressed,
in spite of himself. "Get on with your work."

One of the other natives guffawed. But it *was* his work, this native
thought. In prancing up and down like that, in the dough, Mletshwa
was only doing his *work*. And here was the boss angry with Mletshwa
about it. Surely, the ways of the white man were strange.

It was only a little later that the night foreman noticed what other
effect the violent exercise had had on Jim Fish: he was sweating like a
dozen niggers; the sweat was pouring off Mletshwa as though from a
shower bath. Which was something that Mletshwa had never had in his
life – a shower bath or any other kind of a bath.

This time the night foreman swore.

"Get out of that tub, you black son of a bitch," he shouted. "That's for cake for white people to eat, you bloody ——. Look at all the sweat running off your —— backside into white people's cake."

Mletshwa's was a temperament that was easily cowed. In a moment the sound of the night foreman's voice had changed him from a bloodthirsty warrior to a timid bushveld thing trying to escape from a trampling rhinoceros among rhinoceroses. In a split second he was out of the tub and halfway across the bakery floor towards his khaya in the back yard.

He had to return to the tub, however. The night foreman saw to that. The night foreman also saw to it that Mletshwa scraped all the dough off his feet and other parts of his person, and stuck it back where it belonged.

"Trying to bugger off with half the confectionery dough sticking to him," the night foreman said to the mechanic who was working at the motor, working to get it started again. Then the night foreman addressed Mletshwa once more.

"Cha-cha," he shouted. "Inindaba wena want to steal lo wet meal, huh? Come on, put it all back. That lump between your toes, too. It's cake for white people to eat. You meningi skelm, you."

Gideon van Blerk and Robert Murray walked back along the road that led between the minedumps.

They neither of them mentioned Pauline. But they spoke about their future. Maybe this topic was not totally unrelated to their meeting with Pauline. Perhaps, also, the fact that the new year was only a week off made them pause to take stock.

"I think I'll go on the mines," Robert Murray said. "In five years where can't you get on the mines? Pen-pushing in an office can't get you nowhere. What you say we both try the mines? Your father's got a good job on the mines. He'll be able to get you fixed up. I mean he may be able to get us both fixed up, that's what."

Gideon van Blerk shook his head.

"I'd like to work on a newspaper," he said. "But there's no chance for a South African. I know, I've been round to ask. But it's no good. They bring them all out from England. You can't show me a newspaperman here in Joburg that's a South African. I don't think it's fair. I think maybe I'll go back to university for another year. Perhaps they'll take me on, then. But I'll talk to my father about getting you fixed up on the mines."

Something made Gideon van Blerk take a swift look at Robert Murray in the darkness. Something made him wonder whether Robert Murray would get far in the world. There was a certain stolid quality about Robert Murray that you couldn't miss. And Gideon van Blerk had heard of that sort of person getting on.

But all Gideon van Blerk could see in the shadows was a young man of about his own height and build, a young man with good features that were somewhat on the heavy side. And then Gideon remembered that Robert Murray had kissed Pauline. And Robert Murray had kissed Pauline because she had let him, Gideon van Blerk said to himself. It seemed that everything in life was like that. Robert Murray got away with kissing Pauline because he was half English. Young men from Fleet Street got jobs on the Johannesburg newspapers because they were wholly English.

Afterwards, when he parted from Robert Murray, Gideon said to himself that he hadn't really wanted to kiss Pauline. He thought she was nice, and all that, but it wasn't actually a deep sort of feeling that he had for her. And then it also struck him that his keenness to work on a newspaper did not partake, either, of the quality of a passion. Walking home alone he started wondering if it didn't mean that you had to want a thing very desperately before you could get it.

And then he started thinking of Pauline. What would happen if he never saw her again? Supposing she didn't keep the appointment at the Zoo Lake for the following afternoon?

His mind was not able to dwell on that possibility, however. Somehow, he felt that she would be there.

Mletshwa came slinking out of the room in the back yard where Annie Bogodi stayed. He had known her for several months. He had met her on the night when he had danced a war-dance in the confectionery dough and had made up a princely song about himself. It was because he had felt so exuberant, that night, even after the foreman had sworn at him, that he had been able to speak to Annie Bogodi in the street and even to walk home with her to her khaya in that back yard. That was three months ago. Since then he had seen her several times, on those nights when he was free. Tonight, Christmas Eve, was another such night when he didn't have to work in the bakery. He sidled out of the back yard and then proceeded up the pavement in a markedly diffident manner. He knew that this was the season in which white people rejoiced much. So he did not wish to take too many chances. As far as possible, on his way back to his room in the Mai-Mai he confined himself to the dark sanitary lanes that ran at the back of the houses in those days when some of the best suburbs were still waiting to be linked up with the sewerage system.

All the way from Jeppe, past End Street through the City and Suburban, Mletshwa's luck held. It was when he got to near Delvers Street that he realised that he was being trailed. Several white youths were lengthening their stride behind him. Mletshwa broke into a trot. A quick look over his shoulder informed him that the white youths had started running also. Mletshwa made straight for a galvanised iron fence. In those days you could find a galvanised iron fence almost in the middle of Eloff Street – certainly at the lower end of Eloff Street – dozens of them. Mletshwa was over that fence in the twinkling of an eye, sustaining no more injury than having skin ripped off the palms of his hands and a triangular rent in his trousers. He was still running when he heard the white youths blundering into the galvanised iron fence. They helped each other over. By the sound of it, Mletshwa judged his pursuers to consist of half the white youths in the neighbourhood. Actually, however, there were only three of them. In after years, when relating the affair to his dark-skinned cronies over a dagga smoke, Mletshwa indulged in a good deal of unpardonable exaggeration on this and other scores.

Mletshwa was busy climbing over the next fence – having in the interim gained quite considerably on the white youths, who had been delayed by the first fence – when a spaniel with long ears made a leap at him. The spaniel, usually of a playful disposition, smelt sweating kaffir. That changed the spaniel's whole nature. Before he could find a big enough stone to stave in the spaniel's ribs on one side, Mletshwa had parted with some more of his trousers and a piece of flesh out of the back of one calf. But because he was busy running, the Christmas Eve fugitive did not at the time notice the loss of part of his trousers and a piece of his anatomy. If anything, the encounter with the dog did him good, helping him to put on speed.

A large number of things happened, then, all at once, as it seemed. A white man came out blowing a police whistle. Somebody was shouting something about a kaffir bastard killing a white man's black dog with a stone you'd never seen the size of. And he'd murder them all in their beds next. Three youths, with determined white faces, were assisting each other over another galvanised iron fence. They were breathing heavily with the exertion of running and the lust of the chase. Their blood was up. A tram conductor sleeping with the wife of a miner who was on night shift thought that all the noise meant that the miner had come back. So he grabbed his trousers and jumped out of the window. Because of the lateness of the hour there were not many citizens privileged to see a bare-footed man clad only in a shirt sprinting down a street, over his arms a pair of uniform trousers of the tramways department. He covered the best part of a quarter of a mile before he stopped to put them on.

A young fellow, with a girl on his arm, flicked the man blowing the whistle in the face with a paper plume, calling out "Merry Christmas." And the girl on the young fellow's arm flung several handfuls of confetti over the helmet and shoulders of the policeman who came dashing round the corner just after Mletshwa had successfully negotiated yet another fence. In a few moments several dozen people, including children, arrived on the scene in various stages of undress (Johannesburg having at that date not yet reached the dressing-gown stage of civilisation).

Meanwhile, the three white youths' chase of Mletshwa continued. Somewhere near Von Wielligh Street he doubled back on his pursuers. This was legitimate strategy. His hunters appreciated it. Between Mletshwa and the young white men who were out for his blood there became established a bond that partook of the character of a distorted kinship. What went on in the side streets of Johannesburg on that Christmas Eve was team work. Mletshwa Kusane, alias Jim Fish, was as much of, and as important a member of, the hunt as were the three white youths baying at his heels. He was a member of their fraternity when he was scaling a galvanised iron fence, to the detriment of flesh and skin and flannels. He was a lot nearer to his hunters than a nigger that was not being chased. He was a lot nearer to those three white youths than any white man who didn't chase niggers.

But enough of philosophy.

When those three white youths eventually caught up with Mletshwa they made a meal of him, all right. Maybe, if he hadn't given them so much of a chase they wouldn't have given him such a doing. On the other hand, if they had caught up with him earlier, it is possible that they would have had more energy, and that in consequence they would not have – at least, *one* of them would not have – been reduced to the extremity of having to stamp a tired heel over and over again into Mletshwa's left eye when they caught him in a sanitary lane that was within fifty yards of his own khaya.

That was the irony of that particular hunt, of course. In the way that every hunt has its irony. Mletshwa had successfully outpaced and out-distanced and eluded his three grim pursuers through the whole of Jeppestown and the City and Suburban and afterwards the Wolhuter area, only to be overtaken when he was within fifty yards of his own room in the Mai-Mai. Tracked to his lair, in other words.

Actually, he was slowed down so much by the time his hunters caught up with him, that what seemed to Mletshwa like running was nothing more than an ordinary walking pace. And as, for the last time, he stumbled up to a galvanised iron fence, with the intention of scrambling over it, he was so slow that the foremost of his pursuers was able to trip him up before he had got even one foot off the ground.

There was grunting. And there were thuds. And there were no words spoken. And the three white youths walked away, afterwards, each having in turn satiated his bloodlust. And Mletshwa had blood on his face. And one of the white youths had blood on his shoes that he wiped later on a piece of blue and orange streamer that he found in the gutter.

It took Mletshwa a long time to drag himself for that remaining fifty yards that led to his khaya behind the bakery. And he lay on the floor of his khaya for two days with a tattered blanket over him. And on the third day the foreman himself came and had a look at Mletshwa and then phoned the hospital for the ambulance.

But when he was dragging himself back to his khaya that night, after he had got his doing, Mletshwa came across a white man in an even more helpless condition than his own. The white man was lying stretched out at full length on a pavement in the Mai-Mai. The white man was dead drunk. That much was clear to Mletshwa. What Mletshwa didn't know was that the white man had once been an important public figure – had been Deputy-mayor of Johannesburg in his day.

All Mletshwa saw was that the white man was lying there dead drunk, and that the white man would not be able to get up and hit him. Some dog instinct from his kaffir huts by the Molopo where he was brought up told Mletshwa, alias Jim Fish, what to do. He stood over the white man, half bending forward over him, with the pain of trying to keep on his feet. Then he staggered on the rest of the way to his khaya. But the ex-Deputy-mayor was so drunk, lying on the pavement, that he hardly stirred. With his hair and face and clothes soaked in a nigger's urine, the ex-Deputy-mayor went on lying there on the Mai-Mai pavement until it was morning.

Christmas morning.

191

Notes on the Text

I N all cases the sources are either original typescripts held by the Harry Ransom Humanities Research Center at the University of Texas at Austin or versions first published in newspapers or periodicals, mostly held in safekeeping by the Greater Johannesburg Public Library. The previously unpublished "Romance: A Sequence" was fashioned from a set of undated (but clearly contemporaneous and related) typescripts that have been arranged in a sequence. The characters' names in "First Served" were adjusted to fit the rest of the sequence; otherwise the sketches appear here unaltered.

Because attributions to Herman Charles Bosman had to be made in many cases, the pseudonyms under which the various pieces were published have been provided in the listing below:

"The Fowl" (H. C. B.). *The Sunday Times* 1 May 1921.

"The Needle Test" (Will-o'-the-Wisp). *The Sunday Times* 3 July 1921.

"The Dagger" (Will-o'-the-Wisp). *The Sunday Times* 11 Sept 1921.

"Three Phases" (Ben Eath). *The Sunday Times* 18 Sept 1921.

"The Dilettante" (Ben Eath). *The Sunday Times* 29 Jan 1922.

"Fraternal Love" (Ben Eath). *The Sunday Times* 12 Feb 1922.

"A Sad Tale" (Ben Eath). *The Sunday Times* 19 Feb 1922.

"The Watch" (Ben Eath). *The Sunday Times* 2 Apr 1922.

"The Deserter" (Ben Eath). *The Sunday Times* 21 May 1922.

"Caste" (Ben Eath). *The Sunday Times* 11 June 1922.

"Beyond the Beyond" (Ben Eath). *The Sunday Times* 30 July 1922.

"In the Beginning" (Ben Africa). *The Sjambok* 1.7 (31 May 1929): 21-22.

"The Gag" (W. P. Jacobs). *The Ringhals* 20 Oct 1939: 8 (believed first published early 1930s).

"The Man-eater" (Herman Malan). *The Touleier* 1.4 (Apr 1931): 222-225, 227.

"Rita's Marriage" (Herman Malan). *The New Sjambok* 1.2 (25 July 1931): 12-13 and 1.3 (2 Aug 1931): 18-19.

"Heloise's Teeth" (Herman Malan). *The New Sjambok* 1.9 (14 Sept 1931): 12-13.

"A Nun's Passion" (unsigned). *The Ringhals* Dec 1933.

"Romance: A Sequence" ("Romance"; "Wingspread and Bedspread"; "A Blue Cylinder"; "Afternoon Ravishment"; "Solemn Wind"; "Vista of Bees"; "Blunted Weapons"; "First Served"; "Comings"; "Without a Bit"; "Red Cock-crow"; "A Double Night"; "The Bridge"; "Denticulated Space Bloom"). Undated typescripts, Harry Ransom Humanities Research Center; sequencing and title supplied.

"A Shorter History of South Africa" (Ferdinand Fandango). *The Sunday Times* 3 Dec 1922.

"Cricket and How to Play It" (Ferdinand Fandango). *The Sunday Times* 17 Dec 1922.

"Keeping Fit" (Vere de Vere Tornado). *The Sunday Times* 4 Mar 1923.

"From a Student's Diary" (Pedagogue). *The Sunday Times* 22 Apr 1923.

The Canterbury Tales (H. C. B.). *The Umpa: University of the Witwatersrand Student Magazine* Mar 1925: 22.

"Pride of the Reef" (Ben Onion), originally entitled "A Blot on Benoni's Escutcheon." *The Sjambok* 10 Oct 1930.

"The Professor" (Herman Malan). *The Sunday Times* 23 Nov 1930.

"The Artist" (Herman Malan). *The Touleier* Jan-Feb 1931.

"By the Kerbside" (Herman Malan). *The Touleier* Mar-May 1931.

"*The Touleier's* Talkies" (Herman Malan). *The Touleier* Mar-Apr 1931.

"The Recognising Blues." Undated typescript, HRHRC. First published in *The Purple Renoster* 4 (Summer 1960): 27-29.

"Stephen Black" (Herman Malan). *The New Sjambok* 7 Nov 1931.

"*The Hottentot's God*: A Preface" (Herman Malan). *The Touleier* Jan-Feb 1931.

"Masters. . . and Others" (Herman Malan). *The New L. S. D.* from late 1931 up to June 1932.

"Two Unauthorised Biographies" (Herman Malan). *The Touleier* Apr 1931 and *The New L. S. D.* 4 Nov 1932.

"The Urge of the Primordial" (H. C. B.). *The Umpa: University of the Witwatersrand Student Magazine* Oct 1925: 34-35.

"Mara" (Herman Malan). *Mara* [nine poems with "Mara: A Play in One Act"] (Johannesburg: African Publications, c. 1932).

"Street-woman." Undated typescript, HRHRC. First published as an eight-page supplement in *Speak: Critical Arts Journal* 1.3 (May-June 1978).

"Johannesburg Christmas Eve." Undated typescript, HRHRC. First published in *Bosman's Johannesburg* (1986): 87-113.

Grateful acknowledgements are made to the Harry Ransom Humanities Research Center for permission to reproduce manuscript material here. Thanks also to Ronél Smit, Librarian at the Rand Afrikaans University, Johannesburg, for assistance in locating archival newspaper material.